THE EARL OF LONDON

LOUISE BAY

Published by Louise Bay 2018

ISBN – 978-1-910747-551

BOOKS BY LOUISE BAY

The Mister Series

Mr. Mayfair

Mr. Knightsbridge

Mr. Smithfield

Mr. Park Lane

Mr. Bloomsbury

Mr. Notting Hill

The Christmas Collection

The 14 Days of Christmas

This Christmas

The Player Series

International Player

Private Player

Dr. Off Limits

Standalones

Hollywood Scandal

Love Unexpected

Hopeful

The Empire State Series

Gentleman Series

The Ruthless Gentleman

The Wrong Gentleman

The Royals Series

King of Wall Street

Park Avenue Prince

Duke of Manhattan

The British Knight

The Earl of London

The Nights Series

Parisian Nights

Promised Nights

Indigo Nights

Faithful

Sign up to the Louise Bay mailing list at
www.louisebay/mailinglist

Read more at www.louisebay.com

ONE

Logan

I might call my lawyer. See if I could sue the so-called journalist who'd written the scathing piece about me in *The London Times*. I don't know why I hadn't left the newspaper in the office, put it through the shredder. Instead, I was torturing myself. Reading and rereading. This writer guy didn't know me. He'd accused me of making money from destroying the lives and legacies of innocent people.

It was bullshit. I never lied or cheated. I was good for my word. A straight shooter.

"So, beautiful, what's taking you so long?" I called out to the woman I'd met on a negotiation earlier in the week who was about to suck my cock and stop me thinking about journalists trashing my reputation.

Normally criticism bounced off me and I didn't give it a second thought. There were always plenty of people trying to bring you down when you were on top, but I kept replaying the article in my head.

It was as if it had been describing someone else. My

father. Not me. The only thing that might dampen my anger and frustration was a powerful, confident, clever woman, who had almost outsmarted me in business, get on her knees and take my dick in her mouth.

When I was younger I'd had my fair share of models and actresses, but they didn't have the same appeal as a successful woman who liked to dominate in the boardroom, and beg me for their orgasm in the bedroom.

I tipped back the last of the whiskey she'd left me with before she'd disappeared, shrugged off my jacket and slumped on the couch. The wall of floor-to-ceiling windows opposite the sofa was black, speckled with the lights of London's still-busy streets. My reflection ghosted over the cityscape, which meant I'd get a good view of her head bobbing between my knees from two angles.

Nice.

"Just freshening up," she said, striding back into the living room wearing just a black lace bra and knickers. And her six-inch heels.

Very nice.

This woman was my type to a tee. Tall. Cool. Sophisticated. A gym-honed body with tight muscles, golden skin and small, high breasts.

"I could do with a little freshening up," I said. "Come here."

She placed her palms on my thighs, bent over, then slid to her knees between my legs. I leaned my head back, ready to empty my mind of arsehole journalists and enjoy what was coming next. She could warm me up a little by sucking me off and then before things got out of hand, I'd stand, hold her head while I fucked her mouth deep, watching as her eyes watered as she gagged. Nothing better than a female hedge fund manager who oversaw assets of hundreds of millions of euros and was used to putting men in their place letting me do whatever I wanted to her.

My dick strained in my trousers as she ran her nails down the outside of the fabric. A little teasing was okay, but if she didn't have my cock in her mouth in two minutes I'd make her pay for it later. As if she could hear what I was thinking, she unzipped me and clasped her fingers around my length. She'd need two hands.

I groaned as she squeezed, preparing myself for the feel of her tongue when the familiar ring of my phone sounded from my jacket pocket. Shit.

"Tell me you're not going to answer that," she said, her lips poised at my crown.

In most similar situations I would ignore it. Silence it and refocus on what was happening to my dick, but the article had me on edge.

"I have to get this. Stay where you are, on your knees—it suits you. I won't be long," I said, sitting up straighter as I saw it was the number of my real estate agent. Why the hell was he calling me?

"You're an arsehole," she said, releasing my erection and leaning back on her knees.

I grinned as I answered the phone. Well, I hadn't promised her romance.

"Howard?"

"You know way back when we first worked together you asked me to track that house in Woolton Village and to let you know if it ever came up for sale?"

I shifted, zipping up my trousers. Howard had my full attention. "I remember." How could I forget? It was the whole reason behind my success. My ambition and drive came from needing to get to a point in my career where I could afford to buy that house. I'd long had enough money, but the current owners had always turned down my generous offers over the years.

"Well, I just got word that it's going on the market tomorrow morning."

"Badsley House?" I wanted to be sure we were talking about the same place.

I held my breath waiting for his reply.

"Yeah, that's the one. You want me to find out how much it's listing for?"

My hand clenched the phone tighter. "No. I want you to buy it." I'd bought and sold millions of pounds worth of property, built an empire worth billions, but I wouldn't ever feel successful until I owned Badsley.

"Right. Okay. Do you have a ceiling price?" Howard asked.

There was no price I wouldn't pay for that place. It was my opportunity to right the wrongs of the past, to make the only person in the world who I cared about happy. To prove once and for all that I wasn't my father. "No. Just get the deal done. I'll expect to sign paperwork tomorrow."

"You don't want a survey or—"

"No. I want to own that house by the end of tomorrow."

Howard paused before he answered. "I'll make it happen."

I ended the call, wanting to digest what had just happened. Badsley House was finally going to be mine and I couldn't wipe the grin from my face.

I was about to fulfil a lifetime's ambition.

I was about to buy my grandmother's childhood home back.

TWO

Darcy

There was something magical about the English countryside on a spring morning. From the dew-covered spiders' webs to the early sunshine encouraging the snow-drops and crocuses out of hiding until they were riotous blots of color that bloomed despite the odds of winter. It was my perfect paradise.

My favorite thing to do on a Sunday morning was to ride across the Woolton Estate. It was land that had been in my family for generations and was now my responsibility to maintain for the future Westbury family. I'd lived here almost my entire life. It had been the constant when first my father, and then my mother, abandoned me and my brother to our grandparents. It was home, a safe and happy place where I could forget anything bad in the world existed. And I did my best to keep it as it always had been. I wanted to honor the people who had done it before me and preserve it for the people who would come after me.

It was a huge responsibility. Not just because of the

generations who would follow, but also the livelihoods that depended on it now from gardeners to gamekeepers, stable staff and then all the people who maintained the house— Woolton Hall. Their families trusted me to provide work for their loved ones. I saw it as an honor as well as my duty. And on days like today, it was a complete pleasure.

As we pulled up at my favorite spot, I dismounted from Bella. It had rained overnight, so although it was dry now, the ground was covered in slippery, muddy grass. Technically, I was checking out the boundaries of the estate and ensuring everything was how it should be, but really I just loved the view from here.

"You're going to have to hold me upright, Bella," I said, holding her reins tight and guiding her toward the view. "Look at that. I reckon you can see a hundred miles." In the distance, the rolling hills of the Chilterns broke up the horizon and a patchwork of fields were divided up by hedges, trees and church spires, as if cars and people didn't exist. Birdsong floated toward me on the breeze and I closed my eyes and breathed in the fresh morning spring air. I was so lucky to live in a place this beautiful.

Out of the corner of my eye I caught movement in the trees. Had one of our deer wandered into the woods?

Squinting, I realized it was a person. A man. A very tall man who seemed to be focusing on the phone in his large hand while headed in my direction. I watched as Bella and I went unnoticed. In his mid-thirties, in jeans and walking shoes, I didn't recognize him. He swept his hand through his chocolate-brown hair, the edge of his sharp jaw catching in the hazy morning sunlight as he looked up, just to check the ground ahead of him. Perhaps he was an estate agent, or a surveyor. He was on Badsley House's land, which had just gone up for sale since Mrs. Brookely had died. I was torn between wanting to be left alone with my horse to enjoy the view and wanting to know what this man's business was on the border of my family's land. And perhaps I wanted to see whether or not he was as handsome close up as he seemed to be from a distance. He strode toward Bella and me, his head down, the morning mist swirling about his feet. What a shame that he was missing out on the beautiful morning, on this fantastic view.

As he came closer, he pulled at his collar, revealing a smooth, tan neck and prominent Adam's apple. A small ridge burrowed between his eyebrows as if he was irritated by what he found on the screen in front of him—or perhaps was trying to figure out a puzzle. If he lived in Woolton Village, I would recognize the difference between the two expressions on him and for no explicable reason it niggled at me that I didn't know him a little better.

Catching me off guard, the man who by now was just a few meters away from us suddenly looked up and right at me watching him, his blue eyes pinning me to the spot. I wasn't the sort of girl who stared at men. I understood that personality outlasted looks and that what was on the inside was more important than the outside, but apparently this guy's outside had me staring. And I'd been caught. "Good morning," he bellowed, waving.

Before I could decide if embarrassment would stop me greeting the stranger, Bella caught my attention as she whinnied and struggled against the reins. As I tugged the leather to reassure her that everything was okay, she pulled in the opposite direction, breaking free of my grasp. *Shit*. As I charged after her, my foot slipped on the wet grass and I fell, face down into a muddy puddle.

"Bella!" Spread-eagled on the ground, I lifted my head and saw the man running after her. To my considerable surprise and relief, he caught her reins and began to lead her back. It was unlike Bella to do anything a stranger told her, but she must have taken pity on me.

Struggling to my feet, I glanced down at myself, covered in mud. Sloppy, cold water dripped down my face onto my neck. So much for my perfect morning.

I grabbed the reins from him and smoothed my palm over my face, trying to make the best out of the situation.

"Thank you," I said, a little flustered. If I'd been embarrassed at being caught staring at this handsome man, the fact that I now looked like a character from a zombie movie didn't make things any better.

"You're welcome," he said. "It's a beautiful day. I presume you're from around here?" he asked.

Concentrating on Bella, I addressed the stranger without looking at him, unsure whether I'd be able to look away. Didn't he know we were on the Woolton Hall estate? "Yes, and I presume you're not," I said, hoping he'd fill in the blanks.

When he didn't respond, I turned to find him regarding me as if I were a zoo animal. "You're completely covered in mud." He started to laugh.

Perfect. The first good-looking man I'd run into in a year, and I was providing his entertainment. This was just my luck. And why I was single. I just wasn't one of those glamorous girls who men found attractive. I liked being outside too much and was a little too comfortable in the mud.

"I'm sorry. Can we start over? I'm Logan Steele," he said, and held out his hand.

I held up my palms to show him how the last thing he wanted to do was shake my hand, and I certainly didn't want to further embarrass myself by covering him in mud.

"I just wanted to wish you a good morning, what with you being on my land and everything."

"*Your* land?" The clearing before I reached the woodland skirting Badsley House was most definitely *not* his. I squinted, ignoring the mud still trickling down my face. "I think you'll find this is part of the Woolton Estate. The boundary is..." There used to be a small post indicating where our ownership of the land ended.

"Over there?" Logan pointed behind me toward Woolton.

For years, I'd taken no notice of the boundary between Badsley and Woolton. Because the woodland and the stream where my brother and I would play when we were children was right at the edge of Badsley House's land, it provided a natural fence, but technically, the three or four meters this side of the trees also belonged to Badsley. I winced and then realized what he'd said. "You've bought the place? I thought it only went on the market yesterday?" This tall, handsome man was going to be moving into the village? Great first impression I was making. First falling over and getting covered in mud. Now I was trespassing.

"I don't think it technically went on the market. I signed the paperwork yesterday afternoon."

"Oh," I said. I was pleased Badsley hadn't laid empty for too long but it was a bit of a shock to find the place had already been sold. And to someone like the man in front of me who, looked more like he'd be at home in a London penthouse rather than a country house. "So, you're all moved in already?"

He shook his head, grinning at me while I searched my pockets for a tissue so I could wipe my eyes clear of mud.

"Not yet. Three days ago, I didn't know the place was

coming up for sale." He held out his scarf. "Use this if you want to wipe your face."

I smiled but shook my head. "Thank you. But I wouldn't want to ruin it." It looked expensive. "I'll just ..." I pulled taut the sleeve of my riding jacket and wiped around my eyes. Could I feel any more ridiculous?

"You decided quickly about the place then?" I asked. "Had you been looking in the area long?"

"Sort of." He shoved his hands in his pockets and tilted his head. "So, you said you were local, do you ride over here often?" he asked.

"I'm sorry, I wasn't meaning to trespass. The previous owner didn't mind me—"

"And I don't either," he said. "It's a beautiful view." He glanced over toward the Chiltern Hills.

So he *had* noticed his surroundings a little.

"It really is. And with the stream just over there," I pointed to beneath the trees to the place where my brother and I used to play. "This is my favorite spot in the village."

"It's beautiful. Any other places I should make sure I visit around here?"

"Well, it's all beautiful. You'll have to explore and decide," I said, trying to ignore the fact I was covered in mud. "It's so peaceful up here. It's good to get away and escape. But you might prefer...something else." By the looks of him, he spent a good deal of time in the gym.

"Well, perhaps next time I run into you at one, I won't spook your horse and you won't end up covered in mud." For the first time since I'd fallen over, I was grateful for the muddy camouflage. I hoped it was covering my blush at the mention of seeing him again. I always complained about there not being enough single men in the area, and here it seemed Badsley House had planted someone right next door.

"It's fine. At least you caught her." Normally, I'd be furious that someone wasn't more thoughtful around my horses but I could hardly chastise someone new to the village. "Do you ride? Or your...wife?"

He chuckled. "No, I never learned. And I'm not married."

"Oh," I said. "That's a shame." Now I sounded like I wished he was married, which definitely wasn't the case. "That you don't ride," I corrected. "It's a wonderful way to get out into the countryside."

"I see that. Maybe I'll learn." His eyes sort of twinkled and I couldn't tell if he was making fun of me or it was just his normal charming way.

"Well, I'd better be going," I said, feeling a little awkward and out of my depth. I was used to being neither. I needed a hot shower and not to be talking with a ridiculously handsome man looking like I did.

"I didn't get your name," he said.

I'd rather have slunk away without introducing myself. That way, maybe the next time I saw him, he wouldn't recognize me without the mud and I could have a do-over. "Darcy," I muttered.

"Good to meet you, Darcy. I hope I'll see you again."

"Woolton Village is a small place, I have no doubt we'll run into each other again. Hopefully I will be a little cleaner."

He grinned, and those eyes did that sparkle thing again. "What's a little mud between friends?"

I looked back toward Woolton Hall, unsure of what to say. "Well, nice to meet you."

"See you soon, I hope," he replied.

I turned and began to walk away, trying not to fixate on the fact he'd just said he hoped to see me soon. Because he was just being polite. Neighborly.

Glancing over my shoulder, I saw he was still in the same spot, watching me as I led Bella back to Woolton. Crap, I should have worn my magic jeans that made my arse look half the size it actually was. I also shouldn't have fallen over into the mud. Or trespassed on his land. But despite all of it, I did find him a little bit charming. And more than slightly handsome. And I didn't run into men like that very often. I could think of worse neighbors to have.

THREE

Darcy

After my ride had been cut short, it was still early when I got back from the stables. The edges of the Woolton Estate faded in and out beneath a layer of shifting mist. Even so, I knew what the sun would reveal when it burned away the fog. The lawns, all neatly mowed. The trees, perfectly pruned in autumn, were now bursting to life. The roof of the stables had been replaced and the flooding driveway fixed.

I might be covered in mud, but things on the estate were under control. And I had unexpected news about my morning. I couldn't wait to tell Aurora whose car was in the drive.

"Hi there," I called as I kicked shut the oak door of the boot room and negotiated the expanse of coats hanging on the wall on the left. Given I was the only one who lived at Woolton full time, I was pretty sure there should be fewer than three thousand coats hanging on the wall. I'd forgotten the members of the Women's Institute were over, using the kitchen today. I think they said they were jam-making.

I grinned at the rumble of excited voices the other side of the door. I loved the sound of the house full. Since my grandfather died, the house felt ten times as big and I missed my brother even more, even though he visited from the U.S. just as often. I felt the loss of family sharply, as if memories of those days after my mother abandoned Ryder and I were made yesterday, not a lifetime ago.

"Darcy," someone called.

"Coming," I said as I struggled getting my riding boots off. I was just about to win the one-legged battle to rid myself of my footwear when I lost my balance to a roar of thunder, fell against the wall of coats and then slipped completely over on my bottom. How was it possible to fall over twice in one day? At least Logan Steele wasn't here to witness my clumsiness this time.

What the hell was that noise?

"Darcy?"

I looked up and found Aurora, my best friend since I was four years old, shaking her head at me as if I were purposefully floundering around on the ground beneath a mountain of wool and tweed.

"What are you doing?"

"Oh, just playing hide and seek. Help me up?" At least in the kerfuffle my boot had released my leg.

"What's all the commotion?" Mrs. Lonsdale asked. The five ladies from the village bustling about the kitchen were like family to me. They'd known me since I was still in nappies and I'd watched them bake, sew and share their lives with each other for as long as I could remember.

"Darcy fell over," Aurora replied for me. "And she's covered in mud."

"You need to be more careful." Mrs. Lonsdale wiped her hands on her apron as she regarded me, shaking her head.

"It wasn't my fault. Did no one else hear that noise? It sounded like a passenger jet flying about fifty feet off the ground."

"More like a helicopter," Aurora said.

"Whatever it was, it was loud," I replied, washing my hands at the sink, muddy water trickling into the drain. Most of it had dried, but I still must look a fright.

"It might be your new neighbor," Daphne said as she continued to chop the rhubarb that Glenis had washed at the sink, then transferred to the table.

Were they talking about the man I'd just met? It was difficult to be sure as we didn't really have neighbors in the usual sense. On a clear day, Woolton Hall owned the land as far as the eye could see.

"Yes, from Badsley House," Freida announced. "It sold already. Didn't you know?"

I felt a little smug that not only did I know Badsley House had been sold, but I'd also met the new owner. But I was a little surprised Freida knew as she was always the last to hear about village gossip.

I shrugged and poured myself a glass of orange juice from the fridge—I wasn't about to confess that I'd met Logan Steele because then the tables would turn and *I'd* be the one who was questioned. No, I wanted to hear what people already knew about my handsome neighbor. Did he have a girlfriend? Was I blinded by mud or did everyone think he was as good-looking as I did? And I wanted to know why they thought he'd be flying a helicopter over the estate.

"Some city people bought it, apparently."

"City people moved to the country?" I asked hopefully as I collapsed into one of the free kitchen chairs, watching the women of the Woolton W.I. and their makeshift assembly line of strawberry and rhubarb jam-making.

Mrs. Lonsdale snorted. "If you count being here on a Saturday and Sunday moving."

My shoulders dropped and the excitement I'd felt on my walk home faded as quickly as birds chased away by the bark of a dog. So Logan Steele wasn't really moving in at all. I knew he didn't look like he was the country type. "Weekenders?" The last people I wanted in Badsley House were those who had more money than sense, took no part in village life and went back to their penthouses on Sunday evening. People like that sucked the life out of a village. Badsley House needed someone who was going to spend money in the shops, come to the village fête, and carry on the local traditions. Weekenders got upset by the smell of cow dung and thought owning a Barbour jacket and a Land Rover made them country people.

I knew Logan Steele had been too good to be true.

"He might be persuaded to stay for longer than the weekend if he has reason to. I've heard he's handsome," Freida said.

Whoever he was, someone needed to tell him he couldn't fly over Woolton Hall.

"And single," Freida offered, casting me a look.

"And in his early thirties," Aurora said with a wink as she added an endless stream of sugar into one of the large saucepans.

"You knew about this and didn't tell me?" I asked her. Aurora and I told each other everything.

"I just found out," she replied.

"I heard that they've kept Mr. Fawsley on, so hopefully they'll maintain the garden." Freida knocked her wooden spoon on the side of the pan.

Despite being irritated that I didn't have the scoop on Badsley House having been bought—by weekenders no less —I took some solace that Logan hadn't fired the gardener. Mr. Fawsley'd devoted his life to the place. His daughter had been married in the grounds.

"It was such a shame that place had to be sold," I sighed. Mrs. Brookely had died just a few months ago, and her family had been forced to sell the place in order to pay the inheritance tax. The place was beautiful. Smaller than Woolton Hall, obviously, but still substantial, with some surrounding woods that I loved riding through.

"But new life in a village can be a good thing. Especially for a young family," Mrs. Lonsdale said.

"He'll have to find a wife first," Freida said.

So, he was single at least. But that didn't help the fact that he wouldn't be at the house full-time. And he was happy to disturb our peaceful existence with his helicopter.

"Okay, out with it," Mrs. Lonsdale said before I had to. "How are you the source of all this information? I'm usually the one telling you everything."

Freida shrugged, keeping her eyes fixed on the chopping board as she tried, unsuccessfully, to stop the corners of her mouth from twitching. "This knife is blunting," she said.

"Freida," I said, taking the knife from her and heading toward the sink to wash it. "Tell us your source."

She let out an exasperated sigh and plonked down her rhubarb. "If you must know, my daughter's best friend's grandmother's best friend's grandson is the new owner."

I frowned, trying to follow that tangled thread. "Who?"

I mouthed at Aurora, but she just shook her head. I pulled out the knife sharpener from the second drawer down and set about my task.

"So, what do we know about him? What does he do for a living? New money, no doubt," Mrs. Lonsdale said.

"He was profiled in *The Times* this week," Freida said. "I might have a copy in my bag." There was no might about it. She'd just been waiting for the right moment.

"He's very good-looking." Freida pulled out the paper and handed it to me, casting me a pointed look. There were disadvantages to having known these women my whole life —they all felt as if they had a stake in my love life. "Handsome. Charming. And very successful in business."

I abandoned the knife sharpening and took a seat, unfolding the paper.

"Page eighteen," Freida said.

I turned the pages and saw the sharp jaw and twinkling eyes of Logan Steele staring out at me. He had the kind of face that was difficult to turn away from. As I began to read, I glanced up at Freida. The article set out how Logan was the most successful of a number of corporate titans who, the journalist reported, made their money by destroying businesses. I'd expected it to be a super-flattering puff piece, but it was anything but. The article argued that Logan's approach to business was stifling innovation, that he only cared about profit and that his methods would eventually lead to a shrinking economy if people followed his lead. "This says that he's destroying British industry. Closing down businesses and putting people out of jobs," I said. "It paints him as quite the villain."

"Yes, yes, but you know what these papers are like. You can't believe everything you read," Freida said. "And he's very good-looking in the photograph. And the article says how rich he is."

Why did Freida think I could be interested in a man, even if he was wealthy and handsome, if his whole focus in business was destruction? A man's values were more important to me than a pretty face.

"And I did hear that in person he's incredibly charming."

"Not *that* charming, if he's flying so low that if I'd been outside my hair would be several centimeters shorter," I replied, placing the paper on the side and picking up the knife again to sharpen it.

"You've got to get with the times," Freida said. "This is how rich people travel these days."

I winced at the sound of steel against steel. "My brother is both rich and occasionally lacking in charm, but he wouldn't dare turn up to Woolton in a helicopter."

I fixed Aurora with a glare that said that she'd be wearing the saucepan of rhubarb and sugar if she told the room that Ryder had once suggested he take a helicopter from the airfield to Woolton. Luckily for me, our grandfather had said no and Ryder hadn't reopened the debate since my grandfather's death. I might worship my brother and there was little he could do that would irritate me, but that was a line in the sand for me.

"Hopefully, the helicopter is an occasional thing," Mrs. Lonsdale said. "It would be very disruptive if that's how he travels regularly."

"I hope he doesn't turn out to be like the last people who bought a weekend place in Woolton." I paused, not wanting to be drowned out by the collective groan that followed. "Exactly," I said. "The Thompsons' extension took three years of scaffolding, drilling, skips and builders swearing like sailors. For what? So they could turn around and sell the place at a profit."

Alice Thompson had charmed us all at first. She'd joined the W.I. and explained how the extension to her newly acquired village cottage was needed to accommodate her growing family. Then as soon as her planning application had been granted, we'd been dropped like proverbial hot bricks and she'd headed back to her London home, leaving us to put up with building works, clogging up the high street and disturbing the neighbors for three long years. For the Thompsons, buying a property in Woolton had been a financial investment. For me, the investment in Woolton was all emotional.

"Not everyone is going to be like the Thompsons," Mrs. Lonsdale said, lugging over another huge pan and placing it onto the table.

"What about that couple who bought the old rectory for weekends? The Foleys," I said. Surely they couldn't have forgotten the police cars in the middle of the night and Mr. Foley being arrested for beating the crap out of his wife when he was drunk as a skunk?

"That was years ago," Daphne said. "Not everyone who grew up somewhere other than Woolton is bad, Darcy. And you'll have nothing left of that knife if you keep sharpening it."

"I know, but that doesn't mean we should trust them right away either." For a few minutes, I'd been charmed by the new owner. Taken in by his handsome face and warm smile. And now I felt like an idiot.

"Do you suppose the new owner will allow us to see the garden?" Daphne asked. "That would be a good gauge of how well our handsome new neighbor will settle in." Mrs. Brookely used to let any local in to visit. In fact, the rose garden that sat behind Woolton Hall beyond the croquet field had been planted after my grandmother had seen the rose garden at Badsley House. I hoped it would continue to provide inspiration to the village.

"Perhaps you could ask him when you visit, Darcy," Freida said.

"Visit?" I asked, rinsing the knife under the hot water before drying and passing it back over.

"To welcome him to the village, of course. You could take some of this jam if you like," Mrs. Lonsdale said.

After this morning's debacle and embarrassment, and the article I just read, the last thing I wanted to do was turn up on Logan Steele's doorstep. Apart from anything else, he might think that I was...interested in him. Romantically. He probably had every woman he met eating out of the palm of his hand. But not me. I'd been briefly taken in by him this morning, but I was over it. The article had ensured that. "There is no way I'd impose on him like that. And given he's used to city life, I'm sure he'd find it quite odd."

"It's what your grandparents always did for any newcomers," Mrs. Lonsdale said.

I sighed. She knew my weak spots. I loved to uphold the traditions and history of the village—keep the place as special as it always had been—and honor the memory of my grandparents. But there was no way I was turning up on Logan Steele's doorstep with a pot of jam.

"It would be a perfect match, you know. A rich, handsome earl and a duke's granddaughter," Freida said, clearly having given up on not-so-subtle hints. "This house needs more life in it."

"An earl?" Mrs. Lonsdale said. "It doesn't mention it in the article."

"No, he doesn't use the title anymore, for some reason.

But if you ask me it seems like fate, Darcy. An earl moves in next door to you—that can't be coincidence," Freida said.

"Titles don't mean anything these days," I said, ignoring the six pairs of eyes on me as I stood and tipped a large pan toward Freida's board. She slid in the chopped rhubarb. "It's the person not the position that's important." I carried the saucepan to the sink. "Can't we talk about Aurora's love life?" Every W.I. meeting I held at Woolton seemed to end in a discussion about my love life. Now that my ever-single brother had finally married, it seemed the grandfather clock in the hallway got louder with every passing day, chanting *sin-gle, sin-gle, sin-gle*.

"I've decided I need someone foreign. Greek maybe. Or American," Aurora sighed.

"Since when?" I asked.

Like some Tennyson character, she stared wistfully into space, and I decided not to question her.

"That reminds me," I said. "When Ryder, Scarlett and their little rascals come next month, we're going to start planning the summer garden party. So, any ideas, let me know."

"And you'll go to Badsley this week?" Freida asked.

I sighed. "No, why would I?"

"We'll leave you an extra pot of jam," Mrs. Lonsdale said. "That will be a nice welcome. And you might take some roses—they're looking beautiful, Darcy. You can tell him the story about how your grandmother planted them because of the roses at Badsley."

These women didn't know how to take no for an answer.

I'd sooner take a pitchfork than a selection of my grandmother's roses. At least that way I could threaten to slice and dice the guy if he flew a helicopter over Woolton again.

As much as I might have admired his outside earlier today, his ethics and attitude were much more important to me. I'd devoted my life to Woolton Hall and the traditions of our village, and I'd do whatever it took to ensure Badsley House's new owner didn't disrupt any of that.

FOUR

Logan

I'd finally done it. At last, my grandmother was back in the home she'd grown up in. The house that she'd given up for me. I was finally able to repay her sacrifice in a small way.

Holding a tray of tea, I opened the French doors with my elbow and stepped out onto the terrace. I'd spent the last few days working from home while we got settled in our new house, which meant afternoon tea on a Wednesday was part of my day when ordinarily the afternoon would pass in a blur of conference calls, meetings and briefings.

"There you are. I thought you'd got lost," my grandmother said as I placed the tray down in front of her.

"I'm still finding my way around." My grandmother may have grown up in a place like this, but I hadn't. The two of us had lived in a two-bedroom terraced house when I was growing up. Technically, I might be a member of the British aristocracy, but I'd learned quickly that titles didn't provide anything I needed growing up. And they absolutely were no guarantee of financial success—that was all down to hard work and focus.

I took a seat facing the neatly manicured gardens. The land immediately surrounding the house was divided into various sections—a walled area full of herbs and vegetables just outside the kitchen, one to the west that was nothing but roses, and three additional sections that—according to the gardener—were divided by color, although it was too early in the year to see. The terrace overlooked steps down to a pond and various raised flowerbeds. I could see why my grandmother had loved this place.

"It's a huge house. I'd forgotten quite how big. You really didn't need to do this," she said, shaking her head. "You know I was perfectly happy at my little bungalow."

"I wanted to do this." More than *wanted*, I'd *needed* to do this.

My grandmother sighed and patted my hand. "It was never your mistake to fix."

"This house was yours and was taken from you. I'm just giving it back—making things right for you in the way that you always made things right for me." I placed the tea strainer over the rim of her porcelain cup and poured her a strong cup of oolong. "Anyway, you always told me that a man's greatest strength was his ability to adapt—it will feel like home in no time." I added a dash of milk to her cup but kept mine black.

"Yes, but I meant to hardship," she replied.

She'd given up this place for me but never complained, never even mentioned it.

"It works both ways, Granny." I'd vowed to ensure that one day she'd get back the gardens she used to describe in my bedtime stories as a child. It wasn't until I was older, looking through an old family photo album, that I realized how much she'd missed them. Things had come full circle now. She was back in the place she'd called home for so many years. I'd expected a sense of victory, but it was more a calming realization of this was how things were meant to be.

She squeezed my hand. "It's still a beautiful house and the gardens are no less spectacular all these years later." She let me go and picked up her tea. "We're lucky Mr. Fawsley agreed to stay on." The previous owner's gardener had been delighted when I'd asked him. He clearly enjoyed his work.

"Have you met any other neighbors?" I asked, thinking back to the mud-soaked girl I'd met on Sunday. She'd said she was local.

"No, but it's early days, and as you know, I can't get out much."

"I saw a farm shop at the far end of the village. I'll take you down later in the week if you want."

"That's a nice idea, but you can't spend all your time with me. I want you to make friends around here, you hear me?"

I chuckled. "Yes, Granny. In fact, I ran into a woman when I was out walking around the boundary on Sunday."

"Was she a neighbor?"

"I think so. She seemed to know about the area."

"Was she friendly?"

She hadn't been unfriendly but she hadn't been as pleased to see me as I might have expected. "I think she was a little distracted. Her horse bolted when I approached and she fell face first into the mud."

"Oh dear. This is a very different life to the one you have in London. Are you sure you're ready?"

My grandmother was right. I'd never had to hold a conversation with someone who was dripping in mud—

apart from that one time in Vegas...That night had ended messily, but there hadn't been much conversation involved. Darcy had the body for a little mud-wrestling, but I wasn't sure she'd have the inclination. "I'll still be in London most of the week. I think I can handle a little mud at the weekend."

"Was she pretty?"

I paused, remembering her sodden hair and the way she'd refused my offer of my scarf to wipe the rivers of muddy water that ran down her face. "I guess." There was no doubt Darcy was pretty—beautiful, even—with glossy brown hair that I'd spotted before she fell, deep brown and a great body. But she wasn't my type. She was a lot shorter than the women I usually fucked. With a bloom to her cheeks and pale skin, she looked like the archetypal English rose. Her body, while phenomenal, wasn't the usual gym-fit type I'd go for when looking for a girl for the night. She was softer, her arse a little bigger. And she seemed less into me than I was used to.

But there had been something about her that drew me in and had me wanting our conversation to continue. I wasn't sure if it was the unfamiliarity of her, or something deeper that had me hoping I would see her again and have the chance to...I wasn't sure what. Touch her? Talk to her some more? Watch as her warm smile took over her face and warmed everything in its orbit?

"I bet you're the talk of the village. Rich, successful, handsome and without a wife. I can't imagine there's many men like you around these parts."

"I think you're a little biased, and anyway, I told you—you don't need to worry about my love life. I do fine."

"I'm not talking about sex," she said. "I want you to find someone you can build a life with. When I'm gone—"

"Granny," I growled, interrupting her. "I don't want you talking like that. You know you're going to live forever."

"I certainly hope so, but I'd like to see you settled down. You're not getting any younger."

"You're hitting me high and low with the compliments. Give me a break. I'm thirty-five."

"Yes, exactly. You've had plenty of time to play the field. It's time, my boy."

"You don't need to worry, I'm putting down roots," I said, lifting my chin toward the gardens. I didn't spend time and energy playing at anything. I didn't take on things I didn't know if I could make work, but once I committed to something, it got my undivided attention. That approach had made me a lot of money, which was what I'd been aiming for. But it also meant that anything personal was a distraction. Women were simply a way of blowing off steam. Buying this house was the biggest personal commitment I'd ever made and was ever likely to make.

"That will have to do for now. But don't make this lady wait too long for great-grandchildren. This house is plenty big enough."

Great-grandchildren? Getting the semi-regular lectures about not having a wife was bad enough. "I've told you before, children aren't on my horizon." Fatherhood was something I'd do everything to avoid. It wasn't the kind of man I was. The only family that mattered to me and the only family I'd ever have was sitting right before me. "I'm sure this garden will keep you plenty busy enough."

"It *is* beautiful," she said. "But not more beautiful than a family."

That hadn't been my blueprint growing up—my family had been anything but beautiful. It had been sad, turbulent and chaotic and everything I didn't want to repeat. "And you're sure that you don't mind me using the land out of the view of the house?" I asked, changing the subject. Beyond the gardens there were twenty-two acres of land, woodland and unfarmed fields. The stables and the surrounding area had long been abandoned, and the place was waiting for me to breathe fresh life into it. And that was what I planned to do.

"You keep talking about the land—since when have you been interested in that kind of thing?"

"I'm interested in anything that will make me money, Granny. You know that."

"You've always been the same," she replied. "I hope you're not still brooding over that newspaper thing."

I set my cup down. "I'm not a brooder," I replied. "I'm a do-er." I didn't believe in signs from the universe and the stars aligning, but I was perfectly happy to take full advantage of a coincidence. The article in the *London Times* about me destroying entrepreneurship by rewarding destruction rather than new ideas and risk-taking had come out on the same day that Badsley House had come up for sale. And I had an idea percolating of how to use Badsley to prove that journalist wrong.

"You shouldn't let that sort of thing affect you. It's just some self-righteous journalist who's jealous that someone with a 'useless title' has created an empire."

"Hardly an empire," I replied.

"What would you call it? You're thirty-five, and despite the fact that you started with nothing, you were just named one of the richest men in England."

"But like that journalist said, I don't build anything. In fact, I've made all my money doing the exact opposite—they were right about that." The article had got under my skin and stuck. I couldn't shake it off. The criticism reminded me too much of the legacy my father had left behind—destruction. And I'd spent a lifetime proving I was more than my father's son.

I'd thought buying Badsley would fill the hollow inside me that sometimes echoed in the middle of the night. And although there was no doubt seeing my grandmother here had satisfied some kind of need in me, there was something still missing.

"You've done nothing to be ashamed of. You saved countless jobs by ensuring companies don't go into bankruptcy."

"Liquidation," I corrected her. "But yes, there's no doubt that any of the companies I've bought wouldn't have survived otherwise." There was value in what I did—my grandmother was right, I saved jobs, pensions and most of all I made money—but I couldn't help shake the reality that I'd never *built* a business. I'd just broken up other people's. I was hoping that I might change that.

I'd start small, out of the glare of London's spotlight and away from the reputation I had for being cutthroat and hard-nosed—I'd build, produce, create. My father had destroyed his family and his family's legacy. I would do the opposite. Buying Badsley had just been the first step in undoing the hurt he'd created, but I had a long way to go before I'd completely rewritten the harm he'd done and the pain and resentment he'd carved into my history.

FIVE

Darcy

I loved this time of year when the ground underfoot seemed to bounce with new life and the grayness of winter finally gave way to shoots of green. I closed the gate at the top of the farm shop car park and clicked the padlock shut. Having a private path to the Woolton Hall farm shop was an owner perk. The place had opened six months ago, but I still got a thrill whenever I visited. I waved as I spotted Aurora waiting in front of the gray clapboard building on the other side of the gravel car park. The shop sat on the outskirts of the village on a piece of Woolton Hall land that had previously housed a derelict barn. The location meant the shop attracted passing traffic, but was far enough away that it didn't draw any stray customers toward Woolton Hall.

I greeted Aurora with a hug and a blast of color caught my attention. "Oh, they've started doing the hanging baskets I suggested. That's so cute." I crouched to take in the baskets of begonias and miniature daffodils. "They look adorable."

"You've done an incredible thing setting up this place," she said.

"I can't take any of the credit." I linked my arm through Aurora's and we bundled inside.

"You're ridiculous. If you can't take the credit, I don't know who can."

"This guy," I said, high-fiving Rory as we stepped inside. As manager, Rory had done a fantastic job attracting local farms and craftsmen to display their products, and the shop had provided another full-time position and three part-time summer jobs for locals. The small profit that it was projected to make would support the Woolton Village charity, which provided help for the elderly village residents. It was exactly what I'd envisioned. A self-sustaining local shop, providing employment for local people.

And—bonus—it sold plenty of things I liked to buy. "We're running out of honey. Is there anything you need?" I asked Aurora.

"I don't think so. Are you going to create a basket for Badsley House? It would be a nice village welcome, don't you think?"

I paused in front of the two types of local honey the shop stocked. "You think I should?"

"You were considering not taking a gift?"

I didn't want to go at all, but clearly Aurora was horrified at the idea that I wouldn't take a welcome present, so I couldn't admit that. I thought I'd been clear the other day in Woolton's kitchen.

"And anyway, we've already met, so it seems unnecessary to go and formally visit," I said.

Aurora's eyes went wide and she grasped my arm. I

shook her off. "Tell me everything! Is he as handsome as they said? Is he tall? Was there chemistry?"

"Good grief. No, no and no. Why would you think there might be chemistry?"

"I like the idea that you met and it was love at first sight, or at least lust at first sight."

I snorted. I had been covered in mud. And although before I'd found out more about him I'd thought he was attractive, it had just been a fleeting moment. What mattered was who people were on the inside, not how hot they were on the outside.

"Hardly. Anyway, he's absolutely not my type—you read that article. Being a weekender, he won't be around much anyway." I examined the label on a jar of lavender honey.

I spotted a stack of wire baskets by the door and went to grab one. I put the honey in my basket. "I could never even be friends with someone who didn't want to improve the world around them," I said. "Clearly all he cares about is money." In my experience, men like Logan just wanted to be better, richer, more successful than the next guy at all costs. Those things weren't important to me and they weren't attractive to me in others.

"But so does Ryder," she replied as we wandered toward the eggs.

"I don't think money is all Ryder cares about. It was important to him to make his own way in the world, that's all. Anyway, I don't get to pick my family."

She laughed. "But this new guy clearly likes the country, even if he didn't grow up here."

"The man flies in to *experience* the country in a helicopter."

"That just means he's wealthy, not that he doesn't like

the country. And you know what these journalists are like. They might have some kind of ongoing feud. The writer might just be jealous."

"You're grasping at straws." Aurora was nothing if not a romantic.

"But didn't you say he was handsome?" she replied as if she hadn't read the article and didn't know how little his looks would matter given his character.

I shook my head and guided us toward the "New in Store" section. "Definitely not. He looked like a fish out of water, and worse, a tourist." There was no real doubt that he *was* handsome, even if he wasn't what I'd normally go for, but admitting that would be adding fuel to Aurora's fire. He was too direct, too confident. And he was taller than most men I'd dated. And broader. Like maybe he hadn't given up playing a lot of sports since leaving university.

"And he spooked Bella."

She winced, knowing how much I believed that horses were the ultimate judges of character. "Not a horse person?" she asked.

"Not by the looks of it," I replied, which was a little unfair. Logan had raced after Bella, and to my surprise, caught her and managed to bring her back to me. Bella was always a little skittish, and it had caught me off guard that she'd responded to him.

"Well, like it or not, he's a villager now. And even though you might be disappointed that he's not as handsome as you'd hoped, you really should call 'round and welcome him."

I spun to face her. "Wait, what? You think I'm disappointed he's not handsome?"

Aurora shrugged. "I thought you wanted to meet someone special."

I'd settle for some sex—but yes, of course I wanted to meet *the one* at some point in the future. "I'm not desperate, Aurora."

"I see how you are around Scarlett and Ryder's children, and I know you think Woolton is a little empty with just you living there."

My heart sank at the thought that I would be living at Woolton on my own forever. I loved the place and never wanted to leave—it was where I'd made all my good memories from childhood, and almost all of my adult ones. But at the same time, Aurora was right. I wanted to find someone to share it with.

"That might be so," I replied. "But I never thought that the new owner of Badsley might be suitable." Maybe I'd thought about it for the thirty minutes between meeting him and reading that article. But I couldn't get away from the facts.

"You really need to try and be a little more open-minded," Aurora said.

"About what?"

"About new people moving into the village."

"I'm just protective. I just want to preserve what's special about the place. If our new neighbor destroys everything in his path, I don't want Woolton Village to be next on his list."

"You're being so dramatic. I know you want things to stay as they always have been. And you're not good with change, but I just think—"

"I don't know how you can say that—if it wasn't for me, this farm shop wouldn't exist."

"True enough. But I think sometimes you're clinging on to an idealized view of how things *should* be, instead of how they are. All I'm saying is, be open to new ideas. New people."

I welcomed new people. Scarlett had been welcomed into the family, and she was an outsider. An American. And Scarlett's sister, Violet, had become a close friend. Aurora wasn't looking at the facts.

"Did you ever think you're writing this new guy off because he's just not familiar?"

"Aurora, seriously? You read that article. Does he seem like the kind of man I'd be attracted to?"

"But when's the last time you dated?"

"What's that got to do with anything? I'd happily date someone if I met someone I liked."

"Really?" she asked, her raised eyebrows and tilted head calling me out as a liar.

"Really. And you're a fine one to talk."

"If you remember, I went on a date last week."

"Dates in London don't count." It wasn't as if she could get serious about someone who lived in the city any more than I could.

"Darcy, we're an hour and a half away from the city. We're hardly in the Outer Hebrides."

"I'm just being practical."

"So unless someone you like moves in next door, you don't want to date them, but if they *do* move in next door, they're not good enough because they're a weekender, or they're tough in business or their wellies aren't muddy enough."

"You're being ridiculous."

"Am I? So you weren't considering avoiding the new owner of Badsley House?"

"I didn't say that."

"You should have already been by," she said, elbowing

me in the ribs. "You might even find out the newspaper was wrong about him."

"Don't be ridiculous."

"Whoever they are, they're not going to disrupt anything in Woolton, but even if they do, maybe that's a good thing."

Aurora must have a short memory. "How can you say that? Every time we get newcomers in the village, disaster strikes."

"Disaster? You're exaggerating."

"I am? What about the Thompsons and the Foleys? And when Mr. Jenkins got run over by that Aston Martin?"

"But the driver was a friend of Mr. and Mrs. Lonsdale. It wasn't anyone in the village."

"Exactly. People from the city don't understand life out here. They don't know that Mr. Jenkins can't get to the other side of the road as quickly as most people because of his arthritis. They wouldn't think to slow down. They're less compassionate, less thoughtful."

Aurora sighed. "Woolton can't exist in some kind of perfect bubble. Sometimes change can be a good thing."

She would never convince me of that. I'd had far too much change growing up. My mother wandering in and out of our lives as it suited her. My grandmother dying. Then my grandfather falling ill and dying a couple of years ago.

Woolton was the constant. It had always been the life raft I could cling to when everything was falling apart. My world was returning to a new normal, and I just wanted the normal to stick around for a while. I wanted to preserve the village so it was the same place my grandparents lived in, the same place that provided mine and my brother's safe and happy haven. I wanted to maintain it for them, for me, for all the people who would need Woolton

Village as much as I had. That wasn't such a bad thing, was it?

"You know your grandfather would want you to visit the new owners of Badsley."

I sighed. Aurora was right. I really should probably go and introduce myself when I wasn't trespassing and covered in mud. And a basket would be a nice touch. "Okay, you win. Help me pick out some things you think they'd like and I'll go and visit tomorrow."

"You never know, he might get involved in village life— he could be an asset to the village."

"Helicopters and everything," I said, putting some organic asparagus in my basket.

"Keep an open mind," she replied. "He might be a breath of fresh air."

"We have plenty of that." But I'd go and welcome them. At the very least, I could make a plea for him to stop flying over the village.

SIX

Darcy

Visiting my new neighbor at Badsley House was the last thing I wanted to be doing. I tightened my grip on the basket I was carrying and pressed the brass doorbell. Glancing around, the house looked just like it always had. The wisteria that crept up over the door was about to bloom and the box hedging around the driveway was neatly cut.

At the sound of movement on the other side of the door, I pulled my shoulders back and my mouth into a wide smile.

A woman in her mid-fifties smiled back. My mind flicked through possibilities, a housekeeper? No, she was wearing a nurse's uniform, Logan's mother? Was someone ill?

"Hello," I said.

She nodded. "Good afternoon."

"I'm a neighbor—Darcy Westbury. I just popped by to drop this off and welcome you to the village."

"Ahhh, Mrs. Steele is in the garden. Let me show you through."

Mrs. Steele? Did she mean Logan's mother or did the ladies of the W.I. have it wrong when they said Logan was single? "I don't want to impose if someone is unwell. I can come back another time, or just leave this," I said offering the basket of food and gifts. When I was ill, I wanted to curl up in bed and watch reality TV. I certainly didn't want to entertain strangers.

"Mrs. Steele is perfectly fine. Please follow me."

I stepped inside the house and glanced around. There were fewer pictures on the walls, and it looked like the place had been recently decorated, though I hadn't noticed any workmen in the village.

I followed the nurse through the flagstone hallway to the back of the house where the orangery opened up onto the terrace. I'd always loved this room.

The nurse walked ahead of me and up to someone sitting at one of the tables on the terrace. "Mrs. Steele, your new neighbor, Darcy Westbury, is here to see you."

"How delightful," she said, craning her neck to see me. This elderly woman was Mrs. Steele? So not Logan's wife then. Did she live here? With Logan? I had exactly a thousand questions.

She started to stand, but I stopped her. "Please don't get up. I don't want to impose. I just came to drop this off and I will let you be—"

"Nonsense," Mrs. Steele said. "You must stay for tea. Julie, would you see to that?"

Julie beamed. "Certainly. I'll be back shortly."

Mrs. Steele indicated the chair next to me. "Now, come and sit down. You're the first new friend I've made in this village and I won't let you leave until I know all about you."

I laughed and took a seat. It was the kind of thing my grandfather would have said, and despite not knowing anything about Mrs. Steele, I decided I liked her.

"So how are you enjoying the garden?" I asked.

"Isn't it wonderful? So many memories. And do you know, the gardener has agreed to stay on with us? I'm so pleased."

I grinned, thankful that Mr. Fawsley's talents were recognized. "Well, that was very nice of him. So, you're here on your own today? With Julie?"

"Logan's in London, but will be back shortly. Really, he shouldn't be spending so much time with his grandmother, but there's no telling him what to do. I think he's trying to make sure I'm settled, although he'd never admit it. He's such a thoughtful young man. I'm so proud of him."

The way she described him suggested a very different person than the one described in the article in *The Times*, but my grandfather used to dote on me like Mrs. Steele clearly doted on Logan. I missed that feeling of having someone completely on my team.

"So you live here? With Logan?" The man I'd met didn't strike me as the type who lived with his grandmother.

"Well, he insists it's my house." She shook her head. "That boy. But yes, this is my home and Logan's at the weekend. And you're from the village, dear?"

"Yes. At Woolton Hall."

"Oh my—you're the Duke of Fairfax's granddaughter?"

"Well, sister now." I'd been the Duke of Fairfax's grand-daughter for most of my adult life, and it still felt odd to think of my brother as the duke.

"Yes, I heard about your grandfather. I'm so sorry. He was a good man. I liked him very much."

"You knew my grandfather?"

She nodded. "A lifetime ago. Oh, we had such fun. Your grandfather was very mischievous when he was young. The ringleader of our crowd. Although marriage tamed him somewhat, I do think your grandmother was the perfect match for him. She seemed to encourage his spark in the right direction."

Joy and confusion bloomed in my chest at her memories. "My grandmother loved his mischievous nature," I replied. "How did you know each other?"

"Didn't I say? I grew up in Woolton Village. In this very house." She glanced around. "Not much has changed."

"You used to live here in Woolton? But I've been here since I was a small child." Mrs. Brookely had lived here for as long as I'd been alive.

She sighed. "I left over three decades ago. I have such wonderful memories from the place. And I think over the years I must have talked about the place to Logan more often than I should have."

I was so taken aback, I hardly knew what to say. "And you used to know my grandfather." If only he was here. They could swap stories, share memories. "Did you know each other well?"

"Yes. Very well. I knew your grandmother too. We all moved in the same circles, even more so when I married. Back in those days the British aristocracy was like an exclusive little club." So Logan *was* an earl. He hadn't introduced himself that way. "My husband's ancestral home was up in Scotland and that was never my favorite place. When he died, I moved back down here to my parents' place to help out with Logan after he was born." I thought I caught a look of sadness in her eyes, but almost as if to make up for it, she smiled widely. "I suppose this is the third time I've come back. Some places are just special, I guess."

Mrs. Steele wasn't an outsider. She'd known the village longer than I had, understood how wonderful it was. "Welcome back. It's so wonderful to meet someone who was friends with my grandparents."

"Thank you, my dear. It's good to be back. Anyway, enough about me. I heard your brother lives in America. Is it just you up at the house?"

I didn't want to talk about me. I wanted to hear more about Mrs. Steele and my grandparents when they were young. But I would have to be patient. "Well, just me and everyone else who helps look after the place."

"So you're not married, dear?"

I shook my head.

"Do you have a boyfriend? You're very pretty. I'm sure you must have suitors lining up."

I laughed. She was nosy, but sweet. I couldn't be offended. "There's no line. And no boyfriend."

"I don't know what it is with you young people. Logan's the same." She sighed as Julie delivered our tea, then disappeared again. "No girlfriend and doesn't seem to get any closer to having a family with each passing year."

I didn't respond, unsure of what to say. I got the feeling Mrs. Steele's comments were deliberately aimed at me, but given we'd just met, she couldn't be suggesting that I should take an interest in her grandson, could she?

"Will you be mother?" Mrs. Steele asked, inviting me to pour the tea.

"Of course. It would be my pleasure." I set about checking the strength of the tea and arranging cups and saucers before pouring us both a cup.

"So tell me why such a lovely, pretty girl like you doesn't have a boyfriend, or a queue of waiting men." Without looking away from me, she took a sip of her tea.

I smiled at her. "I'm married to the estate. It's my family's legacy and I really enjoy making sure it's ready for the next generation. It doesn't leave time for much else."

"Gosh, my Logan's just the same. Work, work, work. But he always has time for me."

The distant sounds of a helicopter echoed above us. My gut churned. I really didn't want to run into Logan again. My conversation with Mrs. Steele was so confusing. Instead of confirming that Logan was just some city type who was spoiled and entitled with no love of the countryside, he had some kind of right to be here. And he'd bought this place to keep his grandmother happy. I needed a chance to rearrange my thoughts.

"Is it me, or do you hear a helicopter?" Mrs. Steele asked.

There was no mistaking it. "Yes, it sounds like your grandson is on his way back."

"Perfect. You'll get to meet him. I think you two are going to get along famously. How old are you, Darcy?"

"Twenty-eight."

"Excellent," was all she said.

What was excellent about being twenty-eight? It was far too close to thirty for my liking. Before I got a chance to ask, the overwhelming sound of the helicopter prevented any more talking. We watched as it landed and Logan stepped out.

He grinned and waved at his grandmother before turning his attention toward me. I offered a wave in return as my heart began to thunder through my blouse. I hadn't remembered quite how handsome he was. As he came toward us, warmth travelled through my body and I couldn't help but smile.

Today, he wore a navy-blue suit without a tie and he

seemed even taller than I remembered. His square jaw had a day's worth of stubble on it, and his broad chest and confident walk fought for my attention. This man knew he was attractive. Enjoyed it. And I couldn't blame him. Aurora was going to think I was full of crap when she saw him in the flesh. Perhaps I shouldn't have been so quick to dismiss how good-looking he was.

From the confused look on his face, it didn't look as if he remembered me. Perhaps that was just as well.

"Logan, so wonderful to have you home early on a Friday," Mrs. Steele said, a smile on her face as wide as the sky. She clearly adored him.

He took the three steps up on to the terrace and bent and kissed his grandmother on the cheek. "Well I couldn't let you enjoy this beautiful day on your own a moment longer. But apparently, I needn't have worried," he replied, glancing at me, his eyes sparkling. I couldn't tell if it was curiosity as to what I was doing there, or general pleasure at being home. Either way, I couldn't stop staring. Who was this man? Every time I heard something more about him, I had to change my mind about who he was. From horse-whisperer to corporate raider to granny's boy and back.

"Let me introduce my new friend, Darcy. She lives up at Woolton Hall, which is her family's estate."

I smiled and held out my hand. "Hi," I said, still unsure whether or not he recognized me.

"Nice to see you again," he replied, taking my hand in his firm grip, his voice vibrating across my skin. Apparently, I didn't look that different, clean or muddy.

Out of the corner of my eye, I caught Mrs. Steele glancing between us. "You know each other?"

A small grin curled his lips as he held my gaze. "I met Darcy last Sunday on my walk around the boundary. I think

I mentioned it. I'm afraid to say, Granny, that I don't think I left a very good impression."

"Oh dear. What did you do?" She patted the seat next to her and Logan sat—directly opposite me.

"Nothing." I shook my head, feeling the intensity of his stare as I addressed his grandmother. "Nothing at all. It was me. I was covered in mud and I was trespassing—I've gotten far too used to the previous owners of Badsley House being very relaxed about me riding on their land. I'm sorry."

"You have no need to be. You were right. It is a beautiful view," he replied. "Shall we start again from now?"

Heat rose in my cheeks as I nodded. I needed a fresh start with him, perhaps I'd judged him too harshly. "Sure. Fresh start."

"Darcy brought us this beautiful gift," Mrs. Steele said. "She's such a thoughtful girl, and devoted to her family's estate, isn't that right? Sounds to me like you deserve some time off. Do you go out anywhere in the evenings? Perhaps you'd show my grandson what young people do in the village. I don't want him getting bored, sitting in with me all weekend."

Logan chuckled. "I could never get bored beating you at gin rummy, Granny."

"Beat me? As if. I taught you everything you know."

"True enough."

It was lovely to see Logan and Mrs. Steele interact, but it made me a little sad that I wasn't able to tease my grandfather anymore, that he wasn't able to scold me for running about the house in bare feet. I wonder if there would ever be a day when I didn't miss him.

"But I go to bed early anyway—you really should find out what goes on in the evenings. Darcy, what kind of thing do you get up to?"

"I wish I could tell you some scandalous stories, or even just a few interesting ones. I'm a homebody, so I enjoy being at Woolton with my grandfather's library and a hot bath."

Logan's eyebrows pulsed upward. "Now that does sound potentially scandalous," he said.

I straightened, a little embarrassed by his reaction. I hadn't meant to be flirtatious. "It's anything but. Since my grandfather passed away I live a very quiet life, although sometimes my best friend and I go into the village because the pub serves great food, and we can catch up with people. My family has a house in London, so I tend to save socializing for when I'm in town."

"Where's your place in London?" Logan leaned back and his legs crept toward me as he stretched out.

"Hill Street, Mayfair."

Logan looked confused and I couldn't tell if he was trying to remember where Hill Street was or if he was surprised that a country bumpkin like me stayed in town. I might feel more comfortable at home at Woolton, but that didn't mean I couldn't handle London.

"Logan's used to life in the city. I don't want him to get bored out here. It's enough that he's made it possible for me to come home. He shouldn't have to spend all his time with me. You'd be doing me a tremendous favor by getting him out and about, if you wouldn't mind?"

"Now, Granny, I fear you're getting a little mischievous. Darcy doesn't want to have to babysit me."

He had a charming way of getting himself out of a tricky situation, which I rather admired. He made it sound like it would be a burden for me, though we both knew he didn't want to go.

"Quiz night's on Thursdays—there's usually lots of villagers there. It would be a great place to meet more people. And Mrs. Steele, you might consider joining the local chapter of the Women's Institute. They're a fixture of Woolton Village and hold their meetings at Woolton Hall from time to time."

"I've never thought of myself as a W.I. kind of woman, but I'm keen to get to know the village."

"And I hope you don't mind me mentioning it, but Mrs. Brookely, who lived here before you, opened her gardens the first Saturday each month to the village. And I know the villagers are very fond of Mr. Fawsley's work, so you might want to consider doing something similar."

Mrs. Steele threw up her hands. "Of course. We must do that. I had no idea, did you, Logan?"

Logan grinned as he shook his head, his chest expanding as he leaned back in his chair, his eyes still fixed on me so that every time I glanced at him our gaze met. "We can make that happen."

"I'm so pleased you mentioned it, my dear. I know how difficult it can be to move into a new place and I want to make sure we do our part as members of the community, isn't that right, Logan?"

"Absolutely," said Logan.

"But I should leave you in peace," I said. "I'll let you know about the next W.I. meeting, Mrs. Steele."

"Thank you, and Logan, will you be able to make the quiz meeting this Thursday?" she asked.

Logan frowned. Did he think an evening with me so burdensome? Not that I had any desire to babysit him, as he put it.

"I'll be in London," I replied so he didn't assume there'd be any enforced time together. "But of course, do go on your own. People are very friendly." I was having dinner with my brother, who would be on a layover from New York to Beijing.

"Well, that is disappointing," Mrs. Steele said. "But another time. I think you two have so much in common. Both young, good-looking people devoted to their family. You should get to know each other."

Mrs. Steele might be elderly, but that didn't stop her playing at being a matchmaker.

"Grandmother," Logan growled in warning. "I'm sure Darcy can arrange her social life without your help. And I know I can."

Mrs. Steele shrugged and took a sip of her tea as if she hadn't quite heard her grandson's admonishment. And I tried to hide my blush at Logan making it clear, so charmingly, that he wasn't interested in spending any time with me. Not that I was with him. But still.

I stood and thanked Mrs. Steele for her hospitality.

"I'll see you out," Logan said, grasping the sides of his chair. We walked out, Logan following me.

"It was good to see you again," he said, his voice low and gravelly. I almost jumped as his large hand briefly touched my lower back just as we reached the front door.

I glanced up at him and I blinked, trying to formulate an appropriate response which I knew should have been easier, but my mind was blank. I nodded, unable to come up with anything.

He tilted his head. "No mud today. But still the same smile."

"No mud," I said pressing my mouth into a self-conscious straight line. "Have a good weekend."

As I got to the gate on the other side of the drive, I glanced back to find Logan watching me. What was he thinking?

If I hadn't seen him here today, I wouldn't have imagined him as the sort of man who came home to spend weekends with his grandmother playing gin rummy. From what I'd read about him, I would have thought he was more the type who had a different date every night, went to all the top bars and restaurant openings in London, and had some office in a skyscraper where he barked orders at people and made a ton of money while destroying people's businesses.

Which Logan Steele was the real man underneath the custom suit and the charming smile?

SEVEN

Darcy

As soon as I saw Ryder, I squealed. I just couldn't help myself. It was always good to see him, but since Grandfather had died, I needed our time together even more. I scurried toward him. "It's so good to see you, even if only for dinner," I said as I held his face in my hands.

He kissed me on the cheek, then extracted himself and indicated the chair opposite him. We always ended up coming to this place, which was a relaxed local Italian restaurant around the corner from the Hill Street house. How it survived amongst all the Michelin-starred restaurants in this area, I had no idea, but I was pleased it did. The staff were friendly and the food was always incredible. "I saw you on FaceTime two days ago when you were gossiping with my wife. It's hardly like we are strangers."

"First, I can't squeeze your cute little cheeks on Face-Time." I reached across the table to grab another handful, but he backed out of reach. "Second, we weren't gossiping, we were talking about the summer party. It's important."

"Whatever you say."

"Exactly right."

"So what's going on in your world?" he asked. "Any village scandal I should know about?"

"We have some new villagers. Well, sort of new. A Mrs. Steele. She used to live in the village when she was young, apparently. She knew Grandfather and Granny. I guess she wasn't Mrs. Steele back then. She married an earl and moved away ..." I paused. Had she told me why she'd left the village? She'd come back after she was married, but why had she left again? "Anyway, she's back. And her grandson bought the place and he comes down on weekends."

"Do you recognize her from before?"

I shook my head as I patted the napkin on my lap. "No, she moved away before we were born. Thirty years ago."

Ryder was trying to act interested, but I could tell he couldn't care less. "Mrs. Brookely died, right?"

I rolled my eyes. "Yes. Anyway, they've agreed to keep the gardens open to villagers on first Saturdays, so that's a good start."

"They sound very accommodating. I'm not sure I'd like strangers wandering about in my house."

The helicopter wasn't so accommodating, but I wasn't about to mention that in case it gave Ryder ideas. "People won't be wandering about in the house. It's just the gardens. And they're so beautiful—don't you remember?"

Ryder shook his head. I'd only ever left Woolton for university, but Ryder hadn't lived there since. Maybe that was why he didn't have the pull toward the village and the way of life, or even toward Woolton Hall, that I did.

"Do you remember how we used to play in the Badsley woods there?"

"Sure. We were so little. I can't imagine letting my kids

wander off on their own before their twenty-first birthdays. You were barely out of nappies."

Good memories from that time were few and far between and the ones we had were made together on days in Badsley's woods or the grounds of Woolton. And eventually the good blotted out the bad.

"I know. I guess Grandfather and Granny felt we were safe. And they were right."

"Safe once she'd finally left us," he mumbled, referring to our mother. I learned later that it was that summer when my grandfather put his foot down and told his daughter that her children needed a full-time parent, and that although she was welcome to visit us, we would live at Woolton Hall from then on. Her visits were infrequent and grew more so over time.

At the beginning of that summer, Ryder was the only one I spoke to. He'd been my interpreter. My protector. The only one I trusted. But that first summer at Woolton opened me up, cloaked me in warmth and consistency and eventually over dinner, I began to help Ryder tell our grandparents the stories of our daily adventures. The four-leaf clovers we'd found, the dens we'd built, the trees we'd climbed. Woolton had helped me find my voice that summer.

"I'm glad she left us," I said.

Ryder sighed. "I just don't get it. Not then, but especially not now that we've got Gwendoline and Toby."

"I know." I reached across and squeezed his hand, my heart tugging at his reference to my niece and nephew. Ryder was a workaholic control freak, but he worshipped his children and his wife, and I knew would stand in front of a bus for them. And for me. To him, that's what family did. That's what our grandparents did for us when they kept us at Woolton Hall.

He glanced over my shoulder. "Hey," he mouthed, greeting someone across the room. The reason I liked this restaurant was because Ryder didn't run into business associates. "I'll just be a second." He stood and placed his napkin on the chair.

"I've not seen you in forever," he said, greeting one of the endless number of people Ryder knew.

"Not since that conference in Vegas," a familiar voice said, and I snapped my head around as realization dawned. Logan grinned back at me. "I've seen a lot more of your sister. It's all starting to fit into place now. Hi, Darcy." Logan bent and kissed me on the cheek.

"You two know each other?" Ryder asked, sinking back into his chair.

"My grandmother and I just moved into Woolton Village. I'd not realized that Woolton Hall was your family's place."

"You bought Badsley House? What a small fucking world, we were just talking about you," Ryder said.

"No, we weren't." I said, shooting Ryder a look.

Ryder pulled up a chair from the empty table next to us. "Well, join us, sit down."

Wait, what? I didn't want to make polite conversation with a near-perfect stranger. Especially one I hadn't figured out yet.

"That would be great," Logan said. "My meeting just got canceled, so I was about to enjoy the steak alone."

"Darcy was just getting me caught up on the Woolton gossip."

"She seems to know everything about what goes on," Logan said. "I'm learning the ropes. Pub quiz on Thursdays.

Open gardens on the first Saturday of the month, right?" He grinned at me.

I couldn't tell if he was teasing me. But why would he understand what a special place it was? "The village is a lovely place to live and the people are wonderful and kind. We care about each other."

"So far so good." He held my gaze as if trying to see beyond my words and into my mind. "The farm shop at the end of the village is fantastic. I took my grandmother there on Sunday."

"That was all Darcy," Ryder said.

"It was your idea?" Logan asked.

"Not just her idea. She did the business plan, got the bank loan, planning permission, sourced all the suppliers. Picked a team to run it. My sister is a force of nature." If I didn't know better, I would have said my brother was proud of me. "I told her I'd fund it, but she insisted on doing it herself."

"That's very impressive," Logan said.

"I know it's small fry compared to your billion-dollar deals, but it's not just about a farm shop," I said. "It's about sustaining local producers and supporting village life. It was a passion project."

"Starting a business, big or small, takes a lot of hard work and courage. And I find approaching something with passion always leads to better results."

It wasn't the reaction I expected. I thought his approach to business would be cold hard facts and numbers, given the article I'd read. I couldn't help but wonder what *he* approached with passion. "I don't know how to approach things in any other way but with my heart."

Ryder's phone buzzed and he excused himself from the table.

"So here we are again," Logan said his eyes twinkling, his jaw no less sharp.

"I'm not sure we've been here before," I replied.

"You and me. We keep running into each other."

"It's a small world, I guess."

He shrugged. "Maybe. So what's next for you now the farm shop is up and running? Any more passion projects?"

"I'm sure I'll find something. But I have plenty to keep me busy in the meantime." Logan stretched out his long legs under the table brushing against my thigh. But he didn't shift. Or apologize, he just kept his gaze steady and focused directly on me. Was he waiting for me to react to his touch, to elaborate on what I'd been saying? He seemed so comfortable with the silence.

My heart tripped in my chest and I stuttered. "There's always so much to do. There's the full-time staff, the stables and then a regular cycle of things that go wrong at the house —it's never-ending."

The corners of his mouth twitched and his lips spread into a slow, wide smile as if he'd discovered a secret. "I'm sure. But you make time for Ryder."

"He's important. My family. Of course I make time for him. But it's fine. I got caught up on a lot of paperwork this past weekend so I could steal some free time now."

"And you visited my grandmother. That was very thoughtful."

I blushed. Not at his compliment, but knowing how close I'd been to not going. "The village is my passion project."

"Well, she really appreciated it. I did too."

"I'm surprised you have the time to spend in Woolton."

"Like you said, she's my family, and that's what you do."

I tried to bite back a smile. Maybe Aurora had been

right and the person who'd written the article about Logan had some kind of personal vendetta. I prided myself on being an excellent judge of character, but there were so many conflicting sides to Logan, it was difficult to see who he was at his core.

I couldn't decide what to make of him. The guy was clearly a player. Too good-looking, with his perfect hair, sparkling blue eyes and hard body. I was sure he got his own way personally and professionally because of the subtle flirting. His confidence, the article in the newspaper. It all painted one picture. But then his relationship with his grandmother—the way he'd bought her childhood home for her. And the way he talked about approaching business with a passion? That was something entirely different. It was as if he'd broken my people compass and I couldn't find north anymore.

"Tell me more about the shop," he said, and when I glanced back up, I found him looking at me. He was asking me about something I was certain he had no interest in. Was he being polite or condescending?

"Nothing much to tell. I do what I can to preserve village life. It helps local suppliers, but it's good for the village because it draws people in from the surrounding villages and they spend money in the pub and at the post office."

"And you went to university, right?"

"Kings, London," I replied.

He nodded. "Smart girl. But you didn't want to go somewhere more rural? I had you pegged for someone who might go to a Scottish university."

"Are you interviewing me for a job I haven't applied for?" I asked. Where were all his questions coming from?

He chuckled. "You're funny," he said. "I don't normally

look for funny in a woman." He glanced at my mouth and I found myself taking in his perfectly shaped cupid's bow.

"What do you mean you don't look for funny?"

He frowned and shifted in his seat and for the first time he seemed like he wasn't in complete control. "I'm just trying to...Never mind. I'm just trying to get to know you, that's all." Was I as confusing to him as he was to me? "It's interesting that you're so passionate about Woolton."

"It's where I grew up, so of course I'm passionate about it."

"But that doesn't always follow, does it? Lots of people move away from where they grew up—Ryder's based in New York."

"Why would I move away when I'm happy? It's a beautiful place—peaceful and calm. I enjoy my life there."

"You never get bored?"

Irritation prickled at my neck. I couldn't tell if it was from the fact that he assumed that being in Woolton was boring. But also because the answer wasn't a flat-out no. I'd never told anyone, but my reasons for getting the farm shop up and running was for all the reasons I said it was, and one more. I'd wanted the challenge. Since university, I'd been slowly taking over running Woolton Estate, but I'd still expected my grandfather's death to bring more issues. But those had been emotional more than anything else. I'd needed something more. "Do you ever get bored doing what you do?"

His gaze flitted behind me, then back. He grinned. "What, flying all over the world, meeting new people, doing deals, running a multi-billion-pound company?"

"Yeah. Doing the same thing every day, whatever it is, can be boring." I never understood the appeal of being behind a desk or chained to a telephone all day. I couldn't think of anything duller.

"Of course, I don't get bored," he said, his words a little more clipped than usual. He ran his hand through his hair. "Jeez. You have a spiky side."

I let out a genuine laugh. I couldn't doubt that he was saying exactly what was on his mind. "Just trying to figure you out. Maybe I'm pushing your buttons a little, seeing how deep the charm goes. I can't quite decide about you."

His mouth curved into a grin and he shook his head. It was as if we'd both revealed a different side to ourselves. He thought I had a spiky side. I didn't know what to make of him. It was as if we'd been circling each other, trying to work the other out and finally we'd put our cards on the table.

"You're right. I was being defensive. I'm trying to figure you out too." He owned his response and I respected that. He'd been honest with me. "But I think I like you. I don't have enough people in my life who call me on my bullshit." He shot me a grin and took a sip of his wine. "And, you know, it's always nice to hear a woman tell me I'm charming."

"Yeah, I love being told how people *think* they like me. Let me know when you've made up your mind." I grinned.

His eyes flickered down to my mouth and back up. "I think I just did."

My pulse began to throb in my neck and my skin tightened. I rarely got flustered, and I couldn't ever remember having such a physical reaction to a man. I blinked once and took a deep breath. "What I was trying to say was at the end of the day, I have people counting on me. Livelihoods that depend on the estate. That's a responsibility that I can't afford to be bored by." That was the truth. "Every day is different and there's always some kind of fresh disaster or problem that needs solving. But yeah, I can sometimes yearn for something more. I think the farm shop was part of that." I'd not told anyone that. Why him?

He pulled in a breath and held my gaze. "I get that. I *totally* get it. I guess it doesn't matter if I'm travelling all over the world doing God knows what, you're right—I can still get bored. No matter the size of my balance sheet, I've been feeling lately that *something more* is exactly what I need."

If I'd thought I was confused about Logan before, our conversation was just making it worse. Tonight, he wasn't a corporate bad boy or a charming granny's boy. He was still charming and a little flirtatious, but he seemed honest, almost vulnerable and far more interesting to me than he had been since I'd first met him. I couldn't deny it any longer—I liked him. Even if my mind tried to deny it, my body betrayed me. I had a growing crush on the man sitting in front of me.

EIGHT

Logan

I'd made up my mind. I liked this girl. More so every time we spoke. That first day when she was covered in mud and she'd taken it all in her stride and smiled so wide I almost couldn't look away. Then when I saw her, sitting on the terrace with my grandmother—she seemed to embody an English summer, all lightness and sunshine. Everything I discovered about her made me want to know more.

But the pull toward her was all so inexplicable, because it was 180 degrees from my normal M.O.

She'd called me out on being condescending and even though I'd been a little taken off-guard at first, I found I liked her for it. Other than my grandmother, I couldn't think who else I knew who would do that.

"What?" she asked, and I realized I was staring at her.

"Nothing. Just taking it all in."

"Taking what in?"

"You."

She rolled her eyes, which made me want to pull her onto my knee and slide my hand up her skirt.

What was happening to me? She wasn't any more my type now than she'd been ten days ago when I'd first met her. In fact, she was probably *less* my type. I liked high-powered female executives who crawled across the room to earn my dick in their mouth. Not women who spent the day in Wellington boots and gave me shit across a restaurant table.

Until now.

She wasn't impressed with my money, my status or the company I'd built from scratch. She saw all that for what it was.

"I find people interesting. Is there anything wrong in that?"

"You mean you find trying to figure out how to get women to sleep with you interesting."

I chuckled. "You think I'm trying to figure out how to get you to sleep with me?" She wasn't wrong, and I admired how confident she was.

"Are you?"

"I like to understand what makes people tick—men and women," I replied. "But yes, I suppose I am."

She grinned. "Men too? I didn't have you down as—"

"I'm not into men." I looked her right in the eye. There were some things I didn't joke about. "Not sexually. I'm saying I like to understand how men and women work, what motivates them, irritates them. I see a lot of the same kind of people, and I get used to being able to figure them out really easily. I guess I got a little lazy. I've made assumptions about you that I shouldn't have."

"Yeah?" She paused and pulled her bottom lip between her teeth. "Well, maybe I did the same to you."

I grinned. I liked the thought of her wondering about me. Of her trying to work me out. "Right. Tell me what assumptions you made about me, and I'll tell you if you're right."

She laughed. "As if. You'll just tell me what you believe I want to hear."

"That's not who I am."

"Never?"

"Right now, I can't think of a situation when I would need to do that."

"You're saying you don't tell women what they want to hear so they'll sleep with you?"

I was definitely attracted to her, which I was still trying to figure out. And I definitely wanted her to *want* me to seduce her. There was nothing more flattering. But if she took the bait, would I close the deal?

"You think I need to tell a woman what she wants to hear in order to sleep with her?" She clearly underestimated how many horny women there were in this city. I was handsome, successful, and kept myself in shape—I didn't have to work for it.

"I guess it depends on your appetite." She glanced away, perhaps not ready to see that appetite reflected back at her. She was so bloody cute.

I paused, waiting for her to look back at me. "Is that right?"

She shrugged. "I'm sure it's easy to find willing women, looking like you do. Up to a point." She looked right at me and my heart began to thud against my rib cage. "Depends how often you like to...fuck."

A lot, baby. A hell of a lot. "I don't have to try very hard," I said, keeping things deliberately ambiguous.

Who was I kidding? Of course I'd like to close the deal

with this woman. I might have done business with her brother, and we might be neighbors, but I was rarely intrigued by a woman. If she was up for it, I'd definitely like to explore that. Explore *her*. See how those curves moved when they weren't covered up–having a type meant I'd been indulging in the same body over and over for the last couple of years. Perhaps fucking Darcy would keep things interesting.

She narrowed her eyes and I held her gaze, willing her to challenge me. I liked her spirit.

But Ryder interrupted us as he came back to the table slicing through whatever that had been building between us. "Darcy, don't hate me, but we have to go. There's been a security alert at the airport and they're requiring an early check-in." He sighed. "I hate flying commercial."

"Really?" She looked devastated. "Since when did you start flying commercial?"

"Trying to fly private into China is ridiculous. Come on, I'll drop you off on the way."

She glanced at me, and for a moment my heart lifted in my chest. Was she going to stay with me? But her gaze didn't fall on me, it went to the plate of pasta that had just been delivered.

My seduction technique clearly needed some polishing up, but it was probably for the best. Going home for the weekend to see my grandmother might get difficult if something was to happen with Darcy. I had no idea if she'd have some kind of expectation of me beyond sex. And there was nothing to expect of me in that regard.

"Stay and eat," I suggested out of nowhere. "I can see you home."

"It's just around the corner. I can see myself home."

Darcy glanced at Ryder and then back at me. "But I'll stay and have dinner. No point in it going to waste."

"Good idea. I know how much you like your pasta," Ryder said.

"I'll see you and Scarlett in a couple of weeks?" Darcy said.

"Yes, we're bringing the kids. We'll have plenty of time then, more than just a rushed half dinner."

Darcy's shoulders sank. "Okay," she said slumping back into her seat. "Don't miss your flight."

"Good to see you, Darcy, and Logan," he said, looking at me. "Don't let her walk home on her own."

"Absolutely on all counts," I said and shook Ryder's hand. "She's safe with me." That was a blatant lie. Thirty seconds ago, I'd been imagining his sister naked, her large breasts swaying as I thrust into her from behind. Shit. I swallowed. "I'll make sure she gets home safely." I nodded and tried to look serious.

"You look a little flustered," Darcy said when Ryder left. She picked up her fork and began to twist it in the strands of pasta.

"Me? I don't get flustered." Thinking about a business colleague's sister, naked and panting while shaking his hand, was as close as I'd ever gotten to flustered. I clearly needed to get laid. I should drop Darcy off and find a bar somewhere. Something to take this edge off.

"So, you seem close with your grandmother. What's that about?" she asked, then popped a forkful of spaghetti into her mouth.

That was an easy way to shut down my imagining what was under her jumper, how much I'd like to peel off her jeans. "What do you mean? She's my grandmother."

"But you seem close. She lives with you, or you with

her. At the weekend, at least." She sat back and narrowed her eyes, studying me as if she thought I might be a closet jewel thief.

"We've always been close. We're a small family, and I'm her only grandson. I like to look after her."

"Where are your parents?" she asked, slipping another forkful of pasta into her mouth.

My family background was nothing I wanted to get into. "Wanna know my blood group?"

She shrugged. "It's called conversation—you're not used to it?"

I chuckled. "You're just direct." I didn't talk with the women I fucked. There was no need. And I didn't have women friends I took to dinner. I was unprepared for whatever it was we were doing.

"I guess. I'm just interested. There's a lot of things about you that add up, but living with your grandmother on weekends isn't one of them."

"What doesn't add up about it?"

"Well, you're a guy, who's what, thirty-five?"

I nodded. Jesus, was that just a guess?

"You're rich, good-looking..."

Yes and yes.

"Cocky. Clearly a player."

"Now that's not very nice," I said.

"Do you prefer 'confident' and 'likes women'?" she asked, grinning.

I grinned. "Much better." This girl.

"But you don't spend your weekends in London partying, entertaining, or enjoying the good life. You're home having tea on the terrace."

"I can enjoy the good life while drinking tea on the terrace. Badsley's gardens are beautiful."

She laughed. "But you get my point."

"Well, maybe I'm complicated."

"Maybe not." She grinned at me and then beckoned over the waiter. "Can I have the bill, please?"

Apparently, she was done. "How was your pasta?" I asked, wanting our conversation to continue.

"Good," she said, her eyes flashing—carefree and enthusiastic in a way I'd not seen before. "How was yours?"

The waiter delivered the bill. "I'll get—"

"You absolutely will not." She snatched it out of my reach. "This is my treat."

I grinned. It was something my grandmother would say. "Darcy," I warned. "Let me pay. What would Ryder think if I let you?"

"He'd think it was the twenty-first century and I could afford a bowl of pasta and a steak." She handed over her credit card and punched her PIN into the machine.

"Not many women have bought me dinner."

"Probably because you don't deserve it," she said, smiling at me as if she'd paid me a huge compliment. "Well, it's been enlightening, neighbor, but I have a big day tomorrow, so I'm going to have to get my beauty sleep."

"Darcy, you picking up the bill is one, but there's no way on Earth I'm going to let you walk home on your own."

"It's just around the corner. I'll be fine."

"I'll just walk behind you, and that's just going to look as if I'm following you—I could get arrested. You want that on your conscience?"

She stood and pulled on her jacket. Her jeans clung to her hips in the most delicious way and her jumper that, although it wasn't low-cut, made her breasts look bigger than I remembered. It took all my willpower to keep my eyes on her face.

"You okay?" she asked as she pulled her bag off the back of her chair.

"Yes," I said, indicating I'd follow her out. How did she manage to look so sexy without any effort? I liked that she hadn't dressed up. Sure, she'd been out with her brother, but still, she was confident enough that she didn't have to put on a ton of makeup or wear a provocative outfit. Did she realize she was just innately sexy? Did she know that ninety percent of the men in this restaurant had imagined her naked? "Let's go," I said, blocking her, territorially. I could look at her without dribbling. Just. But I wasn't sure it would be true for all the other guys in this place.

We climbed the steps in single file and when we got to the top she paused, glanced at me over her shoulder and smiled a small, sweet, private smile that pulled all the breath from my lungs.

"You're beautiful," I spluttered before I could help myself.

She laughed and pulled up the collar of her jacket. "You make it sound like that's a problem. I thought you were supposed to be this smooth player."

I chuckled. "You're right. I'm an idiot. It's just…"

She ignored me and started up the road, so I strode after her until we walked next to each other, our hands burrowed into our pockets.

"I don't normally tell women." That wasn't true. I told women they were beautiful all the time, but in a way that was unthinking. As if I was talking about the weather or my commute. Not that they *weren't* beautiful. I just didn't focus on it. But with Darcy, it came out cack-handed because it was true. I knew it and I meant it. "Not women I'm friends with."

"We're friends?" she asked. "Since when?" Her eyes danced mischievously under the overhead streetlights.

I nudged her with my shoulder, trying to bite back a grin. "You're hard work, Miss Westbury."

"I'm just immune to your player ways. That's what growing up knee-deep in mud and climbing trees does to you."

"Inoculates you from being seduced by inappropriate men?"

"This is you trying to seduce me?" She stopped walking, the streetlight behind her, catching on the stray strands of hair, lifted by the wind. She was more than beautiful. I stepped closer to her and she took a step back, so she was flat against the wall of one of Mayfair's grand townhouses.

Women I normally spent time with were glossy and primed, with perfect bodies and sharp minds. Darcy was like a fresh, floral breeze that had floated in and made every other woman I'd ever known seem like they were trying a bit too hard.

I moved closer again and swept a strand of hair away from her face. Her breath hitched and my eyes dipped to her mouth, down to her full breasts and back up so our eyes locked. She was edible. I wanted to sink my teeth into that soft, milky-white skin, slip my hands under her jumper, and squeeze and pull at her nipples until she groaned and begged me for more.

She reached up and trailed a finger along my jaw and I blinked, enjoying the warmth of her touch.

I placed my hands on either side of her head. "I'm going to kiss you."

We both stared at each other, heat building between us as we savored the moment before I leaned forward and pressed my lips to hers. She smoothed her palms up my chest and I tried to savor the feeling each place our bodies joined. She tasted of summer meadows and rain, and I wanted to treat her like glass and fuck her into next week at the same time.

I broke off, uncertain about whether I could stop myself if I stayed as close for any longer.

"Hey. I'm not done yet." She beamed up at me.

I growled, and pressed up against her, my hips pinning her to the wall, showing her who was in charge. "You don't get to say if we're done or not."

She braced her hands against my shoulders and tried to hold me back. "I don't get a say?"

Hearing her reaction to it, my comment sounded brash and unnecessary, but I was so used to running things in my sexual encounters. But there was nothing normal about what we were doing. Not for me. She was a neighbor. She knew my grandmother. I was likely to run into her all the time. She was definitely not someone I should be taking to bed.

But that didn't mean I couldn't kiss her once more.

She gasped as I ran my tongue over her lips and delved inside. She tasted perfect—warm and soft—but I couldn't stop thinking about how her pussy would be sweeter. It was the last place I should be letting my mind wander to, but her fingers were tightening in my shirt and her short little breaths were pulling at my patience and hardening my cock.

Before I gave in and pulled her legs around my waist and ground against her knickers, she broke off our kiss, and ducked under my arm. "Yes, well. I think that's quite enough." She cleared her throat and smoothed down her clothes. "This is me," she said, avoiding my gaze and nodding at the door. "Thank you for walking me home."

It was as if she'd stopped herself before she wouldn't be able to. Before she lost control. Before she enjoyed herself too much.

"It was very much my pleasure," I replied, wondering if she was the same in bed. I imagined she didn't get much opportunity to let loose. Those country boys probably thrust in and out a few times, never giving her pleasure a second thought. I'd like to fuck her until she had no choice but to come—sweaty, screaming and desperate.

"Goodnight, Mr. Player," she said, trying to bite back a smile as she turned the key in the lock and went inside.

I repressed a smile. She was just so bloody adorable. But thankfully, she'd not invited me to come in. I would have said no and hated myself for it. Or worse, I'd have said yes and hated myself for it.

Either way, Darcy Westbury was a lose-lose situation. And I couldn't help but wonder when I'd see her again.

NINE

Darcy

It still didn't feel quite right to be hosting people at Woolton Hall. My grandparents had been natural hosts. But I'd have to get better at it—the summer party would be here before I knew it. I straightened the last row of chairs in the dining room just as Aurora came in, carrying a tray of sandwiches.

"Perfect," I said. "Just put them on the table." I'd pushed the dining table against the back wall to make room for the fifteen chairs I'd arranged in three rows. As well as the Woolton W.I. chapter, a number of other local groups had been invited along to listen to the speaker today.

"What time are they arriving?" Aurora asked.

"Any moment," I replied. "But I think we're ready." I could have used a number of rooms at Woolton for the W.I. meeting, but this one wasn't too big and held wonderful memories.

"What's the speaker talking about?"

"The economy and whether or not we're about to hit another financial crisis."

"Cheery," Aurora said. "I think I prefer jam-making."

This was my opportunity to tell Aurora about Logan. We'd done our preparations and were ready for people to arrive. "I have something to tell you," I said, straightening the tablecloth even though it was already perfectly straight. "About a guy."

Aurora wore a huge smile as if I'd just offered her wine and ice cream at the same time. "Are you dating someone?"

"Gosh, no," I said, removing an invisible piece of lint from the cloth. "But I did kiss Logan Steele and it's no big deal. It's not that I like him or anything, don't get the wrong idea. It was just the circumstances and before I knew it, it just happened."

"Darcy, stop babbling."

"I'm sorry. I shouldn't have—"

"You absolutely should have. This is amazing news. When, where, how? Tell me everything!"

I shrugged and pulled my bottom lip between my teeth.

"Ryder and I ran into him when we were in London," I explained. "He walked me home when Ryder headed off. It just kind of happened."

"I caught a glimpse of him in the farm shop the other day," she said. "He's very handsome." She pretended to fan herself with her hand. "So, was it just a kiss?"

"Of course it was."

She sighed as she twisted the corkscrew into a white wine bottle. "Shame."

"Aurora!"

"Seriously, you need to get laid. How long's it been now?"

"Too long," I mumbled, remembering the last time—I'd known I was going to end things with Henry, so it had been a little sad.

"You don't think I'm crazy?" I asked. "He's a neighbor. And that article."

"Ignore the newspaper—you have to make up your own mind. And I think you're crazy not to have slept with him." She shrugged and began pouring wine into the glasses lined up on the table next to the sandwiches.

"I'm not going to just sleep with every man I meet, Aurora—don't act as if you're sleeping with every guy you have dinner with."

"No, you're right, I'm not, but I'm not having dinner with men that look like Logan Steele, either."

That was for sure—there weren't many men who looked like Logan. Echoes of his hard body as he'd pressed against me, his firm grip and intense stare set goosebumps off over my skin.

"I'm delighted for you."

"It's not like anything else is going to happen. He's not my type."

"Just relax about who is and isn't your type and go with it. You should definitely fuck him, even if it's to find out if he's really hung as well as someone that good-looking should be."

I didn't tell Aurora about the grinding. I was pretty sure he didn't have a problem with penis size. Ego size? That was a different matter. "I just don't think he needs me feeding his ego by being all into him."

"I'm suggesting you sleep with him." She pulled out the cork with a satisfying pop. "You don't have to fall in love. I know things have been tough. But you always cope with throwing yourself into work—protecting the Westbury legacy or something. Maybe try a different tactic. Have some fun."

Kissing Logan had been fun. And I found him interesting. I hadn't given him enough credit. He was more than some wealthy idiot who was obsessed with money and success.

"You think I'm the sort of person capable of just having a casual affair?" I'd half-expected Aurora to tell me I was being an idiot and men like that didn't go for girls like me. The fact that she was so encouraging opened a door in my brain and allowed me to remember how perfect the kiss had been and how a second one might be even better.

"You won't know until you try. And what's the worst that can happen?"

"An STD?"

"Use protection."

We laughed.

"Maybe you're right." The press of his palms against mine, the scrape of scruff and the growl of his voice. Would I get a chance to feel it all again?

Luckily, the doorbell chiming down the corridor distracted me from thinking about when I would see him next. How I'd shivered when he'd said I didn't get to tell him when we were done. How I'd felt a little giddy as I'd said goodbye and gone inside. About how I wanted him to kiss me again. And soon.

"Hello, Mrs. Lonsdale," I said, forgetting my nerves at being hostess. "There are sandwiches, cordial, water and even some wine on the table."

"The perfect hostess, just like your grandmother."

Maybe I was spending too much time trying to be the perfect hostess, looking after Woolton, doing things I was supposed to do. Perhaps I *should* have a little more fun. It wasn't as if I was about to marry Logan. But kissing him had been...nice, and doing it again would be nicer. Sleeping with him might be even better. It was just sex.

Exercise. Endorphins. It wasn't like I was going to fall for him.

Everyone began to arrive and I went out into the kitchen to top up the cordial.

"Darcy won't be happy," I heard as I nudged the door open with the tray of drinks that I'd brought through from the kitchen.

"What won't I be happy about?" I set down the tray and scanned the faces looking at me.

"It's about Logan," Aurora said.

Oh God, was he married? Gay? A serial killer?

"You haven't seen the plans he's submitted, I assume?" Mrs. Lonsdale asked.

"Plans?" I frowned.

"He wants to open a nightclub in the village."

I burst out laughing. That couldn't be true. We were a sleepy village in Chilternshire. It wasn't a nightclub-going sort of place.

"Well, not quite a nightclub," Aurora said. "More of a private members' club. A country retreat for people in the city who don't have a place in the country."

Were they serious? This didn't make any sense to me. "What do you mean?" Someone must have crossed wires. Why would he want to ruin his grandmother's family home? The village where she'd clearly wanted to come back to?

"He's submitted plans to the local council to build on Badsley land," Freida said. "Wants to create a bar and restaurant and some rooms—a small hotel complex for members."

My head spinning with a combination of disbelief and disappointment, I fell into one of the chairs. "But this is Woolton. He'll ruin the place. What was he thinking?"

"I don't know," Mrs. Lonsdale said. "Some people are saying it will be good to bring jobs to the area."

"How can you say that?" Freida puffed out a breath. "This is the beginning of the end. If the Council allows this, then what next? Look at Kingsley. That used to be a beautiful village before they relaxed the planning laws." Murmurings of agreement rumbled through the women. Kingsley had been almost as pretty as Woolton but now most of the locals had moved out as developers swooped in and bought up the village houses, ready to rent them out to tourists. A huge supermarket had opened just on the outskirts, attracting other chain stores in to replace the locally owned boutique stores. The soul of the place had been lost.

"And what about the years of disruption before it opens?" Freida asked. "Have people forgotten how the Thompsons took three years to develop their place and that was just a house?"

"And that beautiful countryside that he wants to build on. They'll have to bring down trees that are hundreds of years old." My childhood had been all about getting lost in Badsley's woods all day with my brother, coming back with scraped knees and matted hair. Those adventures that Ryder and I had together had allowed us to be children, to live without worries. We built up our confidence after bearing the scars of our parents not wanting us during those days. And our grandparents let us play without concern. They knew we were safe. We didn't have to worry about running into strangers. We knew everyone who lived locally. Would the children of Woolton have to be confined to their backyards?

If the plans were in then Logan had been thinking about this since before he'd moved here. You couldn't just shit out blueprints, they took time and planning. He clearly wasn't just some nice guy who bought his grandmother's childhood home so she could relive her memories. It had been far more calculated. Badsley was a business opportunity for him. Every time I thought I had him figured out, he fooled me again. No more. "Well, there's no way the Parish Council will allow it. They have to preserve the village. They've learned their lesson from Kingsley," I said.

Mrs. Lonsdale raised her eyebrows. "From what I hear, Mr. Steele has been on a charm offensive. He's been doing his best to tell Parish Council members all the benefits of the scheme. Employment. Putting Woolton on the map in a sophisticated way—"

"We're already on the map."

"We'll have to band together. Form an opposition group," Freida said. She was right. We would have to get organized if we were going to go against Logan who would have the best lawyers and consultants helping him. But right at that moment, it was as if I was paralyzed by disappointment. In him and in myself for kissing him. The fight had left me.

"Darcy Westbury?" A tall woman in her thirties who looked as if she'd just stepped out of the city stood at the entrance.

Swallowing down my sadness and frustration, I introduced myself to the evening's speaker. "Yes. You must be Constance Reed. Welcome." I smiled tightly. I'd never been very good at faking pleasantries. I took a deep breath, pushed down my devastation and tried for a more genuine smile. "We're all very excited to have you here."

She looked slightly out of place with her blue skirt suit, patent heels and carefully made-up face, and exactly like the sort of sophisticated woman who'd look good with

Logan Steele. I gritted my teeth at the thought of him and tried to distract myself as I ushered everyone to their seats.

As much as world economics interested me, the only thing I could think about was how just a few minutes ago Logan had been a man I hoped might become my lover and now was someone who was set on destroying the place I cherished most in the world.

TEN

Logan

As the sounds of the helicopter drew closer, I grabbed my jacket and keys. One of the perks of commuting this way was I could stay in the country on a Sunday night and still get into the office early on Monday. I glanced at my watch. I had an important call with China at ten, but I should just make it. I pulled the door shut behind me and headed toward the helicopter that had just landed.

I ducked beneath the still-rotating blades and out of the corner of my eye, I spotted a figure approaching over the lawns. I squinted through the wind and realized it was Darcy. I took a few steps toward her, the artificial breeze relenting slightly.

I hadn't seen her since our kiss last week. I supposed a part of me had wanted to run into her this weekend, but another part had been relieved I hadn't. I couldn't remember the last time I'd kissed a woman without fucking her. And although I knew that I shouldn't be fucking Darcy, there had been something about our kiss that had left me far from satiated. I was used to deciding what I wanted and following through. But I couldn't want Darcy. It just wasn't practical. But something about that fact had rankled and left me irritated.

I waved. "Hi," I bellowed.

As she marched toward me, her furious eyes came into focus. In one hand she gripped some papers, the other was fisted by her side.

"What the hell do you think you're doing?" she screamed. She didn't slow down as she neared me. When she reached me, she shoved at my chest and I had to step back to stop myself from falling. What the hell was her problem?

"What's the matter?" I asked, completely confused.

"What's the matter? Are you serious?" she shouted, making herself heard above the noise of the helicopter. "You're about to ruin this village and you ask me what's the matter? You know full well what you've done."

I tried to focus on what she was saying rather than the way her hair lifted in the breeze, or the smear of mud on her left cheek. Neither one was adorable. I liked disciplined, glamorous women. Not screaming banshees.

"Darcy, I really don't have time for this." I glanced toward the helicopter.

"I bet you don't. You don't give a shit about anyone but yourself or anything but money."

What the hell had her knickers in a knot? I didn't have time to stop and talk to her. I had a meeting as soon as I landed followed by a jam-packed calendar, but I couldn't leave her so...unhinged.

She waved the papers in the air and shouted some more about how selfish I was, but I still had no idea what she was talking about and I wasn't about to be late. Darcy Westbury would just have to come with me, but there was no way she'd agree to that.

There was only one thing to do.

Before she could ask me what the hell I was doing, I bent and tossed her over my shoulder. I kept my grip tight around her legs as I strode toward the waiting helicopter, Darcy kicking and screaming all the way. I tipped her into the interior of the Sikorsky, and followed as she scrambled to her feet and tried to open the door on the other side. "What are you doing, you maniac? You can't kidnap me."

I pulled her away from the door and placed her into one of the eight seats. She continued to struggle until we started to take off and then she grabbed my arm, fear in her eyes, which at least meant I got the opportunity to fix her belt and mine.

"Just calm down," I said, sitting back in my chair.

She narrowed her eyes. "I'm being kidnapped. Why would I be calm?"

I gripped the armrests of my seat, trying not to laugh. "I'm not kidnapping you, for crying out loud. I just don't have the time for you to shout at me in Woolton. You'll have to yell while I go to the office. I have a meeting."

"Oh, you have a meeting. What if I have a meeting?"

I sighed. "I thought you wanted to speak to me?"

For the next few minutes I got the silent treatment.

"I can't believe you kissed me," she mumbled.

I was totally confused. "You're angry because I kissed you?"

"Given the circumstances, I want to cut your bollocks off."

"Have I missed something?" This girl was making my head spin, and not for the first time. "What circumstances? I thought we'd had a nice evening." Kissing her had been phenomenal. The way she'd gasped as if she couldn't quite believe what she was feeling. The way her smart mouth had yielded under my tongue. It hadn't been an ordinary kiss. It was the kind you carried with you your whole life, trying to find another that lived up to such promise.

"But it was all a sham. You were just using me."

"It was a kiss. Using you, how?"

"Just trying to soften me up before you dropped this fucking bomb." She tossed the few remaining papers she had in her hand at me.

I scooped the crumpled white sheets from my feet and recognized the planning application for the private members' club I'd lodged. I'd planned to bring the glamour of London to the country and provide a country retreat for people in the city who didn't want the responsibility of a second home. It would be the first business I'd ever started. The first one that I'd built myself.

It was small but personal, and hopefully wouldn't be too distracting from my day job. I needed this to prove to myself I could build something. The scale wasn't important. And Manor House Club had been percolating in my mind for ten years. I'd seen how wealth and opportunity was concentrated in London—that's where people who could provide opportunities and had wealth spent their time. My idea was to attract these people outside of London in the hopes that their wealth would seep into the community. That they would find and provide opportunity outside the city.

"What has Manor House Club got to do with me kissing you?" I asked.

"Well, presumably you were hoping to make sure I didn't object to the planning. Otherwise, why wouldn't you tell me? Especially when I was talking about how passionate I was about Woolton."

"Did it work?" I asked. I was being deliberately provocative, but this woman? She was equal parts beautiful and crazy.

She just glared at me.

"Look, I didn't realize I had to give you a rundown of my five-year plan in order to kiss you."

"You're an arsehole."

"Darcy, kissing you had nothing to do with these plans. Running into you was a complete accident."

"Was it?"

"As much as I might have made the effort to do it on purpose, I can promise you that it was a coincidence."

"Then why didn't you tell me? I'd never have kissed you had I known."

A dull ache gnawed at my stomach as she confessed her regret. "It didn't come up. Manor House Club will be a phenomenal thing. It's going to attract all the best people, have them experience a beautiful place, provide employment in the area, customers for the shops in the village. Why would you be devastated?"

She folded her arms as she stared straight ahead. "It will completely ruin village life as we know it. Think of all the pollution from the visitors, all those trees you'll have to chop down, plus all the building works that will make our lives a misery for years. Not to mention the way the community will be watered down with tourists who think they're better than the rest of us." She blew out a breath as if she was trying to stop herself from crying. "We've seen this before. We've had outsiders come in and tell us how they will improve things, only for the village to suffer. The Thompsons' renovations lasted three years. And then they just flipped the house—it was just an investment for them. Woolton is special."

"I can promise you that the works won't take three years. I want the place open and making money within twelve months." I'd expected some local opposition to my plans. There were people against change whenever you tried to make improvements—I came across it all the time in business. I'd move into a new company, start asking questions about their processes and come across the phrase, "because that's how we do it" too often for me to even be surprised anymore. Most people's automatic reaction to change was to assume it was bad rather than to embrace the opportunity it brought.

"You see? It's just about money for you. You don't care about the impact you'll have on the rest of us. You won't get away with it—there's no way those plans will get through the Parish Council."

"You want to ban any building works in the village? What about when Woolton Hall needs a new roof or—"

"Don't twist my words. That's not what I'm saying, I just want to be respectful of our way of life, of our history."

It was my job to sell people on a brighter future and that was what I'd planned to do with Manor House Club. I was pretty sure I could convince the Parish Council that it would be a great thing for Woolton. "Well, I guess we'll see. Some people have broader minds than you might imagine," I replied.

"What does that mean?" she asked, shifting next to me so she could look at me. "Are you planning to try and bribe people?"

I chuckled. "Are you drunk? Of course I'm not going to bribe anyone." I might have a reputation for doing whatever it took to succeed, but I never broke the law, let alone did anything my grandmother would be ashamed of me for.

She sighed and sat back in her seat. "That's not what it

sounded like to me. You seem too sure to be leaving anything to chance."

"I think that says more about your Parish Council members than it does about me. Do they take bribes often?"

"How dare you!" she snapped. "The Parish Council would never succumb to such dirty tricks."

"Then why would you assume I'd been successful in bribing them?"

"What? Don't twist my words again."

"I'm not. I'm following their logical conclusion."

"Whatever."

"Which I interpret as 'You're quite correct, Logan. I accept that our kiss had nothing to do with your plans for Manor House Club and that you're not committing criminal offenses by bribing public officials'."

She rolled her eyes and shook her head. Darcy seemed clever and running the Woolton estate took a great deal of skill, but this girl was acting as if she'd lost her mind.

"Can't you drop it?" Her tone lowered.

"Drop what?"

"Your plans. They would ruin everything I worked so hard for."

I didn't see how Manor House Club would ruin anything for the Woolton estate, and it would breathe fresh life into the village, bring opportunities to those who weren't as lucky as Darcy. "It's important to me, Darcy. Try to look at all the positive things it will bring to the village." As much as I liked and respected her, and as much as I'd enjoyed kissing her, I wasn't about to abandon Manor House Club just because she wanted to remain in a time warp.

"Is that a no?" she asked.

"I'm afraid so," I replied. "Once I'm committed to something, I follow through. It's how I'm built."

"Then game fucking on," she said lightly, her tone not matching her words at all.

I wanted to ask what she meant, but the helicopter began to descend and I needed to focus on my meeting rather than whatever trouble Darcy might be planning to stir up.

"I'm sure we can work together to make it a great opportunity for the village."

"How am I getting back to Woolton?" she asked, ignoring my attempt to move forward on a positive note.

"The helicopter will take you back."

"You see? You don't even realize what a scourge on the village you helicoptering in and out is. It's deafening. It scares the horses, tears the leaves from the trees. We all hate it."

No one had said anything to me. "You can't make time stand still. Why do you want to put obstacles in the way of progress, Darcy?" What made her want to live in the past?

She didn't respond, didn't look at me. She just stared ahead, her eyebrows pinched together in a determined scowl.

"Let me take you through the plans next weekend," I said as we landed. "I can show you how beautiful it's going to be. How it will be in keeping with the surrounding areas. You're assuming the worst, but when you have all the facts, you might find you like it."

I sighed when she didn't respond. It was like dealing with a toddler that I couldn't put on a naughty step.

"I have to go," I said as the door opened. "I'll be back in Woolton on Friday. Let's talk then."

I got no response, so I left the helicopter and headed

toward the entrance to my building. Darcy might be distracting, beautiful and refreshingly open, but she was also infuriating as hell. She had my attention completely diverted from what I should be thinking about and instead wondering what "game on" meant, and whether she really did regret kissing me.

What was the matter with me? I needed to get a grip. Kick arse on my call and maybe reward myself this evening by blowing off steam with an uncomplicated fuck.

ELEVEN

Darcy

"It's official, we're at war," I said as I opened the door to Aurora. I'd asked her to come over early before the Parish Council members arrived. I was on a charm offensive that would outdo Logan's.

"With the Parish Council?"

"No, of course not. With Logan Steele."

"War? I'm not sure we should be *at war* with any of the villagers."

I sighed as I spun around. "He's not a villager," I replied. "Not really. He's been here five minutes and it shows." I led her into the glass-roofed sunroom which was all set out, ready for tea.

"This looks nice," she said.

"Yes. W.I. jam, of course. We've tried to use things from the farm shop. I hope it's part of the subliminal message." We took our seats on two of the upholstered cream chairs that faced the door, therefore giving the Parish Council members the view of the gardens.

"And you're sure we should be doing this?" Aurora asked. "You don't think we're meddling?"

How could she have any doubt? As soon as I'd returned from my kidnapping, I'd called around the members of the Parish Council and invited them over for tea. Although I was reasonably confident that they would reject Logan's plans, I wanted to be sure. So at tea, I'd ensure they were all planning to vote against the plans and then give them the Westbury's full support of their decision. The Westbury name still meant something around here, but Logan Steele was wealthy and influential in his field and I didn't want the Parish Council intimidated.

"Of course, I'm sure. We want the Council to know they have our support. And I want to ensure they've thought of every way Logan's plans could be disastrous."

"I'm surprised you want to go against Logan."

"This isn't me against him, it's *us* trying to maintain our beautiful village."

"I just thought that, you know, since you kissed him and everything. Going to war with him doesn't seem the natural first step in a relationship."

"Please don't remind me." I guffawed. "And a relationship? That was never going to happen." I'd considered having sex with him, but dating? He wasn't at all husband material as far as I was concerned. "Anyway, he was probably just trying to get me on side so when he announced the plans I wouldn't object."

"You think he deliberately engineered bumping into you at the restaurant?"

"Don't you start. He denied it vehemently, of course."

"Well, to be fair, I don't think he tricked you into kissing him."

Aurora was right. I didn't really think Logan engineered

our run-in. I was just disappointed with the way things had turned out. I'd enjoyed his company at dinner and his kiss even more. I was annoyed at myself for thinking that maybe there might be something more. Something after the kiss. How could I have let myself like him?

"Probably not," I conceded.

The butler, Lane, interrupted us. "Miss Darcy, Mr. Dawson and Mrs. Beadle," he announced and I bounced to my feet to greet my guests with a double kiss. I'd known both of them since I was a child and they'd always been kind to me. Despite my ulterior motive in inviting them over —which they were bound to have guessed—it was genuinely good to see them.

"We were just saying that we haven't been to Woolton Hall since the Duke died. Are you finding it terribly lonely?" Mrs. Beadle asked.

It was as if an icy breeze curled around my heart at the mention of my grandfather. I still missed him terribly. "I still feel his loss every day. But this year, the summer party will be back. The last couple of years were just too much, and I know he would have scolded me for letting the tradition lapse, so I'll have to make it up to him this year and hold the best party that Woolton has ever seen." The Woolton Hall Summer Ball had been the party where he'd met my grandmother, the place where I'd first seen my brother in love. And I knew he'd have been disappointed that we'd skipped it to tend to our grief. I wanted to make it up to him.

"I'm so pleased to hear that," Mr. Dawson said. "You know how much everyone enjoys it."

"As do I. And it's so important to keep these traditions alive. It's what we all try and do, after all. What kind of tea would everyone like?" I asked as Mrs. MacBee entered the room, bringing with her the other three council members, Mr. Newton, Miss Price and Mr. Adams.

With tea ordered and everyone in their seats, I decided to take the bull by the horns. "Speaking of keeping up traditions, I was surprised to see the plans that the new owner of Badsley House had submitted," I said.

"They're certainly ambitious," Mr. Adams said.

I held his gaze, willing him to add to what he'd said. I wanted to know whether or not he thought ambitious was good or bad, but before he could say anything more, Miss Price interrupted. "I can't think of anything worse," she said. "All those awful city types stamping through our little slice of heaven."

My heart swelled. I knew Susan would understand. We were on the fundraising committee for the local mobile library and we both cared passionately about the community.

"I think it would be a real shame to turn Woolton into a huge tourist town," I said, leaning forward to move the vase of peonies, ready for the tea that Mrs. MacBee would bring through, and trying to seem relaxed, as if the plans for Manor House Club had just come up in casual conversation.

"But at the same time." Mr. Newton tapped his finger against his leg. "Logan makes a good point about providing local employment for the village."

I turned to Susan to see if she'd fight our corner, but Mrs. Beadle spoke up. "Yes, there will be construction jobs, but they're not likely to be local. So, long-term, he means a few bar and restaurant staff. I'd prefer to see another restaurant opened in the village than some exclusive club that won't be open to villagers unless we pay thousands of pounds of membership fees."

"That's an excellent point," I replied and glanced at Aurora, wondering why she hadn't joined in yet.

"I don't like the exclusive nature of it either," Mr. Dawson said. "It will be a huge part of the village, but exclude local people. That doesn't sit right with me."

I shook my head. "City people." I sighed.

"Well, maybe we can talk to him, get him to give free membership to residents of the village," Mr. Newton said.

"Do you think he'd do that? I'm not sure how exclusive it would be if he started handing out memberships to us villagers." I shrugged.

Mrs. MacBee brought in the tea and set it down. I set about pouring drinks for everyone while I listened to everyone's opinion. I wanted to know how hard I was going to have to work to get Logan's plans defeated.

"You know the thing I'm worried about?" I said in a lull in the conversation. "The drinking and what that does to people. Remember the Foleys?"

"I don't think it would be like that. That was a specific issue with that couple. And remember, Mrs. Steele grew up in this village. She doesn't want it ruined any more than we do." Mr. Adams smiled as I handed him his tea.

They had to understand that Mrs. Steele probably didn't have any control over Logan's plans. Surely she would have already persuaded him to change his mind if she could have.

"That's a good point," Miss Price murmured. "My mother knew her when she lived here after her husband died. She seems like a very nice woman. One of us."

I nodded. I couldn't disagree with her. Partly because it was true, and also because as much as I might want to win this battle with Logan, I didn't want to do it by trying to tarnish his grandmother in any way.

"And I suppose I'm a little concerned that Woolton will suffer the same fate as Kingsley. Once the floodgates are open, there's no going back."

"That's exactly what I said." Susan took a sip of her tea. "It's the beginning of a slippery slope."

Over the course of the conversation, the pile of sandwiches in front of us was replenished three times. It was pretty clear the Parish Council was split. Mr. Newton and Barry Adams were the most open to it. And Susan and Mrs. Beadle were set against it. Mr. Dawson seemed to change his mind, depending on the last thing that was said. At least now I knew where I stood and who I had to persuade.

Logan Steele might have a brilliant business brain, but he shouldn't have underestimated me. He should have taken more time to understand the importance of tradition and connections in a village like Woolton.

TWELVE

Logan

I hadn't expected to crave the countryside. I was looking forward to seeing my grandmother this weekend, but more than that, I wanted to be surrounded by trees, grass and blue skies rather than brick, glass and tarmac. The air was cleaner, the pace slower—colors seemed brighter, the smiles more genuine.

The week in London had taken its toll, and by Friday afternoon I couldn't wait to get back to Badsley House. The helicopter landed in the gardens and the stress of the day began to slip away. It was also nice to get distance from my business. I left Badsley more focused, and found I looked at problems with a fresh perspective when I returned to work.

I waved at my grandmother, who was sitting out on the terrace. It was good to see her so happy here. After Darcy's visit, she'd had a number of visitors drop by and she seemed to be enjoying being back home.

Dipping my head, I headed over to the terrace from the

helicopter, I saw my grandmother had a visitor. But it wasn't Darcy Westbury this time.

"Hello, darling, come and join Patricia and me for some tea," my grandmother said as I approached, kissed her on the cheek, then shook hands with our visitor, a slight woman who I'd estimate was in her early sixties.

"Delighted to meet you, Patricia," I said.

"And you. I've heard so much about you, so it's nice to be able to put a face to a name."

"Patricia's come to ask us a favor," my grandmother said.

"Really?" I asked. "What can we do?" I asked, pulling up a chair.

"Well, I'm chair of the local fundraising committee for our mobile library, and I was hoping for your support."

"Of course, how can I help?" I crossed one leg over the other, letting the sun soak into my face, the week's strain chased away by the warmth.

"We have a fundraising target of fifteen thousand pounds this year. Those funds go toward maintenance of the truck that transports the books and payment of the driver."

"I'm happy to donate. I can let you have a check. But what can I do that's more practical? I have a contact at one of the big publishers. I can see if they have any books that might add to your stock."

Patricia set her teacup down. "Well, that would be simply wonderful. Our readers tend to enjoy fiction, especially cozy mysteries, but anything would be a bonus. Thank you. Of course, we'd love to have you on our committee if you can spare the time."

The cogs in my brain started whirring. Since I'd last seen Darcy, her words *"game on"* had echoed in my brain. There was little doubt that she didn't like the plans I had for

Manor House Club, and although I'd already decided to try to talk her through what I hoped to achieve, I wasn't convinced I'd have her on side by the end of it. I expected opposition and knowing who my opponents were and why they took the position they did helped me form an offense and defense. I needed to get to know some of the Woolton villagers better. But I didn't have the time and I didn't make commitments that I wasn't sure I could fulfill.

"That's very kind of you, but I'm not sure I can commit to a position on the committee. I have a number of members of my team who I know would jump at the opportunity and are even better than me at coming up with creative solutions to problems."

Her cup at her lips, Patricia froze, her eyes wide. "That's a lovely thought, but we only have local people on the committee."

She probably thought I was an arsehole for trying to delegate a place on the committee, but realistically, there was no way I could be a regular attendee at meetings. And I didn't half do things or say I was going to do something and then let people down. That was my father. Not me. "Well, perhaps I could come along as your guest, Patricia. Not a member, but just someone who might be able to help. Every six months or so."

"Wonderful," she said. "We need fresh ideas on the committee, and we're thrilled you want to be part of our village. There's a meeting tomorrow morning at ten if you're free."

"I'll make sure I am." Darcy wouldn't expect me to get to know the villagers. She'd count on having more influence with them, but if I made an effort to get to know them, I could at least communicate my point of view. Maybe even gain a few supporters. I'd had the best lawyers draw up the application to the Parish Council so I'd have the best possible chance of fulfilling any technical requirements, but I also understood that the first step in any planning process was easily influenced by the non-technical.

"I'll take you down to the farm shop before the meeting, Granny. Then drop you back."

"Oh, that's so nice that you support our village farm shop," Patricia said.

"Of course. We're a big supporter of local producers. We want to be a real part of the village."

Patricia beamed. "Well, I'm excited for you to get involved."

"As am I. Now, if you'll excuse me while I change into my comfortable clothes? I never feel quite like me in a suit." Perhaps I was laying it on a little thick, but I wanted to be sure there was an alternate argument in circulation when Darcy began to paint me as a corporate monster.

"Of course. I'll see you tomorrow."

"I'm looking forward to it."

I slipped into the house, ready for a hot shower. I always felt dirty when arriving back at Badsley from London, so I hadn't really lied about being uncomfortable in my suit. I'd never found myself feeling that way before spending my weekends in the country. But I found myself wearing ties less and less often, even when I was back in London. Here in Woolton, I was more comfortable in jeans and a shirt. And I was genuinely pleased to help out the fundraising committee. And if it made the likelihood of the village accepting Manor House Club, then all the better.

THIRTEEN

Darcy

There was nothing like an explosion of fresh color to brighten people's moods. The farm shop was no exception. "There," I said, placing a jug of hand-picked lilacs onto the counter by the till. "I knew that would cheer the place up." I came down to the farm shop a few times a week. Rory was an excellent manager, so I didn't need to supervise him. But still, I wanted to show my support, so I always bought a couple of things and caught up with a few neighbors.

"Darcy," someone called from behind me. I turned and found Mrs. Steele using her walking stick as she ambled through the door.

"Mrs. Steele," I said, racing forward to help her before I realized Logan was behind her. "So nice to see you down here. Can I help you with anything?" I avoided looking at Logan. He hadn't so much as apologized for kidnapping me and I wasn't a Stockholm Syndrome sufferer. He'd been completely out of line. That man was far too used to everyone in his orbit being at his beck and call.

"We're just here to browse, although we're nearly out of that lavender honey I like so much," she said, heading toward the jams, marmalades and chutneys section. "You are looking very pretty today, Darcy," she said. "Isn't she, Logan?"

"Please, Mrs. Steele. I don't have a scrap of makeup on, and these jeans have a hole in them."

"She always looks beautiful, grandmother," Logan said, and I did my best not to roll my eyes.

"You must drop by while Logan is home for the weekend." Mrs. Steele tapped me on my arm. "Perhaps you'll join us for dinner one evening?"

Mrs. Steele was clearly still trying to play matchmaker. Little did she know there was little prospect of Logan and I being friends, let alone anything more.

"That is so kind of you, but I have a packed schedule this weekend. Perhaps next week? You'd be welcome to come up to Woolton for supper. I can collect you," I said.

She turned to Logan. "Are you free for supper with Darcy or are you in London all week?"

My stomach churned. Why did she have to assume that the invitation extended to her grandson?

Out of the corner of my eye, Logan's gaze flickered to me. "I'm sure I could make a mid-week trip for dinner with you and Darcy."

My heart sank. The last thing I wanted to do was be polite to someone who didn't think twice about turning the lives of an entire village upside down. Someone who didn't give it a second thought before hoisting me over their shoulder and dragging me to London against my will. Someone I'd *kissed*.

"Perfect," Mrs. Steele said. "Then you just tell us when,

Darcy, and we'll be there. I'd love to see the house, and from what I hear, your gardens are simply fantastic."

"Excellent," I said through gritted teeth. "Wednesday works for me, if that's convenient," I said, hoping the middle of the week wouldn't work for Logan.

"Sounds perfect," Logan said.

"Well, I must be going," I said, still refusing to look at him. "I have a meeting to get to." The mobile library fundraising committee meeting didn't start for twenty minutes, and it was only a ten-minute walk, but I needed to leave before I got into any more trouble. Inadvertently, I'd managed to ensure that I was going to have to entertain Logan in my own home this week. I dreaded to think what I'd do next if I didn't get out of there.

"Well, it's very nice to see you, my dear, and I look forward to Wednesday."

"Yes," Logan said. "Wednesday will be a complete pleasure."

I managed to stay silent at his sarcasm, but he winked at me as if he had the upper hand. Well, he might have won this battle, but our war over Manor House Club wouldn't be one I lost.

"I can't wait," I said, matching his sarcasm. I said goodbye and headed out, turning left down the high street. Logan Steele was all charm and smiles on first glance, but upon a closer look, he was trying to destroy everything I'd worked so hard to preserve.

Well, I saw right through him.

I blew out a breath and started toward the church hall.

"Darcy." Glenis waved from the other side of the road. I slowed to a stop as she headed over to speak to me.

"Hi Glenis. That's a pretty dress." Glenis had a thousand pretty dresses, but this one of purples and pinks suited her more than usual. "I've not seen you since the jam-making. How are you?"

"Wonderful. I finally met our new neighbor. Just as charming as I expected. Have you two been introduced?"

"Unfortunately," I replied.

She frowned. "You didn't like Logan?"

"I think his grandmother is quite lovely, but have you heard how he wants to develop Badsley into members' bars, restaurants and rooms? He's going to ruin the place."

"But where will his grandmother live?"

I shook my head. "The house will stay as it is. He wants to build new in the grounds."

"I hadn't heard that. Has he got planning permission?"

"Not yet. I'm so worried. He keeps talking about jobs and opportunity and all I can think about is all the trees that will have to be torn down and the way all the guests will overtake the village."

"Gosh," Glenis said. "We don't want Woolton turning into Kingsley."

"Yes, that was supposed to attract investment, but look what happened!"

"So many people moved out. Village life was ruined for them."

"I know. I'm so worried that the same will happen to Woolton," I said.

"Not to mention how long construction will take. Do you remember the Thompsons?" She gasped. "Three years. It was hell. I have to talk to the rest of the W.I. members." Determination spread across Glenis' face. "We have to oppose this. Darcy, excuse me, I need to go and speak to Mrs. Lonsdale and some others. Good to see you, my dear."

Before I could wish her well, she'd stomped past me, her pretty dress floating behind her, and I turned back toward the church hall. By the time I arrived for our committee meeting, I wasn't early at all. I was right on time.

"Hi, Patricia," I said as the chair of the fundraising committee wheeled a tray of tea into the main room.

"Darcy," she said. "I'm so excited about today's meeting."

I held the door open so she could push the trolley through.

"You are?" I asked. What had got her in such a good mood?

"We have a guest today—you're going to be delighted."

A guest? We never had guests at this meeting. Across the room, the women of the committee were staring up at a man who had his back to me.

"It will be good to have some gender balance as well." Patricia beamed as she spoke.

Oh, so the man who was holding court was our guest. I squinted, trying to figure out who it was when realization dawned.

Oh God. It couldn't be, could it? My gut churned in frustration.

"Logan," Patricia called. "Do you know Darcy?"

What was with this guy? Was he following me around?

Logan made his excuses to the harem of tittering women and turned to us. "Darcy!" he said. "How wonderful to see you. I didn't realize you were on this committee."

"Patricia, let me help you with that," he said, bounding forward and taking the trolley from her. He wheeled it across to the cloth-covered table under the window.

Patricia gasped and blushed as if he'd just presented her with diamonds. "That's so kind of you," she sighed. "So gentlemanly."

I wondered if she'd think him so gentlemanly if she knew of his plans.

"Darcy's really helped my grandmother and I settle into the village," he said as he wandered over to the table where we always had our discussions. All the women gazed up at him with stars in their eyes.

"She's a good girl like that," Maureen said. "And single, you know."

I glared at her. Why did my being single have to be brought up at every single village function? It had nothing to do with Logan Steele, or the library.

I tried not to glance at Logan, but his smug smile bore into me. I bet everyone thought that grin was charming. I knew better.

"Shall we start the meeting?" I asked. The sooner we got down to business, the sooner we'd be done and I could put some distance between Logan and me. I'd wanted to bring up Manor House Club at today's meeting. Not officially, because it had nothing to do with the library funding, but I needed to tell people what he was planning. Now with Logan here, the women already eating out of the palm of his hand, it seemed I was too late.

Next week's Parish Council would discuss Logan's plans, and instead of me encouraging opposition, Logan seemed to be winning people over with his smooth charm, flirtatious smile and over-the-top interest in Woolton Village. This wasn't supposed to be how it went.

FOURTEEN

Logan

Darcy Westbury had me acting like a nerdy teenager, chasing after the most popular girl in school. "Hey, Darcy," I said, trying to catch up as she strode along the main street of the village. It had taken longer than I'd expected to extract myself at the end of the meeting, and it had meant Darcy had left before I'd had a chance to speak to her. Not that I had anything particular to say.

She didn't stop. She didn't even slow down. "Hey," I said as I reached her. "Great meeting. I didn't know you were a member."

"What do you want, Logan?" she asked.

What did I want? To get her attention? To tease her? I didn't know my own mind. "To catch up. Chat. We're friends, aren't we? I certainly hope we are." That was bound to rile her up and get me attention—two birds with one stone.

"Friends? Last time I saw you, you kidnapped me."

I chuckled. She was so dramatic. "You were yelling, and

I had to get to a meeting. I was happy to let you vent, but I needed to travel while you did."

"It's just your world, and we live in it, isn't it?"

"I could have left without you, but I didn't. Because I like you—though I prefer you when you're not shouting at me."

She stumbled as we made our way across the bridge over the river and I grabbed her arm to steady her, catching a strain of her fresh, floral scent, but she just shrugged me off.

"Well, I don't like you."

I wasn't sure if that were true now, but I knew that at one point it had been different. "Didn't seem that way when you were kissing me."

She stopped still on the pathway and shook her head before carrying on. "Money can't buy you manners. No gentleman would ever bring that up." She sounded disappointed in me or herself—I wasn't sure. I preferred her mad.

"Why on earth not? There's no one here but us, and we both know it happened."

"I'd rather forget about it, if you don't mind."

I brought my palm to my chest. "You're breaking my heart."

I wasn't entirely sure, but I thought a small smile crossed her lips. To cover it up, she sighed. "What do you want, Logan?"

"To talk to you. To see you home. I've not had any one-on-one time with you for almost a week." Of course, I was teasing her. But it was sort of true. I found her fascinating. Passionate. Ready to stand behind what she believed. People were rarely so open with me. In business, I had to remove knives from my back on a regular basis, but Darcy had clutched the dagger and tried to stick it into my chest.

It made for a refreshing change.

And she was an excellent kisser. I couldn't remember the last time when a kiss had stuck in my mind so long. Maybe it was the way her body yielded under my touch, the way my skin seemed to ignite when I touched her or the way she smelled of freshly mowed grass and lime blossom. She was all fire on the outside and cool breeze on the inside, and I wanted to dive in and experience it all.

"I'm perfectly capable of seeing myself home, and I've had enough one-on-one time with you to last a lifetime."

"Now that's not a very friendly thing to say," I teased, amused by the way she was trying to get away from me by walking so quickly.

"Well, that's because we're not friends."

"And I can't quite work out why not. There aren't many people our age in Woolton Village. We should at least *try* to be friends."

"I'll be friends with you when you drop these ridiculous plans for your private members' club."

"That's just business. Nothing to do with friendship."

She shook her head as she continued her march back to Woolton Hall. "That's the point. You think the two can be separated. You don't get that your business impacts our whole way of life, and worse, you just don't care."

How could I convince her that Manor House Club could enhance life in Woolton? "It's not going to be a dump, you know. The bar and restaurant are going to be top quality and the landscaping is going to be beautiful. It'll attract wealthy people with money to spend locally. And those same people will hopefully be inspired and invest in the area. Why don't you keep an open mind?"

"Insults, calling me closed-minded—you've got a funny

way of being my friend. Those aren't the kind of accusations friends make of each other."

She didn't let me get away with anything. "Okay, so the deal is we can't be friends unless my plans fail at the Parish Council meeting next week? But if that happens, we can?"

"Why would you want to be friends with me if I beat you?"

I didn't think she'd beat me. But even if she did, I didn't want there to be bad blood between us. And if I offered an olive branch, when I beat her she might let bygones be bygones. I never gave a second thought to the enemies I made in business. But I didn't want to be enemies with someone like Darcy. Yes, she was a neighbor and my grandmother liked her but it was more than that. Wanting to be... friends with Darcy wasn't just practical. I liked what I saw, and I wanted to know more. "I just figure there must be layers."

"Everyone has layers," she said, waving at a woman who was pushing a buggy on the other side of the road.

Always an answer for everything. "You're right. But I'm not interested in most people's layers."

"If I tell you we can be friends if I beat you, will you leave me in peace?"

I chuckled. I really must be irritating her, but instead of that wanting to make me back off, it only made me want to know more about her.

"You'd get a temporary reprieve. How's that for a compromise?"

"I'll take it." She rolled her eyes. "Then yes, we can be friends when I beat you. Now, skedaddle and leave me in peace."

I wanted to reach out, stroke her hair or claim a kiss, but I resisted. "Finally, a consolation prize worth having."

She chuckled and shook her head. "Unbelievable. You need a refund from that charm school you went to. I'm a consolation prize?"

"That's not what I meant." I touched her shoulder, but she shrugged me off. "And if I win? Then what?" She challenged me at every turn—not just on my plans but what I said, how I said it. She was hard work. And I liked it.

"Then I hate you for the rest of my life."

"That seems overly harsh. Murderers normally only get fifteen years."

"Seriously, I don't understand why you want to be my friend," she replied. "And I don't understand why you think I'd want to be yours when you're trying to do something that goes against everything I stand for. Everything I've spent my life working against."

When she said it like that, my actions made no sense. Perhaps I was just far too used to getting what I wanted, and right now, I wanted the development of Badsley, I wanted her. She was the antithesis of my life in London. Of the women there. The perfect English rose—pale skin, no makeup. Jeans with a smear of mud. I bet she'd never seen the inside of the gym. So, what had me so bewitched?

"It looks like that Parish Council meeting will be a win-win for me," I said. "I get Manor House Club, or I get you."

She stopped, an incredulous look in her eyes. "You don't *get* me." She started walking again. "I'm not some kind of object you can win."

"That came out wrong—it was supposed to be a compliment."

"And even if you win, don't think you're going to flutter those long eyelashes and have me dropping my knickers."

Interesting. "So you've been examining my long eyelashes."

"No. I mean. Eyelashes are normally...yours are a normal length."

I chuckled as she struggled to explain. It seemed Miss Westbury's feathers were capable of being ruffled.

"I'm just saying that your flirting won't work on me."

I hoped that wasn't true. I might have to work harder, but somehow I'd find a way to break down her walls. "Hey, you were the one to mention your knickers dropping. I only talked about friendship. Dinner maybe."

We got to a fence with a stile and we stopped. "Good luck with your plans, Mr. Steele. I'll continue the rest of my journey alone, as this is Westbury land." She stepped up onto the stile and across the fence.

"Well, you're welcome to trespass on my land anytime you like. You and your horse, that is," I called as she headed across the field, her tangle of hair lifted by the breeze, her round, firm arse wiggling as she went. "I'll take that as a yes to dinner if I lose at the council meeting."

If the Parish Council meeting didn't go my way next week, dinner with Darcy would likely more than make up for it. With the women I normally slept with, our relationships were as businesslike as any meeting or negotiation, but with Darcy, there was no separation between personal and professional. Her business was completely personal to her. And I liked that. I got it. As much as she thought developing Manor House Club was all margins and money to me, it was the most personal thing I'd ever tried to do. It was why I was determined that the council would approve my plans.

FIFTEEN

Darcy

My favorite thing to do in the whole world was to tuck up under a blanket in my grandfather's study with a glass of red and watch an old film. So, with *The Philadelphia Story* on the TV, and Aurora and I at either end of my grandfather's oxblood chesterfield, a bottle of wine and a worn, gold chenille blanket, I should have felt pretty close to perfect. Especially as Mrs. Steele had telephoned earlier to cancel the dinner we'd arranged. Hopefully we could rearrange another time when Logan couldn't make it.

Except Aurora was being deliberately infuriating.

"How can you say that it's nice?" I asked. "It's clearly to manipulate people into thinking he has some kind of interest in the village." If Logan had fooled Aurora by coming to the library fundraising committee meeting, then would members of the Parish Council fall for it, too?

"Maybe he's had a change of heart. You can't tell me you wouldn't enjoy having a smart bar and restaurant nearby. Plus, I heard he's going to have a pool and a gym on the site and allow people to fish in his lake."

"You can't be on his side!" I said.

"It's not that I'm on his side. Just that if the plans were to go through, it might not be the end of the world."

A pool in the village would be a great idea. But for locals. Not the wealthy elite. That was what was so infuriating—some of the ideas were good. And I liked that he wanted to commit to the village—he was just going about it in the wrong way. "We'd end up divided between the haves and the have-nots. The ones who get to use the pool and eat in the restaurant and those who have to clean the pool and serve up the meals. It would be the end of Woolton as we know it."

"Darcy! Can't you see what a hypocrite you're being? You know you are a duke's sister, and aren't you Lady Westbury or something?"

"What's that got to do with anything?"

"You're complaining like you're a 'have-not' in this scenario, when you're one of the haves."

"Don't be ridiculous. I've never acted like I was better than anyone."

"Maybe not, but you're more than used to flying private. You have a butler and a housekeeper and a cook, as well as all your other staff. Sounds to me like you don't mind the wealthy elite in the village, as long as it's you and your family."

I winced. Aurora's words stung like summer nettles on bare legs. "That's not why I'm fighting Logan's plans. I love this place. It's the only real home I know. It's the only place I feel safe. I'm just trying to hold on to that."

We sat in silence, Katharine Hepburn's portrayal of a

rich socialite getting everything wrong at every turn not as appealing as it had been when we'd sat down.

"You're right," I said. "I'm privileged in many ways, but the most precious thing I ever got was to grow up in this place. Among the solid oak and ash trees, playing hide and seek in the beech hedges, paddling in the stream with Ryder. Knowing these good and honest people. This place saved Ryder and me. It's special. Magic. You know that."

She reached out and squeezed my leg. "I do. And nothing will change those memories. But people do need jobs. And encouraging money out of the city to places like this isn't always a bad thing."

"Maybe that's right, in principle. But why did he have to choose Badsley and Woolton?"

"Were you at least civil?" she asked.

"Of course, I was civil, even though he chased after me as I walked home."

Aurora grinned. "He did? What did he say?"

I blew out a breath and picked up my glass of wine. "Nothing interesting. Just that he wanted to be friends and that his planning application was all business."

"That was nice of him."

She wasn't getting it. "He was just trying to manipulate me. He's doing the same thing to the entire village—he's in the farm shop with his grandmother, at the library fundraising committee, chasing me down at every opportunity. It's all an act so he can make money."

"Maybe, but maybe not. He might actually want to be part of the village. I mean, he comes home every weekend, he's spent a lot of money on Badsley House. You usually give people the benefit of the doubt."

True, but Logan's plans for Manor House Club undermined all that. "Yeah, well, by all accounts, serial killers are normally charming—it's the sociopath thing."

Aurora choked on her wine. "You can't compare Logan Steele to a serial killer."

I giggled. "Maybe not. I'm just saying that he has a hidden agenda for every nice thing he does." I circled the rim of my glass with a fingertip. "For example, he said that if he lost at the council meeting, he wanted to take me to dinner. He's trying to manipulate me. Wants me to be friends with him if he wins. I see through him." If I didn't know better, I might have been taken in by his charm and easy manner.

"Do you think that maybe you like him and you're scared?" she asked.

I frowned. "Don't be so ridiculous." I had liked him for a second or two, but that was embarrassing to admit, even to myself.

"Is that a yes?"

"No! It's a definite no."

"I'm not buying it. This is perfect," Aurora squealed. "He's totally going to lose the vote and then you two can pretend to be friends for five minutes before you fall in love."

"Oh my God, Aurora, you're delirious. I hope he loses the vote, but there will be no falling in love. I told you, I don't even like the man."

She shrugged and placed her wine down on the table beside her. "I'm not sure that's true."

"Of course it is. He's the exact opposite of the man I see myself with."

"He's tall, good-looking and rich."

"Yeah but he's also elitist, self-satisfied and wants to ruin our village."

"He lives in Woolton a huge part of the week. And the fact he's successful on his own merits? That has to be sexy. It is to me."

She had a point. Men who were self-made were far more attractive to me than men who just sat around living off what their ancestors had left them.

"You need to be with someone with money—his own money. That's why it didn't work with Sam." Aurora finished her glass of wine and grabbed the bottle to top us both up.

A talented carpenter, Sam's handmade furniture had appeared in *Elle Interiors*, but he'd found the gap between our situations far too difficult to handle—he thought that it had emasculated him. And truth be told, whoever I married either had to have their own money or not be intimidated by my family's.

"And you don't want one of these guys who just wants to live off you."

I groaned. I could sniff out those particular men a mile off. The freeloaders, the ones completely happy for me to pay for everything. No, there was nothing attractive about that kind of man. Aurora was right. In a lot of ways, Logan looked like a good match.

"Don't you ever think that you might just be looking for reasons to hate Logan? I mean you won't even admit he's good-looking, which is just crazy because he's the hottest man I've ever seen. I think this might be a case of the lady protesting too much."

I groaned and tipped back my wine. "Okay, he's handsome. I'm sure I've admitted that before." He was also a great kisser, but Aurora didn't need to hear that.

"And you admit he's socially suitable?"

I topped up Aurora's glass, then my own. "Yes, yes. I

agree he wouldn't want me to fund his lifestyle or be intimidated by mine."

"So, if the only issue is this planning application, then you have to promise me you'll go to dinner with him if he loses."

"Don't you start," I replied.

"Well, if not, I'll just have to assume you want to be single forever. If you won't even go to dinner with him, spend *one* evening with him, then you deserve to be alone."

I'd wanted to watch a film and get a little drunk, not be taken to task and have my life choices questioned by my best friend. "How can you say that?"

"Because you're missing out on an opportunity to get to know someone who might be perfect for you."

Logan Steele was infuriating, not perfect. Woolton was a steady, happy place that was all about routine and tradition. Since Logan had arrived, every day had been turned on its head and nothing was predictable. I never knew what was going to happen next, what was around the bend. Who knows what would happen if he won the planning vote? Things would only get worse.

SIXTEEN

Logan

The last thing I'd have thought I'd be doing on a Wednesday afternoon would be attending a Parish Council meeting in the Woolton Village Hall. I'd planned to leave the details of Manor House Club to my trusted team. I rarely got my hands dirty with things like this, but I was here for two reasons. First, Manor House Club was important to me—the first business I'd ever start from scratch. And second, I never underestimated my opposition. I knew Darcy would oppose my plans and I didn't want my absence to be fuel to her fire of an outsider coming in and ruining her village.

So I'd come to the meeting in person. Careful not to look too much like a city implant, I'd dressed casually in dark jeans and a blue shirt, and sat with a pack of papers on a table opposite the committee members. At the next table were a group of six villagers who represented the opposition to my plans. Interestingly, Darcy wasn't one of them, which

I could only guess meant that she had enough support that *she* didn't have to get *her* hands dirty.

"Mr. Steele, would you like to address the committee?" the chair asked.

"Thank you," I stood and gave a copy of my presentation to each of the committee members. "I've set out an overview of the benefits of Manor House Club on the first page." The hall fell silent apart from the sound of pages being turned. "You will see that the plans would mean more jobs both in the construction and then ongoing in hospitality."

"And can you guarantee these will be local jobs?" asked the member on the far right, Miss Price.

"I'm very hopeful that most of them will be."

Miss Price rolled her eyes. "'Hopeful' and 'most'? You're not prepared to make a commitment?"

"To provide the best service and facilities for customers, we will want to recruit the best people for the jobs. I have no doubt that a high proportion will be local." It was probable that we'd have to source some of the positions from London. Surely they couldn't expect anything else.

"I see," Miss Price said.

I went through my other arguments, how it would attract visitors to the village, how those people would bring their money with them and boost the local economy.

"And can you tell me your experience with starting businesses like this? What is your track record?" Mr. Beadle asked.

"Well, Steele Enterprises made a profit last year of—"

"I'm not interested in Steele Enterprises generally. Or your profits. I want to know about your experience, specifically, of developing businesses such as this and the impact they've had on the local community."

"With the utmost respect, I believe my general experience with growing Steele Enterprises is directly applicable." I went on to detail the strong financial position of Steele Enterprises and how successful I'd been.

"And how will you address the divide between the members and the non-members who live in the village? The last thing we want to do is encourage an *us and them* culture," said the older lady on the end.

"I would argue, respectfully, that there will always be different people with different backgrounds and resources in any village. Now in Woolton, there are some people who own a great deal of land and have access to a great many resources. And there are those who don't." Darcy might pretend that she was like any other villager, but she wasn't.

"The difference being that here the people of resources are currently part of the village, live here permanently and are committed to village life. What we want to avoid is creating a divide that will cause resentment," Mr. Beadle said.

"I'm open to looking at what areas of Manor House Club might be open to local people at certain times of the year."

"But you make no mention of that in your presentation."

"I'd be happy to consider any suggestion you have." I no more wanted to create a divide among the villagers than anyone else did.

Mr. Dawson sighed. "Do you have anything further to add?"

"I think I've taken you through all the advantages."

"Perhaps. But you've not said anything about how your plans will impact the people. The sense of community. You've not spoken at all about the impact of Manor House

Club on our way of life." Mr. Dawson pulled out the article in *The London Times* that described me as a peddler of destruction. "It's been brought to my attention that you don't seem to measure success in the same way we do. You see, it's not our job to ensure you can make money. It's our job to ensure we don't destroy lives, that we don't unnecessarily destroy beautiful and picturesque countryside with buildings and roads. We need to see clear and measurable benefits for the community. Anyway, we must vote."

My time was up as the committee members turned away from me and began to murmur to each other.

The Times sat in front of all the committee members. Some had tried to hide it. Others hadn't bothered. Darcy might not be here in person, but her influence was clear. That article was following me around, determined to show me as a force of destruction when I'd worked my entire life to be anything but. Manor House Club was meant to be proof that I wasn't out to destroy anything.

I knew the outcome without a vote being necessary.

Darcy had won. I'd been defeated.

It was the first time a business venture hadn't gone right for me in a long time. As I sat there, I tried to convince myself it was a character-building moment, though it didn't feel like it. It felt like the change I was trying to make to my legacy, the move away from destruction to something more positive, had been futile. At least there was no press to witness my defeat.

Already, I was running through ways to appeal the decision. But for now, I was going to sit here, listen to the outcome and look disappointed but dignified.

And then I was going to see Darcy.

"Those in favor, please raise your hands?"

Not one committee member put their hand up.

"And those against?"

Four hands went up.

"I'm afraid, Mr. Steele, your application is denied," the chair announced, finally putting me out of my misery.

I shook their hands and thanked each of them for the time and consideration. I wasn't going to look like a sore loser, and I didn't want to burn bridges in this village.

Ignoring the murmurs of the crowd and the eyes fixed on me, I strode outside, the spring sunshine bright enough to have me slipping my sunglasses over my eyes, and I headed to Woolton Hall.

I needed to pick myself up, dust myself off and refuse to see this as the end, just a bump in the road. And even a lost planning application had a silver lining. Darcy had promised me dinner as a consolation prize, and I was cashing in. I wanted to know how influential she'd been in the planning process. How hard had she campaigned against me?

And I wanted to take the woman to dinner.

I saw her before she saw me. She stood in the driveway, her jeans hugging her arse perfectly, her brown hair tumbling down her back as she looked toward the entrance to the driveway as if she were waiting for something.

"Darcy," I called.

She turned, a look of shock passing over her face as she saw it was me. She probably thought I was a man who'd retreat after a defeat to lick his wounds in private. It was a shame she didn't know me better. But she would soon.

"Hi," she replied, gathering her hair and coaxing it to one side. "I didn't expect to see you here."

She already knew about the planning decision.

"I would have thought you'd be expecting me. I'm here to fix a date for dinner."

She tipped her head back and laughed. "You're serious? I thought this planning thing was important to you. Shouldn't you be devastated?"

I found myself studying every part of her as she stood bare-faced out in the sunshine. Her eyebrows were two perfect arches above her chestnut eyes. She had a small smattering of freckles over her nose that made her look younger than she was. Her ears weren't pierced and I was pretty sure there was a story there that I wanted to hear.

I could stare at her forever.

"Logan?" she prompted when I didn't reply.

"I told you it was just business. I can compartmentalize. And anyway, it means we can be friends now, right? I get to take you to dinner."

"Well, I'm not one to renege on a deal, so sure, we can do dinner. Shall I come over to your place? The three of us could eat together."

"I don't think so." Nothing that was going to happen between us before, during or after dinner was going to be witnessed by my grandmother. "Friday at six. Be ready—and dress up."

She groaned.

"Don't complain. You made this deal."

"But dressing up?"

What was Darcy's problem? "Yes. Black tie. No excuses. I'll pick you up."

"Logan—"

"I don't want to hear it. You made the deal." By the time the evening was over and she was underneath me, writhing, chasing an orgasm I might or might not grant her, she'd have forgotten all about her reservations.

SEVENTEEN

Darcy

"But sequins? *Gold* sequins?" I glanced at my reflection in the mirror. My hair was piled on top of my head and the full-length gown sucked me in all the right places. It had a slit up one side, a deep v-neck and a black fabric belt. I'd bought it for a charity gala in New York last year, but hadn't worn it.

Still, I loved it. It made me feel sexy and slightly dangerous, but I wasn't sure I wanted to feel either when I was anywhere near Logan Steele.

"He said black tie," Aurora replied. "You don't want to be underdressed."

"You don't think it's too much?" I asked as I smoothed my hands over my waist.

"You look sensational," Aurora said. "Logan's not going to know what hit him."

I pressed my glossed lips together. I liked the idea of shocking him. He'd only ever seen me in jeans and no makeup. No doubt, the women he usually took to dinner were super glamorous—designer clothes, never left the house without a blow-dry and professional makeup. "If he's not in a dinner jacket when he arrives, I'm going to look like a complete idiot."

"You couldn't look like an idiot in that dress. You're beautiful. And you so rarely dress up—it's nice to see you like this."

I'd enjoyed getting ready. Taking time with my makeup. Plucking, moisturizing. Not that I was doing it for Logan. Not at all. I just wanted him to know I could compete with the women he was used to.

The doorbell sounded and I heard Lane's footsteps along the hallway. Too late to change now.

"He's on time," Aurora said, handing me my black clutch.

Part of me wondered if he'd just not turn up to try and exact some kind of revenge. It would have been really embarrassing to dress up only to be stood up.

"I've put two condoms in your bag," Aurora whispered. "I'm going to be disappointed if you don't use them."

"I have no intention of sleeping with him. I said yes to dinner because he lost his planning application. It's a deal, not a date."

Aurora groaned. "You might as well kill two birds with one stone—Sam Jones cannot be the last guy you slept with when he was so *lacking* in so many areas." She tried unsuccessfully to hold back a giggle. "I bet Logan Steele is killer between the sheets."

"Have you been imagining him?" I asked, elbowing her in the ribs.

"Uh, yeah—just like every other woman who's met him."

I opened my clutch, pulled out the condoms and tossed

them on my bed. "I absolutely will not be sleeping with him, but thank you for thinking of my sexual health."

"Just think of it as exercise. It's way past when you should have last got laid."

I laughed and headed out. "Speaking of, why are you in my bedroom, handing me condoms on a Friday night? Take some of your own advice."

"I intend to—the guy I'm seeing is due at my place at seven."

Had I heard her right? Aurora hadn't mentioned anything about a guy she was dating regularly. I thought she was on serial dates with different men. "He is?"

"Yes, so *I'm* definitely getting laid tonight."

Was everyone having more sex than me?

"We're in our twenties, Darcy. This is when we should be having all the sex."

I glanced at the condoms, half-tempted to scoop them off my coverlet, but Lane's knock interrupted my train of thought.

"Miss Westbury, Mr. Steele is downstairs for you," he said when I answered the door.

"Thank you, Lane. I'm just coming. Aurora?"

"Have a great night. I'm going to play in your dressing room for a while and then make my way home."

"Have fun," I said.

"Let's *both* have fun tonight—and share the details tomorrow at the Dorchester."

I blew her a kiss and headed down the sweeping staircase. I tucked my clutch under my arm and used one hand to pick up my long skirt and clung onto the old oak balustrade with the other. If I managed to get down these stairs without falling, I'd call tonight a win. I was much better barefoot or in wellies.

Halfway down where the two sets of stairs joined leading down to the hallway, I glanced down to find Logan grinning at me, in a dinner jacket that made him look even broader and taller than he already was. As much as I liked being barefoot in jeans, there was nothing like a man in a dinner jacket to make my pulse race and my stomach flip.

"You look completely breathtaking," he said, shaking his head.

And Logan in his suit looked better than any man I'd ever seen. The man never looked anything but movie-star gorgeous despite his attitude, but in a handmade tuxedo, he took good-looking to a whole new level.

"You said black tie," I replied.

"And you decided on breathtakingly beautiful," he said and held out his hand as I reached him. "But no change there."

I tried to bite back a smile, pleased that he'd said it, even though I didn't believe it.

"Have a good evening, Miss Darcy," Lane said.

"Thank you," I said, grinning despite the fact I was about to share the evening with someone I couldn't even decide if I liked.

Outside the front door, a black Lexus idled, a driver at the wheel. It was a strange choice. He could clearly afford a helicopter, so I was more than a little surprised that he hadn't picked me up in a Bentley or a Jaguar—something a little more showy—but I was pleased he hadn't. He opened the door and guided me inside before rounding the back and joining me. He grinned as we pulled out in silence.

"I thought I might arrive and you would claim to be washing your hair or something," he confessed.

"I told you I would go to dinner with you when you lost the planning application."

Logan chuckled. "When, not if?"

I shrugged and glanced out of the window. I wondered where we were going, but didn't want to give him the satisfaction of asking.

"Seriously, Darcy," he said. I turned and he looked into my eyes as if I was the only thing he was thinking about. "If you really don't want to be here, then we'll turn around. I don't want to take a woman out who has no wish to be in my company."

It was as if my annoyance at him was a balloon and he'd popped it with a pin. The problem was, if I hadn't wanted to go to dinner with Logan, I wouldn't be here. I was turning my irritation on him, when it should be aimed at myself. I'd found myself wanting to spend time with this man since the moment I first laid eyes on him, when I knew I shouldn't, and I couldn't explain it. So I just got angry. "I'm sorry. I'm so used to fighting with you. I don't know how to switch it off."

He swept his thumb under my bottom lip. "Relax. Be yourself. I've never seen you fight with anyone but me, so maybe pretend I'm someone else?" he suggested.

I laughed. "You want me to imagine you're another man?"

"You know, you're the first woman to trample over my ego like it's a worn rug."

I focused on the crinkles around his eyes as he smiled, and that generous mouth of his. I bet women didn't say no to him very often. "Then it's long overdue. Ego shouldn't drive a man."

"No? Then what?"

"Character. Values. The need to make a difference, create a legacy."

He nodded, but didn't say anything, almost as if he was

taking in everything I was saying. "And what about you? What drives you?"

It was an obvious question, but I wasn't sure I had an obvious answer. "I want to preserve the Woolton Estate."·

"But isn't that your brother's legacy? Your grandfather's? What about you?"

"It's my family's legacy. Just because I don't have the title doesn't mean I don't feel the responsibility." I sighed. I should make an effort to be nice at least for the evening. What was I afraid of? "Just because it was my grandfather's legacy doesn't mean it shouldn't be mine. It's really not Ryder's. He's never had the same connection to the estate that I do. Maybe because he went to America when he was right out of university. I don't know. But I love Woolton. I've always loved it. It's always been a sanctuary for me. A safe space." I clasped my hands in my lap. "It's important."

He stayed silent for a few seconds, as if he were assimilating what I was saying. I wasn't used to the men I dated being interested in what I did.

"So it's not a burden? It's such a big place, and it's just you living there."

"I understand how someone might think so, and I can't say that the responsibility isn't huge, even overwhelming at times. But overall, it's an honor." Glancing out at the darkening sky, it looked like we were headed into London. Most men would head into the city if they were trying to impress a woman, but I wasn't sure if Logan was trying to impress me or analyze me. Was I here because he was attracted to me? I was sure there were plenty more attractive and exotic women he could take to dinner who wouldn't trample on his ego.

"I hope you don't mind, but I need to make a brief

appearance at an event on our way into town. My assistant double-booked me."

"You could have canceled dinner."

"And lose an opportunity to spend time with you?" He grinned. "Never."

I didn't know if he was teasing me or giving me a compliment. Perhaps both. "You want me to wait in the car?" I asked as we pulled into a dimly lit North London car park. Jesus, it looked like he was about to meet a mafia contact or make a drug deal.

"I'd like you to come in with me, but do what you feel comfortable with."

I squinted as I looked out of the window. "Where are we going?"

"Live a little. Let it be a surprise."

I peered out at the shabby, utilitarian, box-shaped building that had been built in the Sixties. The paint peeling from the window frames suggested that no one had looked after it since, although a stream of teenagers in school uniforms were filing inside, so it wasn't abandoned.

Logan opened my door. "You want to come in?"

What was going on in there and why on Earth was Logan here? "Sure," I said, stepping out. "Clearly, I'm over-dressed."

"Not at all. You can get dresses similar on the high street, right?"

I laughed. "Yeah." He was probably right, Zara probably did an excellent knockoff of this Gucci number.

I shivered as his hand met the small of my back and he guided me toward the door the teenagers were all going through. Were we volunteering at a youth club or something?

As we drew closer, we caught the attention of one of the

boys. "Hey, Stevie, look! It's Wolverine." His face broke out into a grin and he came bounding up to us, knocking fists with Logan. "We didn't know if you were coming tonight or if Mr. Graham was going to make the announcements."

"Wouldn't miss it," Logan replied.

"I hope you've brought your credit card," another of the boys said as we collected a swarm of boys around us as we made our way inside.

The bright electric lights overhead lit up a large room lined with informational posters about local services and groups. Rows of orange plastic chairs faced a small stage, most of which were occupied by teenagers in uniforms.

Behind the stage, a banner read: *Welcome Young Entrepreneurs* and then beneath in smaller letters, *Sponsored by the Steele Foundation.*

"You okay?" Logan whispered in my ear.

"I'm fine. You making a speech?"

"We'll be out of here in twenty minutes, I promise."

I shook my head. "Don't worry about it. Take your time." He had me intrigued.

Logan smiled and reached into his breast pocket, pulling out some index cards. "You'll get a good view from here." He headed toward the stage where he shook hands and swapped pleasantries with several people.

I took a seat and waited for whatever was going to happen, to happen.

A woman in her early forties sat down beside me. "It's so nice that Logan brought someone with him tonight," she said. "I'm Avril." She held out her hand.

I took her hand. "I'm Darcy. How do you do?"

"He never wants any press or publicity for this. I always think that he should be shouting it from the rooftops. He's helped so many young people."

"How did he get involved?" I asked, pretending I knew what the hell was going on.

I followed her gaze to where it was fixed to the front of the hall in anticipation. "We've all followed Logan's career since he left—it's not often that you have an earl go to a state school."

Logan had been one of these scruffy kids? Surely not. He was an earl. His family must have had money. He would have gone to boarding school.

"But especially not one that turns around and builds a multi-billion-pound empire. Kids from schools like this don't do that. But he defied the odds. And he decided that he wanted his path to be one that created a way forward for others. He passionately believes that these kids just need an opportunity." She glanced at me, but I didn't know what to say. Logan had been one of these children?

Logan stepped up to the podium. "Good evening, pupils of Newham Comprehensive," he began, and I had to bite back a grin. He commanded the room, stood tall and broad and spoke confidently. I shouldn't have expected anything less.

He didn't talk about his story, although the way the pupils were transfixed by him, it seemed most of them knew it already. Instead, he immediately launched into the reason he was here. "We have had some excellent students in Steele Enterprises on our work experience program in the last twelve months. As well as giving practical experience, it's important to me that Newham students coming to Steele Enterprises understand what's possible. I started exactly where you sit now. You need to figure out what you want in life. It's important to dream big. Then make that dream a reality by working hard, keeping focused. Take the opportunities that come your way. Turn rejection and failure into a lesson. And most importantly, never give up."

I felt like an idiot. I'd made assumptions about Logan's upbringing that were clearly completely off. Furthermore, I'd thought his wealth and privilege meant that he didn't care about anyone other than himself.

He went on to speak about the various students who had done work experience at his company in the past year, and then announced the names of those who would be taking the spots for the following year.

"Now, what you've all been waiting for—time to announce who won the investment in their business idea." He talked through some of the ideas that had crossed his desk and how impressed he was. "What I have enjoyed the most about this year's entries is the tenacity of some of the applications. I had ten people apply this year who also applied last year but were unsuccessful. Those students aren't giving up, and I admire that. Others wrote about what lessons they've learned when things haven't gone as they'd hoped. That determination is key to success. Being able to fail and stand up, dust yourself off and try again is the most important thing you can do for yourself. Don't write yourself off. Failure is the foundation of success."

"If it had been anyone else," Avril whispered, "the students wouldn't take any notice. They'd think he was some rich snob from London who had no idea what their lives were like telling them what to do. But because he's an ex-student, they listen. They want to learn from him. Be him."

I nodded. "I can see that." I glanced around at his audience and they were listening like he held all the answers.

"I've decided to invest in three businesses this time around," Logan continued. "All three of these people worked hard, had clear plans that they've followed, adapted and learned from. Most importantly, they've gotten them off the ground without any financial help. The first recipient is Stacey Grant, who started up a dog-walking business and needs money to advertise and expand. She's worked hard, endured failures, but hasn't let them beat her. I'm pleased to be helping her on her way."

Students started whooping and cheering. Avril clapped enthusiastically. "She's focused on expanding. She already has two other girls working for her. It's quite incredible. She's sixteen and two years ago, I worried she'd never hold down a job."

Logan cleared his throat and the laughter died down. "The second investment I'm going to make is to David Road's newsletter app that condenses football news from all over the web for fans who follow the sport internationally. I've been impressed with the way David has learned new skills in order to make his business work."

"Yes," my neighbor said in a loud whisper. "David deserves that. It's so nice that Logan is giving more than one prize. He only committed to one every six months, but now he gives money to any idea that he thinks deserves it."

Who was this man she was describing? The man up on stage was nothing like the one I'd been sparring with all this time. He was generous and thoughtful. Cared about people, wanted to invest in something bigger than himself.

How was it possible to feel so incredibly proud of someone who days ago I'd hated? What else had I assumed about him that I was wrong about?

"I have one final announcement. I've never done this before for a Newham student, but her ideas during work experience coupled with the turnaround in grades and determination to succeed has meant that for the first time, I will have a Newham student working full-time at Steele Enterprises. Julia Simpson has agreed to come and work for me. She's shown time and again her attention to detail and commitment to stress-testing the ideas you put forward. She's attended every single workshop I've run at the school in the last two years and I believe she'll be a great asset to my business."

If Logan Steele had announced that he was in fact Wolverine, I would have been less shocked. He'd turned my view of him around one hundred and eighty degrees. The man I'd agreed to go to dinner with wasn't the one I was with tonight. I'd clearly misjudged him. Underestimated him. Logan Steele deserved my respect and admiration, and I planned to get to know him better.

EIGHTEEN

Logan

Had I upset Darcy by bringing her to the center? Irritated her because I'd put another engagement first? She hadn't said much since we'd walked out. "Dinner?" I asked as I slid into the car next to her.

"Sounds good," she replied, her voice softer than I was used to.

"Sorry, that was a little out of our way, but it was a commitment I couldn't break."

"Of course not," she replied. "I'm glad I got to come. Who knew Steele Enterprises invested in dog-walking businesses?"

I raised an eyebrow. "It was the Steele Foundation. And I want to be encouraging. She was hardworking, organized and committed. That should be rewarded." I fastened my seat belt as the car got moving.

"I wasn't teasing you—you did a great thing. It seems there's a lot about you I don't know."

"Maybe a couple of things." It hadn't been my intention

to show Darcy what I did with my old school. I rarely spoke about it with anyone. Even my grandmother didn't know the extent of my support for Newham Comprehensive. I'd wanted to take Darcy to dinner, but I couldn't get out of the announcements tonight so there had been only one solution —to take Darcy with me.

She didn't seem horrified, and a part of me had wondered if she would be. By my background. By the state of the community center, by the scruffy and sometimes unruly kids. She'd grown up very differently to me—in many ways she was down-to-earth, but there was no way of getting away from the fact that she'd grown up at Woolton Hall as the granddaughter of a duke, at the ancestral estate.

"And here I was, thinking you were all about money."

I sucked in a breath as I fiddled with my cufflink which seemed to be loose. "Don't get me wrong. Money's important to me. Poverty was the best foundation I could have ever had, and a huge motivator."

She shifted slightly so her knees pointed toward me. "I don't get it, though. You're an earl. At some point your family must have had money."

I pulled off my cufflink, which had broken. "My father gambled away all our family's wealth very shortly after he inherited."

"I'm so sorry," she said.

I glanced out of the window, not wanting to see pity in her eyes.

"Do you still see your father?"

I shook my head. "Not since I was three years old. I have no memory of him at all."

"Three? Wow. That's so young. Did he leave you and your mother?"

I blew out a breath. I never shared this story. And

people never asked. My money and power was all people saw. No one tried to dig under the surface. "My mother died when I was two. Meningitis." I never cared that I didn't know my father. I didn't *want* to know him. But my mother? I just had a flash of a memory of her. A single snapshot of blue eyes and soft blonde hair, and it wasn't enough.

"Is that why he gambled? Because he lost his wife?"

I rested my arm on the window ledge. "No. It was all gone by then, from what I understand."

"And so you went to live with your grandmother," Darcy said.

If it had only been that easy. If only my father had wanted to do the right thing by his son. "My grandmother paid my father to give me up, and Badsley was the only thing she had left that was worth anything. He sold me. Took his mother's money. And she had to give up her home." Even though I'd bought Badsley back, the wound hadn't completely healed. My resentment toward my father would last my entire life.

Darcy slid her fingers over the fist I had clenched around my cufflink and we sat in silence. There was nothing she could say that could make it better, and she knew it. And her touch provided comfort that I hadn't expected. Finally, she twisted my wrist so my hand faced up. "I bet I can fix this," she said, taking the cufflink from my palm.

I wanted to tell her to forget it, to link my fingers with hers as we made our way to the restaurant, but instead I watched as she inspected the broken cufflink and then dug about in her bag for something.

"It makes more sense to me now," she said, "you buying Badsley, money being so important. Even the helicopter. Sort of." She pulled a pair of tweezers from her bag and set about tightening one of the screws that had worked loose. "It's like proof or something."

"Badsley's not just a way of me making up for my father destroying his family. That's a big part of it, but I enjoy being there. I like living in Woolton."

She frowned, but didn't say anything. I wasn't sure if it was because she was concentrating, or if she was skeptical that I enjoyed Woolton and Badsley.

"Here," she said, reaching for my shirtsleeve. "All fixed." She slid the silver through the holes and snapped it into place. "Perfect."

"Thank you," I replied.

She smiled, clearly proud of her repair. "Have you done everything you set out to?" she asked. "Even though your father's sins weren't your own, you seem to have taken them on like they were."

"I'm far from done, but I don't think it's about just making money anymore. You using that article in the council meeting was..."

Darcy winced. "I'm sorry. I did whatever—"

"It was a smart move. You went for my Achilles heel. Takes guts. But that article made me reassess. I don't want success for its own sake anymore. I don't need it, and I don't want to have a legacy of destruction. I want to build something of my own. I've always taken on other people's businesses and improved them or sold them, but I've never built anything from the ground up. That's what I want to do with Manor House Club."

She groaned. "I can't regret that it's not coming to Woolton, Logan."

"I know. And there's an upside to me losing that fight— I'm sitting here with you."

The corners of her mouth turned up as she shook her head.

"I mean it," I said as the car slowed to a stop outside the hotel. "Here we are."

I would never have called myself a romantic, but I'd wanted to do something special for Darcy. And I wanted her to know that dinner with me was something to be savored and enjoyed rather than tolerated and endured. As much as she clearly had money, her life didn't seem to involve much indulgence, and tonight I wanted to be a little decadent, indulge her a little. I liked to see Darcy's smile and I'd enjoy seeing her wearing it more often around me.

I opened her car door and guided her to the hotel entrance, my hand on the small of her back. "I don't know if you've ever been here before," I said as we rode up in the lift.

"To Windows?" she asked, referring to the restaurant at the top of the hotel. "I haven't. I heard it has a wonderful view."

I nodded as the doors opened on the twenty-eighth floor. She stepped out and I followed. A member of staff held a tray of champagne as we entered the restaurant. Tonight was a risk. Darcy's comfort zone would be a picnic in Badsley's woods or a home-cooked meal made with products from the farm shop. But I wanted to push her a little. Make her realize that she might enjoy things she'd not properly considered. Including me.

She turned to me when she saw the quiet restaurant. "Are we the only diners?" she asked.

"I thought it would be less distracting if it was just the two of us."

"So you just hired out the entire restaurant?" she asked

as if she thought it was the craziest thing she'd ever heard, but I couldn't tell if under the shock she was a little pleased.

I followed as she wandered farther inside. Floor-to-ceiling windows on all four sides of the circular room gave us the best view in London. "If you look into the distance, the countryside is right there. I thought this was the perfect combination of great food with rural views," I said. "And it's very glamorous. Which I thought would suit you."

"Are you serious?" she asked, turning to face me. "I live in jeans and if I manage to put a comb through my hair most days, I'm doing well."

I paused and pushed her hair behind her shoulder. "Sometimes, I think you're scared of being beautiful. And perhaps a little frightened of letting go and just enjoying yourself. I thought we could both indulge a little this evening. And I'll get to enjoy your beauty even if you don't. This evening you look particularly stunning."

"I just have some makeup on," she mumbled as she scanned the room.

"Stop making excuses for being gorgeous. Have you seen yourself this evening?" I countered. "You're beautiful with or without the makeup, but tonight you're like a Roman goddess."

As I stepped forward, she tipped her head back. "You're right. I'm a terrible compliment receiver, so I'm going to go with thank you."

I swept a strand of hair that had escaped one of the pins away from her face and a blush dusted her cheeks.

Perhaps she didn't think I was such a terrible date after all.

"How is your cufflink holding up?" she asked, glancing down at my sleeve. Her fingers dipped under the cotton and against my skin, sending shivers across my body.

"Holding," I said. "You've always got a solution." I met and worked with a lot of clever, independent women, and though Darcy had never set foot in an office, she was one of the most capable women I'd ever met.

I smoothed my hand up her back and she blinked slowly and then stepped away from my touch. "Let's take a seat," I said.

"But where?" Her grin lit up the room as she twirled around in a circle amongst the empty tables.

"We can move with every course, if you like, to get a different view."

She shook her head. "It's too much. But tonight, I'm going to enjoy it." She chose a table overlooking Hyde Park.

Although I knew money wouldn't impress Darcy, I'd meant to make an impression by hiring out the restaurant. To go beyond what any other man had done on a date. As much as she would have dated wealthy men before, I knew the British aristocracy weren't fond of extravagance—yet it was what she deserved. And I wanted to stand out to her, as she did to me. But I hadn't imagined seeing such delight painted across her face.

It was intoxicating.

She wasn't pretending that she did this all the time. She wasn't trying to make me feel bad for being indulgent or even for bringing her to London. She was enjoying herself, just as I'd hoped. I'd never had so much fun with a woman. Never enjoyed someone's pleasure quite so much.

"You can see the Serpentine, even in the dark. Look," she said turning to me.

It was just possible to see the light catching the water of the lake between the parting of the trees in Hyde Park. "You can," I replied. "And Apsley House, down here."

"Gah," she said. "I love that place."

I grinned, enjoying that she knew it and loved it. "It's my favorite thing to do in London. That huge statue of Napoleon at the bottom of the stairs? I love that Wellington kept his archenemy at the heart of his home."

"It's an interesting way to deal with your nemesis, for sure. Are you going to install something at Badsley?"

I chuckled. "No enemies. None worthy of a sculpture, anyway," I said. She'd been my most worthy opponent.

"I'm surprised you have time to take in the sights when you're in London."

I took a seat opposite her. "I haven't been for a while—perhaps you'll take me."

"Take you sightseeing? I don't think so. I'm a busy girl."

I couldn't remember wanting to touch, stroke, connect with a woman, like I did Darcy. Being on opposite sides of the table created too much of a divide between us. I reached, brushing my thumb under her chin. "I like that about you."

She sat back in her chair and looked at me as if she were trying to see inside my brain. "Is this your general M.O.? With women? Dazzle them with this kind of thing?"

The waiter placed napkins on our laps and left us with the menus.

"No. Normally my M.O. involves no more than a drink and a compliment."

"Then why all this?" she said scanning the room. "It's a lot."

"Too much?" Had I read her enjoyment wrong? Was this a step too far out of her comfort zone?

"If this is what you think you need to do to get me into bed, then yes, it's too much."

"You think I've done this so at the end of the night you'll feel obligated to sleep with me?"

"No, more that maybe you're trying to...seduce me."

"I can't decide whether you want me to reassure you that you're different, or if you're trying to shame my sexual appetite."

"Both, maybe," she replied, tracing the edge of her glass with a delicate finger.

It was the most honest answer I'd ever had from a woman. When I thought about it, Darcy was never anything but honest with me. She never dressed anything up, or paid me false compliments to ingratiate, the way so many others did. I'd never known her to say anything she didn't mean.

"Well, you are different."

"More of a conquest?"

I liked smart women, but Darcy was something else. "I think it's my default setting to see everyone and everything as something to be conquered. And with you it might have started out that way. Getting you here might have been partly me wanting to prove to myself that I could have what I wanted."

"Partly?"

"There's something I like about you that I don't understand, but I'm here to explore it."

"But you can't work out whether or not you want to sleep with me," she said.

I frowned. "No. I'm absolutely sure I want to sleep with you. If I'm holding back, it's because I'm not used to knowing the women I fuck." She deserved the same honesty from me that I had from her.

"And that's a problem because?"

Clearly, she wasn't averse to sleeping together, hadn't balked when I'd been clear about my desire for her. "Because sex is usually just sex. And sometimes I like the woman. Sometimes I don't know her. But it doesn't matter. Because I don't need to know her or like her."

"No feelings involved. No awkwardness the morning after. Well, maybe I'm the same."

I laughed. "You want to use me for my body."

She looked up at me from under her lashes. "It's nice, from what I've seen of it."

"I don't think so. I don't think that's who you are. Not deep down inside." I reached across the table and linked my fingers through hers. She shrugged at my response. She knew I was right. But she was even practical and straightforward about seduction. There was no hiding anything. Nothing unspoken between us. "I'm having a lot of fun tonight. What do you say we just take each moment as it comes and see where it leads us?"

Any other woman and she'd be naked right now. But this wasn't about sex for me. And her pretending it was for her was a defense mechanism. In the same way that she didn't see herself as glamorous or beautiful, she didn't get that I wanted to have dinner with her and get to know her. I wanted to earn it if it happened. And I wanted to deserve it when it did.

NINETEEN

Logan

I wasn't ready for this evening to be over. I couldn't remember the last time I'd talked so much. Listened so hard. Laughed so often. Dinner with Darcy had exceeded every expectation I'd had. As we pulled up at Woolton Hall, I stroked my thumb over our linked hands before releasing her so I could get out to open her door.

I hadn't even kissed her yet, but every molecule in my body vibrated with the need to pull her close.

"Come in," she said as I took her hand and helped her out of the car.

I wanted her and I wouldn't say no despite knowing that if I was being practical, sensible, I should decline her invitation. I wasn't about to make a habit of this evening— not the dinner, not even the sex. Sex was always a one-time deal. But the sensible part of me wasn't the one in charge anymore.

I followed her up the steps, her gold dress rustling as she

walked and drew my attention to the sway of her hips and the smooth skin of her back.

She opened the huge oak door and kicked off her heels as we stepped inside.

"Thank God. My feet," she groaned. "Let me grab some whiskey. Stay here."

She disappeared up the corridor, but returned carrying a decanter of alcohol and two glasses. I took the decanter and she transferred the glasses so she held one in each hand, then pulled up the front of her skirt and ascended the stairs.

She opened the latch of her bedroom door and briefly glanced over her shoulder before she stepped inside. Did she think I might not follow her?

As we stepped inside, she slid the glasses onto an old wooden chest and flicked on the bedside lights.

"So, how do you want to—"

I put my finger over her lips. "Know that I enjoy how independent you are. How you call me on my shit. That you don't let me get away with anything when we talk. Outside of this room we are equals. But also know that when we're fucking, I'm in charge. There's no room for debate. Nothing's up for discussion. You will do what I say, when I say it, how I say it."

Her breath grew short and a scatter of goosebumps rose across her arms. "Logan. That's not me. It's not who I am."

"Maybe it is, and you just don't realize it." I pushed back her silky brown hair from her face.

Her eyes lowered to the floor. "What if it isn't?"

"Trust me. You'll like it better this way." Responsibility seeped through Darcy's pores. She was strong because she'd had to be, practical because that was what was required of her. We'd be perfectly suited in bed because while we were fucking, she wouldn't have to think about any of that.

Everything would be my responsibility. "Do you understand?"

Her eyelids flickered, but she nodded. "I'm not sure I'll be very—"

I circled my arm around her waist and jerked her toward me, pulling her against my throbbing erection. "That's the point—you don't need to worry about anything."

I released her. "Undress me."

She hesitated, then brought her trembling fingers to the buttons of my shirt. Glancing between my face and my shirt, she worked the buttons open and pulled my bowtie free.

"You're a beautiful woman, Darcy. Your tight, generous arse."

She circled me and pulled my jacket off.

"Your tiny waist. Those sparkling eyes."

She undid my cufflinks, placing them carefully on the bedside table, then pulled my shirt from my trousers, her cool fingers trailing over my hot skin as she pushed the cotton over my shoulders. It was as if she was hypnotized by my body as she trailed a finger around the skin above my waistband. She settled in front of me, her fingers fiddling with the opening of my trousers.

"I like every part of you that I've seen. Now I want to see if I like the parts you've been hiding just as much. Is your pussy as soft and hot as I think it will be?" She paused, her fingers frozen as she caught her breath. "Will you moan desperately when I suck and bite your nipples?"

As if need and desperation coursed through her body, she softened and weakened, and she lost her balance. I slid my hands around her waist to keep her upright. She took a breath and released my trousers, looking me right in the eye as she slid down my boxer briefs, kneeling as she did.

"Good girl," I said as she made quick work of my shoes and socks. "Now stand." If she was down there for a second longer, the temptation to fuck her mouth would overwhelm me.

"I'm not sure I like being ordered about."

"Just do it. Don't think about whether you like it."

She rose to her feet, her gaze fixed on my thick, hard dick, already full and throbbing against my stomach.

"Keep doing as you're told and you'll get plenty of my cock. Turn around."

She looked up at me, her forehead furrowed. She ran her tongue over her top lip but she slowly turned.

Jesus, did she realize that every move she made drove me to fuck her into the next universe?

I unzipped her dress and let it pool at her feet, revealing nothing but her naked back and black lace knickers. She was beginning to belong to me.

"No bra," I said, the words almost catching in my throat. "Turn around."

She stepped out of her dress and turned to face me.

"Off," I said, nodding at her underwear.

She hesitated, transferring her weight from one leg to the other.

"I want to see your pussy. Take them off—don't make me ask again."

She sank her teeth into her bottom lip, clearly reticent.

We were at a turning point. Would she surrender? I kept silent as she tried to decide if she was willing to submit.

Her breath grew heavier and pride circled in my belly as she snuck her thumbs into either side of her underwear and slipped them off.

She'd willingly relinquished control. She was mine.

And she'd never looked so beautiful.

As she straightened, she folded her arms, covering her chest. I shook my head. "No." I pulled her arms apart. "This is my body while we are together like this. You don't get to cover it up. It's mine to inspect, to worship, to use, to fuck. You've given it to me."

I trailed a finger up from her belly button to her perfectly ripe breasts, her dusty pink nipples already hard and desperate for my touch. Pinching each one between my thumb and forefinger, she frowned, then tipped her head back on a gasp.

"I get to do whatever I want with you."

"Logan," she whispered. "Don't hurt me."

I wasn't into BDSM in any real sense, though I'd tried it a couple of times, been to a few clubs. What I liked was control. To establish the balance of power. To have someone trust me to give them what we both needed. I released Darcy's breasts and cupped her head in my hands. "All I'm going to do is make you feel good."

Pressing my lips against hers, we stood, our naked bodies brushing, her fingers trailing over my back. I pushed my tongue between her lips and began my exploration.

I pulled back, desire shooting through me as I took in Darcy's reddened lips and her mussed hair.

I walked her over to the bed, my hands full of her arse, and tipped her back onto the mattress, her hair spreading out behind her as if she were underwater.

Pulling her knees apart, I glanced between her thighs. The glistening sheen over the trimmed hair told me everything I needed to know. I was used to women with bare pussies, but I liked that Darcy was different. It suited her. Showed her to be the independent, real woman I was so fascinated by.

Smoothing my hands up her thighs, I pressed my lips to

the soft flesh just beneath her hip on one side, then trailed a straight line to the other. She dug her fingers into my hair and sighed as if she was used to having me between her legs, worshipping her body.

It shouldn't be true, but for some reason the chemistry was easy between us. Perhaps because I'd drawn the lines of responsibility clearly in the sand, or because that was what she wanted. I pressed the flat of my tongue against her stomach and licked up between her heavy, milky-white breasts. Almost every part of her was the exact opposite of the women I was used to fucking, yet I'd never been so turned on. I grazed my teeth over her nipples and she arched, squirming beneath me. I'd bet no one had ever dared fuck this woman properly.

Until now.

Bracing my arms on either side of her, I kissed her, resisting the fingers she curled deliciously around my neck. I rolled to my back. "Sit on me," I said, as I gripped her hips and urged her on top of me "On my face. I want to taste you."

She gasped. "No, I can't..."

I slapped her playfully on her arse. "You remember the bit when I said I was in charge and that there was no room for debate?" I dug my fingertips into her skin, encouraging her forward. "Hold on to the headboard and tell me before you come."

Her pussy smelled of honey as I lowered her onto my tongue. I began to plow a trail through her folds and around her clit, then back down. Christ, I loved going down on a woman, but when she didn't know how good it could be? That was the best. Giving Darcy something she'd never had before was like mainlining power and dominance. She tried to hold in her gasps and moans as I kept her in place, but eventually, she began to twist her hips, thrusting against my tongue as her pleasure built.

I groaned as her wetness increased, coating my mouth and my chin and she began to shudder. "Logan, Logan. I'm...I'm going to—"

I pushed her off my face, flipping her to her back and crawled over her. I wasn't about to let her come on my face. I wanted to be fucking her when she came, so I could see what I did to her when she climaxed. Plus, it was a reminder that her orgasms were mine to give her, rather than hers to take.

"What are you doing?" she asked.

"Fucking you," I said as I slid off the mattress and pulled her to the edge of the bed. "You'll come when I let you."

I grabbed a condom by her pillow. "Expecting someone?" I asked, holding up the square. I spotted another one, just about to fall off the mattress.

She sighed. "My best friend put them in my bag tonight."

"And you took them out?" I frowned. "It's important to be safe, Darcy."

"Am I safe with you?" she asked in a whisper.

"Always," I replied.

I couldn't wait another second to get inside her. I tore open one of the condoms and rolled the latex over my straining cock. "Hold your knees. I want to get nice and deep."

She groaned and did as I asked, displaying herself perfectly for me.

"Good girl," I grunted as I thrust into her, hard and deep. I almost collapsed right then at the perfection of it all.

She was so tight, so wet, her chest heaving, her walls squeezing.

I leaned forward. "Breathe," I reminded both of us. She'd have me coming in ten seconds if I didn't calm down, if I didn't block out how this beautiful, spirited, independent woman was spreading her legs for me, already on the brink of orgasm because of the things I'd done to her.

After a couple of deep breaths, I pulled out and thrust back in, settling into a rhythm that was slow enough to stop me from coming, but good enough that I never wanted to stop.

She gazed up at me and stroked her hand over my cheek. "This is so good," she whispered as if she never thought it could be. "You're so good." She scratched her nails gently down my chest as if she was trying to encourage my orgasm back from where I'd banished it. I knew she'd never been fucked like this before.

I sped up as she reached for me, but I knew her touch would have me coming and I wanted to keep fucking her. I grasped her wrists and held them over her head. Worry passed over her face. "Logan. I'm going to—Logan."

"You can come now, beautiful," I said and watched as her orgasm tore through her, stealing strangled moans from her throat as she pulsed around my cock. I kept my rhythm the same, determined to make her come again before I did.

"Logan," she said, her voice, breathy and desperate. "What are you doing? You. Need. To. Stop."

Her next orgasm wouldn't take long. "No, I want you to come again. You don't get to choose."

She opened her mouth, half-whimper, half-groan as she squirmed underneath me. I released her hands, but kept my rhythm the same as she grabbed at my chest, my arms, bucking wildly underneath me, almost fighting her orgasm, trying to keep it at bay.

Heat coursed through my body as I held back my release, my jaw tightening each time her breasts shifted beneath my thrusts. Sweat collected at my hairline with every swivel of her hips. Her sharp, desperate sounds were like oxygen to the orgasm building and building at the base of my spine. Just as I thought I couldn't last another second, her eyes widened and she wrapped her legs around my waist—I fucked her once, twice, three times before coming like a train. Our eyes locked and all I heard were her breath, her moans, her sighs as she floated back down to earth.

Perfection surrounded me.

Panting, I couldn't tear my gaze from hers; I wanted to sustain this moment of complete perfection and pleasure.

Still fighting for breath, she trailed her fingers over my eyebrows. "Fuck, Logan. I've never..."

"Shhhh." I pulled out and dealt with the condom before gathering her into my arms as I laid back on the pillows to take in what had just happened. I knew she was going to tell me how she'd never come like that, let alone come twice. Or how I was the greatest fuck she'd ever had. She didn't need to—I already knew.

Worse, her confession might lead to one of my own. I could end up telling her she was the sexiest woman I'd ever laid eyes on. How her compliant transformation in the bedroom was the biggest turn-on I'd ever experienced.

How I didn't want to let her go.

I wasn't in the mood for confessions. Especially ones I didn't understand and would come to regret with the sunrise. I knew who I was and what I was capable of. I understood that however amazing tonight had been, this was where it ended. Because it was all I had to give.

TWENTY

Darcy

Shopping had never been my favorite thing to do, especially not after a night like last night, but I'd promised Violet, Scarlett's sister, I'd meet her. And so far, I was still awake and functioning.

"Now mimosas," Violet said as she accepted her card and the Elie Saab dress, all beautifully boxed up from the sales assistant.

"I'm pleased we found something. The purple really suits you." I glanced at my phone. No text messages. No missed calls. Of course there weren't. That wasn't Logan Steele's style.

"Thank you for coming." Violet signaled a cab.

"Where are we going?" I asked. "The Dorchester is just around the corner."

"I know, but I'm in heels and feeling lazy, and we're late meeting Aurora."

It was probably just as well we weren't walking. I wasn't

sure my legs could take it given all the shaking they'd done the night before.

As we sprung out of the cab we almost knocked Aurora over as she headed into the hotel. "Hey, how are you?" I asked.

"I'm not sure if I'm talking to you, since you've done nothing but dodge all my questions," Aurora replied.

I glanced at Violet who narrowed her eyes. "I'm not dodging—I've been shopping all morning with Violet."

"So are you saying you're willing to give a full and frank confession, right now, over tea and champagne?"

"I feel like I'm missing something," Violet said as she pushed through the revolving door into the lobby.

Full and frank wasn't exactly what I was prepared to be—I was pretty sure some of the things that Logan had done to me last night weren't legal, and they certainly weren't the kind of thing you discussed over tea at the Dorchester. "I can tell you how my evening went, if that's what you mean." I headed over to the hostess at the Palm Lounge, gave my name and she showed us to our table. It was in a perfect spot, beyond the serious man in his fifties playing American standards on the grand piano and tucked away from people who might overhear.

The Promenade at the Dorchester was one of my favorite places in London. Decorated as if Lady Bracknell might appear at any time, it felt as if time had stopped in 1892. Palm plants were set against orange marble columns and curtains along each side of the long room. Low, white cloth-covered tables were set amongst the green button-backed chairs, stuffed so full they looked like they might burst at any moment.

"Did you know this room is as long as Nelson's Column?" Violet said as we sat down.

"Are you studying to be a London tourist guide?" Aurora asked, setting her handbag on the low stool provided especially for that purpose.

"No, I just take an interest in this beautiful city," she replied. "You two take it for granted."

"Probably true," I agreed, opening my napkin on my lap, and wondering how long the champagne would take to arrive.

"Anyway, enough of the deflection," Aurora said. "I want to hear about Darcy's date last night."

"Wait." Violet grabbed my wrist as if I were about to bolt. "You had a date? Last night? We've been together all morning and you haven't said anything? I need new friends." She released me and slumped back in her chair.

"Oh good, so I've not missed out on anything," Aurora said. "I thought you two would have picked out the brides-maids' outfits by now and swapped all the gossip."

I leaned back in my chair, resigning myself to the coming inevitable discussion. "Don't be ridiculous. It was a date—no wedding bells are ringing."

"But you liked him?" Aurora asked.

"Who? I'm the last to know everything around here," Violet said.

"Only an earl who moved in next door to Darcy," Aurora said. "A tall, handsome, totally charming—"

"Arsehole who tried to destroy the village," I added.

"Wait a second," Violet said. "You went on a date with someone who tried to what?"

I filled Violet in on the lead up to last night and tried my best not to smile as I told her I'd agreed to the date.

"So tell me everything," she said. "Was he charming?"

I took a deep breath. "Yes. More than I expected." He'd certainly lacked charm in the bedroom, but that had only made him more attractive. I'd been nervous by his demands at first, and I still wasn't sure why I did as he asked. But he was right, I enjoyed it, even though I wasn't quite sure I should have.

"So, what did you do? Dinner?" Violet asked.

I nodded, but before I had the chance to answer, Aurora asked, "Where did he take you?"

"We came into London—to the Hilton actually." I nodded south, toward where the Hilton stood just a few meters away.

"Nice. Did you have the best table?" Aurora asked.

I sank my teeth into my bottom lip, trying to disguise my smile at the memory of realizing we were the only diners. "Every table actually. We were the only ones there."

"What, he hired the entire restaurant?" Violet asked.

I shrugged, trying not to let my grin take over my face. I'd never had anyone do anything so romantic for me.

"Wow. He meant business. He clearly was trying to impress."

I wasn't sure he'd been trying to impress me exactly, but he'd thought about me. The views of the countryside. The way he said he wanted to encourage me to be a little self-indulgent. It was the way he seemed so acutely aware of small things that drew me to him but also made me a little wary of him.

"He has a really nice side to him," I replied, remembering the stop at the community center. I didn't say anything about it because I wasn't sure if Logan would want me to. He clearly didn't publicize it and the woman I'd sat next to had mentioned he'd never brought anyone with him, not even his grandmother. It made me feel more special than it should. I shared something with him that others hadn't. But it had been a diary clash that meant I was there.

It wasn't as if Logan was *trying* to open up and show me a deeper side to him.

"And what about the sex? Was that a nice side?" Aurora asked.

Violet sat forward in her chair, clearly wanting to catch my every word.

"It was..." How could I describe it? It was easily the best sex I'd ever had—and I'd probably never have better. But something about the way that he had me submit to him so quickly had me questioning myself. He'd been right when he said that I'd enjoy it but what was it that he saw in me that had him so confident in my reaction? "He was..." Domineering and controlling and had fucked me like it was his job. "Clearly experienced."

"Well, duh. Did you see him? With a face and body like that, he has plenty of opportunity to perfect his skills." Aurora said. "So how good was it?"

"This is so great!" Violet raised her glass of champagne and took a sip. "I was beginning to think that maybe you were never going to have sex again, and—"

"Good!" I blurted, trying to stop Violet from finishing her thought. "Very good."

"Define 'very'—were you up all night swinging from the chandeliers?" Violet asked.

I fixed her with a stare. "That's all you're getting from me." I wanted to ask them whether it was normal for an independent woman to give that all up for a few hours. Why it felt so good to give up my control, my body to someone else. But it felt too private, too embarrassing to admit.

As our tea and champagne arrived, we fell silent. While our waitress pointed out all the different types of sandwiches and cakes, I couldn't help but wonder what Logan was doing right now. Was he at Badsley? Was he thinking about last night? About me?

"How did you leave things?" Aurora asked.

I tried not to let my shoulders slump in response to her question. I'd woken up late and sped into the shower with barely a good morning. When I'd emerged, he'd been dressed in his tuxedo, ready to leave. "I was running late and he left. This isn't the beginning of some beautiful love story. Sorry to disappoint you, girls."

Part of me had been surprised that he'd stayed over, but given we'd been up most of the night, he hadn't had much of a chance to leave. We could only have slept for a little over an hour. If I hadn't had to rush to get ready to come here, would we have had a conversation about perhaps a follow-up? A second date? And was that something I wanted?

"But you clearly like him. Enough to have slept with him," Violet said.

"You said yourself he's handsome. And I needed to get back on the horse, so to speak. It's no big deal." I wasn't about to confess that if he'd asked me I most likely would have said yes to a second date. Yes to more of his demanding and controlling. Yes to spending Sunday naked and in bed. I wouldn't confess to it because it wasn't going to happen. Men like Logan didn't date. They fucked.

"You said he was charming," Aurora chipped in.

"So?" I asked. "It was fun. No more, no less." I was meant to be cool about it. Meant to think about it as just sex. I may have a desire for more, but if I kept telling myself it was a one-time thing, I might just believe it.

My phone vibrated in my bag, and while I ignored it, Violet and Aurora stared at my Longchamp as if it were a monkey doing a striptease.

"You have to see who it is," Violet said.

"I bet it's him," Aurora added.

"It's probably Lane with a question about thc horses." It would be nice if it were Logan, but he'd made no suggestion of calling me later or seeing me again and my pride wasn't about to let me be a girl who chased after men like Logan Steele.

"Well, there's only one way to find out." Violet nodded at my bag.

They weren't going to stop until I relented, and since I was confident it wouldn't be Logan, I pulled out my phone.

I keep seeing your face when you come. I make fantastic cheese on toast. And I have a bottle of pinot noir with your name on it. How about combining all three? Are you busy tonight?

I sucked in a breath, shocked he'd sent a message, shocked he wanted to see me again and shocked at how his words had me squirming in my chair.

"It's him," Aurora said. "I knew it."

I glanced up to find my two friends staring at me. "No big deal," I said, tossing my phone in my bag.

Did I want cheese on toast, wine and orgasms? I was pretty sure that sounded like a perfect Saturday night, but there was something about Logan Steele and the way I couldn't quite figure him out that had me holding back. Something about how badly I wanted to see him tonight that had me nervous.

"What did the message say?" Violet asked.

"Just to say hi. Like I said, no big deal." I took a bite out of the smoked salmon sandwich, hoping the girls would focus on their food rather than me.

"Are you going to see him again?"

"We're neighbors—no doubt I'll run into him. Now, can we drop this and focus on something more interesting?"

"I can't think of anything more interesting," Aurora said.

My phone buzzed again, and this time it was a call coming through. Was he so impatient for an answer? My heart began to thump against my chest and my fingers twitched with the desire to reach into my bag.

"Answer it," Violet said.

Without looking at the screen, I pulled my phone out of my bag and stood up, wanting to avoid the avid curiosity of my friends. I couldn't remember a time when a man had me so ruffled. It was as if he'd burned down my defenses last night. Nothing about it had been slow and steady, it had been quick and immediate and inevitable. And despite trying to convince myself otherwise, I wanted more.

I got to the end of the promenade and flipped my phone over, disappointed to see that it wasn't Logan at all, it was Lane.

"Is everything all right?" I asked.

"I thought you'd want to know sooner rather than later that Logan Steele has lodged an appeal against the planning decision taken by the Parish Council."

I had to steady myself against one of the marble pillars. "What? When?"

"Looks like it was lodged on Friday. I've got hold of a copy of the appeal. They're not going to give up, Miss Darcy."

I closed my eyes and tried to steady my breathing. I shouldn't be surprised. A move like this was Logan Steele to a tee. Every time I thought he was one man, he showed me another side to him. I wanted him to be the man that took me to dinner last night, had spoken at the community center, had fucked me all night. Instead he was the man who was still trying to devastate the village and memories that I so wanted to protect.

I was angry at him. Angry at myself for letting myself be seduced by him. Furious at the fact I'd been so delighted he'd just messaged me just a few minutes before. Fight drained from my body, chased off by the disappointment churning through my veins.

I'd only agreed to go to dinner with Logan because he'd lost, but he'd planned to appeal and had never said a word.

"Can you email it to me? I'll have my lawyers look over it and we'll see what they can do."

So much for Violet and Aurora's enthusiasm. So much for cheese on toast, wine and orgasms. So much for me enjoying myself last night. It had all turned to ash in a fraction of a second. Everything good about last night had been reversed and rewound. For a moment, I'd let myself relax, let my guard down, allowed someone else to take the reins.

And look where it had gotten me.

TWENTY-ONE

Logan

Darcy Westbury was irritating the shit out of me—even her absence got under my skin. In fact, it was exactly her absence that had me short-tempered and foul-mouthed. I slammed down the phone, cutting off one of my IT guys who was trying to explain why I hadn't had access to the internet for the last hour. I was pretty sure that if I hadn't been his top priority before, I certainly was now.

But the internet wasn't the problem, or at least not the *only* problem. Darcy had been ignoring my messages, avoiding my calls and generally pissing me off since I'd last seen her five bloody days ago.

Our evening had been incredible, the sex better than I could have imagined. And I thought she'd felt the same. Everything had worked between us. I'd confessed things I'd never told anyone and she'd been open and sweet. The next day I'd left her, knowing I should walk away—but in just a few hours, my resolve had disappeared, and I knew I had to have her again. Despite myself, I'd suggested another date, but had no response. For the first time in my life, I wanted more from a woman than she wanted from me.

That was bad enough.

But the fact that she didn't even have the decency to respond to say no was frustrating the hell out of me.

"What?" I snapped in response to a knock at my office door.

"I can come back later if it's a bad time," my head of development said as he poked his head around my door.

"Come in, Malcolm." I should have caught up with him days ago—I needed a way forward after the planning setback for Manor House Club. "I hope you've come armed with solutions."

He took a seat on the other side of my desk. "I need to know if you want to pursue a plan B while we wait for the planning appeal."

I glanced up. "What plan B and what planning appeal?"

"We lodged an appeal as soon as the decision came in from the Parish Council."

"Why didn't I know about this?"

"I spoke to the lawyers—it was their recommended course of action. We appealed the Friday after the decision."

I sighed. No wonder Darcy hadn't returned my calls. "You should have spoken to me about that."

"You're never interested in this kind of detail."

"Yeah, well, this is different. For one thing, it's the first business I'm building from scratch, but more importantly, these people are my neighbors. My grandmother's friends. I need a heads-up before you start making decisions like that." At least now I understood why Darcy had been such a pain in my arse since our date. I just had to figure out how to fix it.

What kind of hold did this woman have over me?

"I'll keep you better briefed in the future. Do you want me to go through possible plan B scenarios?"

I checked my watch. "You have ten minutes."

Malcolm produced a presentation with three worked-out alternative solutions to pursuing planning permission. The first was to abandon the project and invest in a similar business which was looking for funding. That wasn't an option for me. The whole point of this project was that I wanted it to be mine from the ground up. The second involved first opening a location in London to prove my credentials, and the final option was to move the location to a brownfield site about fifteen miles away from Badsley, close to transport links.

"I've not been on the ground, so I'm relying on desktop research," Malcolm explained, "but it looks feasible. The surrounding area is five rural acres that have previously been used for industry but are now abandoned." He produced aerial photos of the proposed site. "The plot has been available for three years, with no takers, and it's already well-priced. I figure we can secure a decent reduction."

"Any issues from the previous industrial use?"

"Nothing that would require anything more than demolition and landscaping."

"What was there before?"

"It's just some industrial retail units—a scheme that was only half finished, but it means roads and water are already in place."

"This is good work," I said, impressed with the idea of the brownfield site. We were less likely to come up against planning restrictions, the site was close to the motorways and we would be enhancing something I imagined the locals viewed as an eyesore at the moment. "When do we hear about the appeal?"

"It's likely to be months—you know what these things are like."

"Arrange a site visit while we wait." Darcy had been able to persuade the Parish Council that the development of Manor House Club would be a curse on all their houses, and I wouldn't underestimate her ability to block our appeal.

My mobile vibrated. "We'll go and see the alternate location next week. Monday morning would work, then I can come into the office from there. Set it up." I picked up the phone as Malcolm stood up and headed to the door.

Darcy's name flashed on the screen and I willed Malcolm to hurry—I didn't want to take this call in front of anyone. Why was she calling now?

He shut the door and I pressed accept. "We need to talk —I didn't know anything about the appeal until a few moments ago."

"You need to get back here," she said, her voice tight and filled with panic. "Get on that stupid helicopter. Your grandmother has fallen—they're taking her to hospital."

It took a few seconds to process what she was saying. I'd expected a barrage of abuse. Or the silent treatment. I hadn't expected her to be calling about my grandmother. "She's fallen? Is she conscious, bleeding?" I asked, heading out of my office.

"No blood and yes, she's conscious. A bit drowsy—concussed, I think, but—"

Jesus. How had this happened? It was why I paid for a

nurse to be on site twenty-four hours a day. "I'll be there as soon as I can. Which hospital?"

"Chiltern Central."

I didn't even know where that was. "Stay with her, will you?" I asked. I hated the idea that my grandmother was alone and vulnerable. I was meant to protect her, keep her safe. "She likes you."

"I'll be here. Just get here. Fast."

TWENTY-TWO

Logan

The worry was overwhelming. The muscles in my body were so tightly strung they felt as if they might snap and I had to remind myself to breathe. "How are you feeling?" I asked my grandmother for the ninetieth time.

"Like I'm going to hit you over the head with a cricket bat if you ask me that again." My grandmother shifted on the bed, trying to sit up. "It was no big deal. You heard the doctor—I didn't break anything."

"Let's wait for the results of the scans before you tell me it's no big deal." I wasn't taking any chances. My grandmother was my only family. She was the driving force behind my success— hell, she was the reason for my survival. If she hadn't rescued me from my father, God knows where I would have ended up. And I would protect her, just like she'd always protected me.

She rolled her eyes at Darcy, who was sitting on a visitor chair by the door.

"I should go." Darcy dropped her mobile into her bag.

The last thing I wanted was for her to leave. She had been so capable, calmly talking to the doctors while I paced and lost my temper every five seconds when no one would give me a straight answer. "Would you wait until we get the results? You speak medicine better than I do."

"You mean Darcy doesn't treat people as if they're conspiring to murder me?" my grandmother asked.

"Maybe." I smiled at her. At least she hadn't lost any of her feistiness.

"Darcy's a very busy woman—she's already spent most of the day here," my grandmother said.

Of course, I was being selfish. Darcy had been here hours, just sitting and waiting, fetching us coffee, encouraging us both. I just wanted her to stay a little longer. I'd missed her in the week since I'd seen her, which was ridiculous, given we didn't know each other very well.

We were interrupted by one of the doctors who looked younger than some of my favorite ties. Surely we should be talking to someone more senior?

"We have the results of the MRI. There's no sign of any bleeding, which is good news. We just want to keep you overnight for observation."

I exhaled. Thank God. It could have been so much worse.

"I told you I was fine," she said, admonishing me as I squeezed her hand.

"I'll be happier when you're discharged," I replied.

"And I'll be happier when you stop looking at me as if I'm about to curl up and die."

"Granny! I'm doing no such thing. I'm just concerned—anyone would be." Maybe I'd overreacted. But she was the only person in the world I cared about. The only person who cared about me. Without my grandmother, I was nothing.

"Visiting hours are over," the doctor said. "And your grandmother is in the best place. There's nothing you can do here, Mr. Steele."

"I don't care if I have to buy this place. I'm not leaving until my grandmother can come with me."

The doctor raised his eyebrows. "I'll let you speak to the nurse in charge."

"Thank you, doctor," Darcy said.

"Yes, thanks," I growled under my breath.

As the door shut behind him, my grandmother patted my hand. "Darcy, will you please take my grandson home? I want to listen to the radio and then have a sleep."

I glanced at my watch. Where had the last five hours gone? "I won't be any bother. I'll just sit over there." I pointed to the chair next to Darcy. "You won't even know I'm here."

"You heard the doctor, Logan. I'll be fine, and you can come back tomorrow morning."

Before I had a chance to reply the door swung open and an older woman in a nurse's uniform bustled inside. "Right, visiting has been over for more than an hour. Please leave Mrs. Steele to rest."

My grandmother shot me an expression I'd seen a hundred times before. Usually when she'd warned me something would turn out badly, but I'd ignored her warning and slunk back with egg on my face.

"You have your mobile, right?" Darcy asked my grandmother.

"Is it charged?" I asked.

My grandmother sighed. "Yes, it's charged, and Darcy put the charger in my overnight bag, too."

I pulled out the phone and the charger from the small bag on the table beside the bed and turned up the volume.

"We're only fifteen minutes away, Logan, and your grandmother does need to rest. It's been a stressful day," Darcy said. "You can't do anything constructive here and you'll only make things worse by fussing." As always, Darcy told it to me straight. Part of my frustration was the fact I was so helpless. But the last thing I wanted was for my stress to spill over and make my grandmother more anxious.

I took a deep breath. Darcy was right. I should leave and maybe my grandmother could sleep. "And you'll call me if you need anything?"

"Yes, Logan. But I'll be fine, especially knowing Darcy is looking after you." My grandmother had great instincts about people and had instantly liked Darcy, making comments all the time regarding what a lovely girl she was. How capable, pretty and clever. None of it passed me by. I knew she wanted me to be happy, and thought me having a wife and family of my own would provide that.

Although I'd never defined my success like that, I understood what my grandmother saw in Darcy. She *was* lovely and capable and clever. Not to mention sexy as hell and breathtakingly beautiful.

"I'll wait for you outside," Darcy said.

"No, you take him with you or I'll never get rid of him," my grandmother said, brushing my hands away.

I chuckled and stood, leaning over the bed to kiss her on the forehead. "Try to behave and don't give the nurses any trouble." I glanced at the formidable woman standing at the end of the bed.

"Stop fussing, Logan."

I would never stop fussing over her. She had been my

world for as long as I could remember. "I love you, Granny," I said.

"I love you, too, my darling boy."

I blew her a kiss and headed out. Having to rely on others to take care of my grandmother wasn't comfortable, wasn't who I was, but making her happy by leaving was all I could do.

TWENTY-THREE

Darcy

I'd never seen Logan Steele so vulnerable. So human. My heart ached a little for him and I hated myself for that. I needed to be building walls between me and this man, not have him smashing holes in my half-constructed ones.

"You really think she's going to be okay?" Logan asked as we headed out.

I stared straight ahead as we headed to the car park, determined that his handsome face wouldn't further melt my resolve. "I really do. Nothing was broken—this could have been a lot worse."

He nodded and scraped his hands through his hair. I imagined he struggled with the lack of control he had in situations like this. I'd felt that way when my grandfather had fallen and broken his hip.

"I just wish I could fix it," he said.

I understood, and despite my disappointment in him, my instincts screamed at me to reach for him and provide him with some sort of comfort.

"Thank you for being there. Were you at Badsley when it happened?"

"No, but her nurse called me and I headed over." I might be trying to protect myself from Logan Steele, but I was very fond of his grandmother, and frankly, anyone in need in the village would have received my full attention.

"I appreciate it. I need to calm down. Distract myself. I know that you're upset with me—"

"Let's just focus on your grandmother—she's what's important right now." There was no point in rehashing what I already knew to be true. Logan Steele wanted to build on Badsley land at any cost. And I couldn't live with that.

The front doors slid open and we stepped into the chilly night. "I didn't know about the appeal when we went on our date, Darcy. It's important to me that you know that."

I sighed, wanting to avoid another discussion about this. "It doesn't change anything."

"I found out just before you called that my head of development filed the paperwork on Friday."

I unlocked my Range Rover and headed to the driver's seat without a word.

Logan climbed in the passenger door and slammed it shut. "You don't believe me?"

"Are you withdrawing your appeal?" I knew that he wouldn't, but I wanted him to understand that it didn't matter if he hadn't known about the appeal if the outcome was just the same.

"I'm looking at several options."

"As I said, just because you didn't know when it was lodged doesn't change anything."

"Darcy, you know how important Manor House Club is to me. I'm not trying to upset you."

"But you have. Let's drop it."

"So we can be friends?"

I pulled out onto the main road and headed back to the village. I didn't want to argue with Logan. He was clearly worried about Mrs. Steele, but at the same time I wasn't about to tell him that appealing the planning decision was okay by me. Because it wasn't.

Silence swirled between us as I navigated the dark, twisty road.

"You'll come in?" Logan asked as I pulled up in front of Badsley House.

"It's been a long day—"

"I know I have no right to ask. You've done more than enough already. But cooking relaxes me and I know I won't bother if it's just me. Can I make you an omelet or something?"

I didn't want to go in, but not because I was tired. My walls were crumbling. I needed reinforcements.

"Come in and eat, Darcy." He stroked his thumb across my cheek.

"You're so bossy," I said.

"And you like it," he replied, clicking open his seat belt and then releasing mine.

As much as I wanted to stay angry at him, he knew how to remind me of the Logan Steele that I liked. The way he made me melt like butter when he touched me. The way he took control in the bedroom. Those deep blue eyes that I so easily sank into. If only he wasn't hell-bent on disrupting our beautiful village.

"You're going to wish you'd never invited me in, you know. Because, while you're making omelets, I'm going to try to convince you that going another way with Manor House Club makes more sense."

He held the front door open and I stepped inside.

"I look forward to it—as long as you remember it's business, and not personal."

"Which means you make a decision based on business sense, rather than emotion." I followed him into the kitchen and took a seat when he pulled out one of the pine chairs around the table.

"Exactly," he said, opening the wine fridge and pulling out a bottle. "If you come up with a better proposition for the development, then I want to hear about it."

"Really?" I held the stem of the glass he'd set in front of me as he poured out the wine. He hadn't even asked me if I wanted a glass, but I did. Perhaps he could tell.

"Really." He shrugged off his jacket and hung it on the back of the chair next to mine. "Like I said, it's just business. Cheese?" he asked.

"It's not personal, it's cheese?"

He chuckled. "Christ, you're adorable." He bent and kissed me on the top of my head. "You want cheese in your omelet?"

"Do you have peppers?" I asked.

"I think so." He took a sip of his wine and set it next to mine.

"So let me give you all the business reasons why—"

"I'd really like to hear more about why you personally are so against it. It doesn't quite add up to me."

"I've been through this with you. The increased air pollution from the traffic, the divide it will create between members and non-members—"

"Yes, I've heard all that. I don't hear you in any of it." He pulled eggs, cheese, peppers and an onion out of the fridge and set them on the counter. "You seem as determined to maintain Woolton in the same way as I was to buy Badsley House back."

"I agree. I'm at least as determined."

"So talk me about why it matters to you. You know how personal Badsley is to me."

Why was he being so difficult? I was giving him good, solid arguments. "I told you. I want to maintain the customs and traditions."

"And why are they so important to you?"

"I've told you. I don't understand why you keep asking the same question." It was as if he were interrogating me. Perhaps he just wanted to be distracted from thoughts of his grandmother.

He turned to me, looked at me intently. "Tell me your first memory of Woolton."

I sighed and slumped back in my chair. He wasn't going to give up. "Probably Ryder and me down by the stream."

"How old were you?"

I shrugged. "I must have been about five."

Logan chuckled. "And your parents let Ryder take you down to the river."

I tried to remember back to that time. "We had a lot of freedom at Woolton. We were visiting. Again. And we didn't want to go home." I smiled at the memory of feeling completely free. The sun speckling through the trees. The cool water of the stream as it ran over my toes. In all my memories of Woolton the sun always shone, and everyone was smiling and happy. "It was the first time I saw a dragon-fly. Ryder told me that it was lucky and that if we made a wish, whatever we wished for would come true. I said my wish out loud. I wanted to stay at Woolton Hall forever."

"And your wish came true," he said.

"Yeah, for better or for worse." Children shouldn't wish

their parents away, but I had, and more than that, I'd been more than happy when my wish had been granted.

"For worse? I've never heard you say anything bad about Woolton."

"And I'm not now. But that time when our mother left us at Woolton, she didn't come back. We didn't see her again for two years." Our mother would regularly dump us at Woolton Hall and go off on some mission to find her inner whatever. "Before that, it had been only a few weeks here or there. I don't really remember. But that time she didn't come back. And my wish came true."

"God, Darcy, I had no idea. Did you miss her?"

Why was I talking about this? I was supposed to be convincing Logan that he should abandon his appeal. "No, I didn't miss her. I had my grandparents and Woolton and the magic of the dragonflies and the endless summer days. I think maybe Ryder did. He was older and understood more about what was going on. And now, looking back, I realize I should have missed her more than I did."

"What about your father?"

Logan's question caught me a little off-guard. I never thought about him. "He left before that. Ryder doesn't even remember him. I have no idea who he is."

Logan abandoned his cooking, wiped his hands on a cloth and came and sat opposite me. "I'm sorry. I think I assumed you lived this privileged life this whole time and—"

"I did in many ways." I picked up my glass of wine. "I had my brother and my grandparents. I didn't lack for food or love and I grew up in this wonderful place." I took a sip, wanting to clear my throat. "Ryder and I just had parents who didn't want to be parents."

I tried to ignore the comfort that Logan's hand on my

leg provided. It was all so long ago, but I had forgotten about the dragonfly. And the wish. "Woolton is a magical place for me. It's a place I've always felt safe in. The sense of community, the values...I've experienced places and people who don't hold those things dear and I don't want that for Woolton. I want the children who grow up here to think it's magical too. To be dragged down to the stream by their big brothers to see dragonflies when they are too young. To have wishes come true. I want Woolton to be a place where everyone feels safe." My voice began to crack and I swallowed.

Logan pulled me onto his lap and brought his arms around me. "Now I get it. The village saved you, so now you're all about saving the village."

I'd never thought about it like that, but he was right. I wanted to protect this place just like it had protected me.

After a few moments, my stomach growled, filling the silence.

"Come on, I owe you an omelet."

I wanted to stay in his arms, but food was a good second choice.

"Do you need a hand?"

"I think I can handle an omelet."

"You don't seem like the kind of man who cooks." I shifted my chair so I could stare at his broad back as he worked. His muscles bunched and released under his shirt, reminding me of how he'd moved when we'd slept together. How every touch had been so deliberate and calculated.

"I enjoy it."

"I'd like to cook more," I said. "I don't get the chance much because it's still very much Cook's kitchen at Woolton."

He turned as he whisked the eggs with the fork. "You have a lot of staff, but it's just you. Is that weird?"

I shrugged. "It's how I grew up, so I don't really know anything else. And of course, Ryder and Scarlett come to stay every six weeks or so. The house is a lot busier then."

"But you can't get into your own kitchen when you want to?"

I wasn't sure if he expected an answer, so I stayed quiet. He didn't understand. It just was how it was done in big, old estates.

"You can come cook here whenever you want." He plated the omelet, which looked perfect. He'd even added some salad. Who was this guy?

I picked up my fork as Logan sat in the chair next to mine. Our knees touched as he sat forward, but instead of moving away, I let myself enjoy it. His touch had a soothing and comforting quality that I wanted to indulge in a little.

He sliced through the omelet with his fork. Last time we'd had dinner it had been at one of the best restaurants in London, and now here we were, eating omelets around his kitchen table. I wasn't enjoying tonight any less, and I liked that he seemed equally as comfortable in both settings. He wasn't one of those men who insisted on being treated like a king wherever he went.

"I have to get to work over the weekend and end up with an alternative site for you," I said.

He chuckled, wiping the corner of his mouth with his napkin. "I look forward to that."

"You're not the only one who's tenacious, you know."

"I'm well aware." He leaned back against his chair and slid his legs between mine.

"The omelet was delicious."

"Something a little more sophisticated next time," he said.

I reached for his plate. "Let me—"

"Absolutely not." He stood, and before I could object had piled everything into the dishwasher.

"I should go," I said, the wooden legs of my chair scraping against the terra-cotta floor as I stood.

In a second he was in front of me, his hands gripping my shoulders. Instinctively, I placed my hands flat against his hard chest, my gaze fixed to the triangle of exposed skin at his throat. He walked me back against the kitchen counter and I gasped when he lifted me onto the granite, but I didn't resist. I wanted this. I wanted him.

He looped his fingers through mine and leaned forward to capture my lips.

His mouth was as warm and strong as I remembered. He transformed my thoughts from *I-shouldn't-be-doing-this* into *please-don't-stop*. He switched seamlessly from an enemy to a man I wanted naked and on top of me.

Sliding his tongue between my lips, he groaned. Heat pulsed between my thighs both at his touch and at the idea that I could make him make those sounds. A man who must have had so many women was at my mercy.

I tried to twist my fingers from his, but he growled, tightened his grip and pulled back to look at me. "Are you saying no?"

"What? I—" I glanced at our joined hands. I wanted to run my fingers over his end of day scruff, trace a line over his collarbone. I wanted to touch him.

"If you're saying no, I'll release you. But if you're not, then I'm in charge—you know how this goes."

My skin tightened and my breath shortened. I did know how it went. And I liked it. More than liked it.

TWENTY-FOUR

Logan

Nothing about this day had turned out as I'd expected, but there was no better way to end it than in bed with my tongue in Darcy Westbury's pussy. She might be spiky on the outside, but she was so fucking sweet on the inside.

Going down on her could become an addiction.

Despite her best efforts to stay still, and my hands curled around her waist, she bucked underneath me. So far, she'd managed to keep her hands above her head as I'd instructed.

"Logan, please," she cried out.

I grinned. Begging me for release already?

I flattened my tongue against her clit.

"You want to come, baby," I asked.

"Don't stop, please don't stop. I'll do anything. Please."

Jesus, her begging had my cock aching, and urging me to get her off and plunge inside. I resisted, took a steadying breath, and made long, steady strokes with my tongue, guaranteed to set her off. Her thighs began to tremble and her back arched as she screamed, "Oh. God. Logan."

I didn't know what was more invigorating, her twitching pussy around my tongue or my dick. I stood, wiped my mouth on the back of my hand, and watched as her stomach rose and fell, her breasts heaving and she opened her heavy eyelids.

"Hey," I said as she looked at me, her face flushed, her limbs heavy.

"Hey." She bit back a smile as if she'd been caught out doing something that she shouldn't. "I'm sorry, was I too loud?"

"You were perfect." I stroked her thigh, then pressed a kiss inside her knee. "I like hearing your pleasure."

She crinkled her nose as if she couldn't bear to remember how she'd begged me to make her come.

"Now undress me, please."

She slipped off the bed and reached for the top button of my shirt. "Why wouldn't you let me before?" she asked as she worked her way down my torso.

Going down on a woman was always better when they were completely naked and you were fully dressed. The balance of power was more pronounced in my favor. "Because I said so."

"You know, I wouldn't put up with that kind of answer if we weren't..."

"But we are and you will." I wouldn't expect her to let me get away with telling her what to do without question under any other circumstances. I wouldn't want to, either. I enjoyed her spirit, her challenge. The way she went head to head with me so openly. In the boardroom, it was much more subtle. Darcy's power outside the bedroom wasn't subtle. And it was the contrast between her in the bedroom and out of the bedroom that had me harder than flint. Her fingers grazed my skin as she pulled my shirt from my trousers.

I couldn't stop myself from cupping her face and kissing her.

Everything about her drew me to her, had me switching everything up. When was the last time I'd taken the same woman to bed twice? Let alone a woman who I knew. Someone who knew my *grandmother*.

She slid her fingers around my waistband and fumbled with my fly. Despite every molecule of my body urging me to strip off and bury myself into her hard and fast, I was determined to continue smoothing my thumbs over her cheeks and working my tongue against hers.

She gasped as her palms brushed over my erection.

"You ready?" I asked as I pulled back.

She nodded, and I grabbed a handful of her perfect arse. "Turn around. On all fours." Despite being desperate to see her on her knees in front of me, my dick in her mouth, I'd explode instantly—I wasn't ready for that.

She climbed onto the bed and looked back at me over her shoulder, as if expecting to be marked out of ten. I avoided her gaze but took in every inch of her body. Her creamy white skin, her glossy brown hair, her breasts swaying gently as if goading me into action.

"Logan?"

"Yes, Darcy?" I didn't stop my inspection of her body, the curve of her back, the roundness of her arse, the goose-bumps along her skin, the way her fingers clutched at the sheets despite the fact that I wasn't touching her. If I could have invented a woman, my imagination couldn't have come up with anything better.

"Logan, please." She leaned back on her knees, stretched her arms and I gave her a quick, sharp slap on her backside.

She snapped back into position, giving me a beautiful view of her swollen pussy. I slid a condom over my straining erection and I kneeled on the bed behind her. Lining myself up, and with one hand on her hip, I pushed inside her. My heart rate doubled and I had to close my eyes against the blinding lights. Jesus, had she felt like this the first time?

"Logan, Logan, Logan," she chanted breathless and desperate.

I took a deep breath. Fuck, I had to get myself together or I was going to embarrass myself.

I tried to block out how good she felt, how soft her skin was, how tight her pussy was. I tried not to think about how this feisty, funny, loyal woman buckled under my touch and pleaded for my cock. Instead, I thrust, my eyes screwed shut, my hands tight against her hips instead of exploring her rounded bottom or her smooth back. I knew it would be too much, so I focused on my heartbeat rather than the perfect sounds of her moans.

She tightened around me and her piercing scream and her fierce climax shattered the fog I'd tried to bury myself in.

I wasn't the only one having a hard time fighting falling over the edge.

I slowed my pace to a standstill as her entire body shook. "Twice already? You're greedy tonight."

"I...I can't help myself. When I'm with you, it's as if my body has been taken over."

While I knew our fucking was the best I'd ever had, it was gratifying to hear this wasn't a one-way street. That I was nothing like her past experiences. "Your body is mine when you're with me."

"Yes," she whispered, bowing her head.

Her agreement took the edge off my desperate need to come. She'd confessed she was already mine—I could take my time in claiming her. I rocked in and out of her, wanting the heat in her to build again. It didn't take long before renewed wetness burst from her and I pushed further each time, one hand curling around her shoulder so I could get as deep as possible. Pleasure shot through me, piercing my body from every angle.

I was so close. But I didn't want to come like this. Something was missing.

My swollen cock throbbed angrily against my stomach as if cursing me for making it wait so long for release, but I wanted more than to just come. I wanted to feel bound and connected to the woman I was fucking.

"Logan?" Darcy asked, her hair flicking across her back as she turned her head to figure out what was going on. Her cheeks were flushed, her barely noticeable eyeliner a little smudged, her hair a little mussed. I'd never seen her look so sexy.

"Turn over," I whispered.

She frowned, as if confused by my request, but complied anyway, shifting onto her back and propping herself up on her elbows, her eyes never leaving mine. I crawled over her, relishing the heat of her body, how soft she was, how perfect she felt against me. I caged her head and dipped to kiss her.

What was with this woman and her kisses? I couldn't get enough.

She swept her hands up my torso and I let out a groan.

How was it possible to squeeze so much pleasure from such a simple touch? Each delicate sweep of her hand was like an invitation to somewhere I'd never been before, into a world that promised a different life.

She brought her knees up, and my dick rested over her slick pussy and pressed against her folds. I pushed inside and had to hold still. How could this feel so good every single time?

I drew back and she stroked her fingers over my eyebrows as I began to slide in and out of her. We stared at each other as my thrusts grew stronger and faster, until we were connected, mind, body and soul.

This is what I'd wanted.

Her beneath me, looking at me, looking at her. For the first time in my life, being with a woman wasn't about getting off—it was more than that. It was about affinity.

Union. Intimacy.

My orgasm descended and I knew I didn't have the power to hold it back any longer. Darcy tightened her grip on my shoulders, telling me she was close to the edge. She gasped and began to shudder just as my climax burst over me.

I groaned into her neck. As much as I set out to claim Darcy, it was as if she owned me in that moment.

What. Was. Happening?

Her small, sweet pants in my ear, Darcy's own brand of smelling salts, brought me back to life. I rolled off her before I crushed her, pulling her with me. I wanted to stay connected every second.

For the first time in my life, coming wasn't the main goal —being with Darcy was. Talking with her, laughing with her, fighting with her, fucking her. It was all I wanted.

She propped her chin on my chest as she twisted her legs between mine. "I'm sure you get this a lot," she said, her lips pressing together when she paused. "But for me, I've never...I mean...it's a ..."

Wrapping my arm around her tighter, I chuckled. I knew what she was trying to say.

"Hey." She slapped me lightly on my chest. "Don't laugh at me."

"I'm not laughing at you. Well, I suppose I am, but not about what you're trying to say." I twisted a strand of her soft hair around my finger, wanting to know her better than I did, wanting to walk through every open door in her brain and charge through every locked one. "I feel it, too."

"Feel what?" she asked, tracing circles on my skin.

"The sex. That's not even the right word. It's more. Something elemental passes between us when we fuck. Something transcen-fucking-dental."

"I've never had that before," she said in a small voice, almost as if she was embarrassed.

"Neither have I. The sex between us—I've never had anything like it. It's different. More intense, more consuming."

"Really?"

I gave her a small smile. "Really." I was in unfamiliar territory and probably should have held back, but there was something about Darcy that made me want to let her in. I wanted to tell her stuff. Talk about nothing and everything with her.

"I wonder what it is?" She shook her head as if we'd been discussing why there'd been an influx of hailstorms this spring.

I didn't have an answer for her. I was in unfamiliar territory and I didn't trust myself not to ask her to spend the rest of the week in my bed. Whatever we had together, I would think about it tomorrow. I'd take it out of my brain like a pebble from my pocket and examine it, analyze it, scrutinize it in the cold light of day. Right now, I was happy to stay here, warm and happy with Darcy Westbury wrapped around me.

TWENTY-FIVE

Darcy

Logan Steele-induced orgasms weren't going to throw me off track. I was on a mission. Lane knew this county better than anyone, which meant he was the perfect man to find an alternative site for Logan's new business venture. "You agree that these two sites are the best?" I asked as we surveyed the plans and photographs spread across our huge mahogany table. I'd turned the dining room into a war room, much to Mrs. MacBee's disdain.

"Yes. I agree. I would have said this one," he said, pointing to my third choice. "But after seeing it, there's far too much unspoiled land surrounding it. I don't want to just move the problem somewhere else."

"I agree. It's definitely between these two, which are already sited near main roads. This one was already a half-constructed commercial site and you can hear the motorway — it's so close that we're not spoiling things. I'm going to talk to the planning office to see if I can get any information about how difficult it would be to get his plans through."

"If Mr. Steele is good for his word, you might have won this fight. Both these sites are better than building on Badsley."

"The only problem is he has to pony up to buy the land."

"True. But he'll save on this plot," he said, pointing at my first choice. "The roads and utilities are already in place."

"That's what I'm thinking. I just wish I had time to figure out the different costings, but I don't know any contractors who I could ask a favor of and I don't want to miss our window of opportunity before the appeal is heard." I wanted everything to be perfect when I presented him with the idea.

"He'll have plenty of people who know that kind of thing, and he'll already have costings for the development of Badsley," Lane said. "There's no point in you guessing those. He says he'll do whatever is best for business, so hopefully when he sees your proposal he'll want to run the numbers himself."

That's exactly what I hoped. Despite running the estate, I'd never run a business, as Logan had. I didn't understand spreadsheets and financial models, but instinct told me that financially, our first choice of alternative site would make more sense for him than Badsley. I hoped I was right.

"Are you going to show him all this?"

"Yes. Today, I hope. He's not been into London all week because of Mrs. Steele's fall, so I thought I'd take advantage of him being in the area and take him to see the site myself."

Although I'd heard from Logan every day this week, I'd not seen him since the night his grandmother had been taken into hospital. Every afternoon, I'd gone to Badsley to check on Mrs. Steele, but I'd deliberately picked the middle of the day when I knew Logan would be wrapped up with work so he wouldn't think I was there to pester him, when I really wasn't. Not that I didn't want to see him, but I didn't want it to look as if I were running after him. He had a life. I had a life. We weren't teenagers.

My phone buzzed and I swiped up to see a message from Logan.

I definitely haven't been thinking about you all week. I want to see you.

I would never have described Logan Steele as cute—but he had a side to him that hinted at it now and then.

I replied.

Good timing. Today at 3 pm. I'll pick you up. Be ready.

MY HEART FLUTTERED in my chest as I pulled up in front of Badsley House. This time, I *was* here to see Logan, although I'd come to see Mrs. Steele first.

"They're beautiful, Darcy," she said as I arranged the bouquet of different-colored roses I'd brought fresh from Woolton in a vase.

"When you're feeling better, you must come up to the house for lunch. I think you'd love the rose garden."

"That would be delightful. I'm sorry I had to cancel on your first invitation." Mrs. Steele cocked her ear toward the open French windows. "Is that my grandson I hear thundering down the stairs?"

The corners of my mouth began to twitch. Had he heard me pull up? It was ten minutes before I said I'd collect him.

I placed the flowers on the wooden table and took a seat,

picking up my cup of tea and focusing on the lawn, rather than who was about to arrive.

"Darcy," Logan said, glancing at his grandmother. "I didn't realize you were here."

"She's come every afternoon, though I keep telling her I'm perfectly fine."

"You're looking a lot better," I said, smiling at her.

"It was very nice of her to check in on you." Logan bent and kissed me on my cheek and it took everything I had not to close my eyes and breathe in his fresh, clean scent. "You're early," he said.

"No, I'm not. I came to see your grandmother first." I turned to Mrs. Steele. "I'm taking him to see a site at three. Hopefully he'll like it enough to abandon his plans to develop Badsley."

"How resourceful of you," Mrs. Steele said. "You two are all business. Perhaps you should stop off and have an early supper somewhere." She glanced between us before taking a sip of her tea. "You know I think you work too hard, Logan. It would be good for you to have a little more time off."

Logan chuckled. "I definitely think you're fully recovered." Did she try to set him up often?

"Well, you two should get going. I'll be fine here with the nurse. Don't hurry back."

"Are you ready?" he asked me, his tone softening to an almost intimate hum.

I nodded and picked up my bag. "And we'll arrange that lunch when you're feeling up to it?" I asked Mrs. Steele.

"I look forward to it."

Logan and I walked silently to the car, the crunch of the gravel and distant birdsong the only sounds between us.

"So we're going to visit a site I've found," I said as I slid into the driver's seat.

"It's good to see you," he said as I pulled my door closed. "I didn't realize this was a professional call, and a field trip at that."

"You said you'd keep an open mind. It's only a few minutes' drive away."

"My mind is perfectly open," he said as I pulled out of the gates. "You look very pretty today."

"I'm all business today." I kept my eyes firmly on the road ahead. I might be focused on getting Logan to commit to a new site, but that didn't mean I hadn't put some thought into what I looked like. Standing in my dressing room this morning, it had hit me how much I liked Logan, so I'd done that thing where you made a ton of effort to not look like you were making any effort. Barely-there makeup that took me an hour. Forty minutes trying on six pairs of jeans to see my bottom from every angle. Not to mention my hair.

And he'd noticed, which I appreciated. But it scared me how much I liked him and that I wanted him to think I was pretty. I was always the practical, sensible girl. I'd never been swept off my feet or lost my head over a man. Logan awoke a part of me I didn't recognize, or hadn't seen in an awfully long time.

"All business," he muttered under his breath. "But maybe dinner afterward." Logan didn't look so bad himself. He was tieless and wearing a white shirt that contrasted with his tanned skin, and his jacket and trousers gave him that casual look that only some men could pull off without looking like they were seventy and lived on a golf course. It had probably taken him ten minutes to get ready this morning and I'd bet money on the fact that he hadn't given me a second thought.

"I guess that depends what kind of mood I'm in when we're done."

He chuckled. "I hope you're not trying to blackmail me."

"Whatever." I grinned. Seeing his reaction to the site would tell me a lot—I'd know if he was just humoring me, telling me he'd keep an open mind. The site I was taking him to was a perfect solution, and one he should consider properly. If he didn't, he wasn't the man he told me he was.

As we pulled into the private road, I saw the real estate agent's car up ahead. I wanted Logan to hear the great things about this site from someone impartial.

I pulled in next to Ivy's blue SUV and snapped on the parking brake. "We're here," I announced, releasing my seat belt.

"I guessed," he replied, grinning back.

Ivy walked toward us, her black curly hair bouncing with each step she took, a huge smile on her face. "Mr. Steele," she said. "I didn't realize you were the person Darcy was bringing for the site visit today."

"You know each other?" I asked. Why on earth would Logan know Ivy? She was an established commercial real estate agent in the area, but she'd lived two villages away her entire life.

"Sure," Ivy said. "I showed Mr. Steele and his assistant the site earlier in the week." She turned to Logan. "I'm so pleased you liked it enough to come back. I thought it would take you longer to work through the financials, but I told you that having the utilities here already makes a big difference to the cost of the build, not to mention the time frames."

So Logan had already been here. I paused and bit down on my bottom lip to stop myself from grinning. Had he really been looking at other sites, as he'd claimed?

He held out his arm for me as Ivy rattled off facts and figures. I wasn't sure I'd ever been as attracted to a man as I was in that moment. He knew this place. He'd been true to his word and he wasn't just waiting around for me to come up with different options—he was actively pursuing them.

"I sent the technical details that you requested to Malcolm."

"Thank you. I know he's working on the numbers and I'm going to go through them with him tomorrow."

"The landowner was excited after your visit—I know he's very keen to sell. Apparently, he applied to the local Parish Council to redevelop the site a little over a year ago, and they approved his plans but he just couldn't raise the finance. Of course, your plans will be different, but I thought it was good to know that they want to see the land redeveloped."

"The fact that there's previously been industrial buildings on the site means the planning shouldn't be an issue," Logan said. "We had that confirmed. And we've done some environmental searches, and they set out what you said about the units here just being used as offices and retail warehousing, which means no cleanup costs."

Logan sounded invested and I had to keep staring at the tarmacked ground to stop myself from grinning like an idiot.

"I hadn't realized that Logan was already considering this site—I'm sorry if I've wasted your time, Ivy."

"Not at all. I think it's helpful to come back and see the place, envisage what you want to create. Did you say it was a hotel?"

"More of an exclusive club with a few rooms." He

looked out over the abandoned industrial units and over to the trees. "The entire place is very secluded," he said.

"The owner was surprised he was given permission to build, but the council has set a precedent now, and at the moment, the place is an eyesore. It needs developing."

Logan nodded as he continued to scan his surroundings. "What was the size again? Just under two hectares, wasn't it?"

"Four point five nine acres."

Logan chuckled and slid his hands into his pockets. He liked details and I figured he appreciated Ivy's specificity. "It's a good size. And the landowner's motivated to sell?"

"Very," she said. "He had an offer twenty-five percent below asking price last year, and I think he would take it if he was offered it again."

"Good to know."

"Would you like to walk the perimeter again?" she asked.

Shit, I hadn't brought my wellies.

"I think we saw what we needed to last time."

"You've already walked through the site."

He fixed me with a stare. "Yup."

"Well, thanks so much for making the time, Ivy." We shook hands then Logan and I headed to the car in silence.

As soon as we were in the car, I expected him to declare business over with and demand some personal attention—which I was more than happy to provide—but before he slid into the passenger seat, he pulled his mobile from his jacket pocket.

"Do you mind if I make a quick call?" he asked, already dialing the number.

"That's fine," I replied, pulling out.

"Head to your place," he said as he put the phone to his ear.

He was *so* bossy, but secretly I was relieved he didn't want to go straight back to Badsley. I'd been looking forward to seeing him before our visit, and now my body was buzzing with need.

"Malcolm, I've just been to see the Planton site again—yeah, I was just passing and wanted to check out a few things. The agent was helpful. She told me the landlord had an offer at twenty-five percent below asking that he wished he'd taken. I know. Plug that into the sensitivity analysis. Yep. Good." He hung up.

"So you've already seen the site," I said, stating the obvious.

"It would seem so," he replied.

"Why didn't you say anything?"

"I did. Ivy did."

"I mean before."

"I said I'd been looking at alternatives."

I'd been looking for excuses not to like Logan. And I'd found plenty. But as I got to know him, they were all fading away and without them I would have to face up to how much I did like him. How much I wanted to explore what we had.

And I didn't know whether to be scared or hopeful. Terrified or trusting.

TWENTY-SIX

Logan

I couldn't get enough of the hot, naked woman beside me.

"I feel like I'm fifteen years old," I said from flat on my back as I stared at Darcy's bedroom ceiling.

She wriggled over to face me and propped her head up on her hand. "Lucky for me you don't have a teenager's body."

I pulled her palm from my chest and placed a kiss on her knuckles.

"It's all this sneaking around." In the last few weeks, Darcy and I had fallen into a routine of sorts. Thursday, Friday, Saturday and Sunday nights I stayed over at Woolton Hall. Regularly leaving the office on a Thursday was a new thing for me but I wanted to spend the night with Darcy. Sometimes she had dinner with my grandmother and me, but we always ended up back at Woolton, and I always headed back to Badsley before my grandmother woke, which meant I was sneaking out of Darcy's bed before sunrise.

"Want to come to dinner tonight?" I asked.

"Only if you're making omelets," she said, then bolted upright, clutching her sheet to her chest. "Shit, no I can't." She looked at me, panic in her eyes. "You have to go." She pushed me out of bed, her heels pressing into my arse.

"It's only just before six. I'll be fine."

"I mean it, you have to leave. I totally forgot that Ryder and Scarlett are about to arrive. They'll be here any second."

Wait, what? She was trying to get rid of me? Our situation was unusual for me, but I'd dealt with it by not analyzing it. Over the last few weeks, I'd just done what felt right. What I wanted to do. Darcy and I had existed in a private bubble where we didn't talk about anything in the future—we'd just agreed not to overanalyze things. It hadn't seemed necessary to talk about what we were doing—but she obviously didn't want her brother to know that we were doing whatever we were doing and it was...chafing.

She squealed as a car door pulled up outside and she rushed to her window, peering down to the driveway. "They're here already. You're going to have to hide." She glanced around. "Maybe in the bathroom or my dressing room."

I wasn't anyone's dirty little secret, but maybe that was how she saw me. "We're not doing anything wrong, Darcy." I wasn't sure if I was talking to myself or her.

She groaned and pulled at my arm, trying to get me out of bed. "Come on."

"I'm serious. Why can't your brother know I'm here?" I couldn't quite believe the words that were coming out of my mouth.

"And what are you going to say to him? Hey, you don't mind that I'm banging your sister, do you?"

"I said I felt like a fifteen-year-old boy, not that I was going to act like one."

She sighed dramatically and headed to the bathroom. "You're impossible. I'm going to have a shower."

I followed her. "Why don't you want him to know about us?" I asked as she stepped under the spray, her toothbrush in her mouth as she tried to multi-task—something she always did when running late.

I'd enjoyed making her late on many occasions over the last few weeks.

She looked at me, water pouring over her face as I watched her from the end of the walk-in shower.

"Why don't you want your grandmother to know about us?" she asked.

"I never said I didn't—it just hasn't come up." She turned away from me to finish brushing her teeth.

"Darcy," I said. I wasn't sure what I wanted her to say— it just felt that we were due for a conversation. I didn't like the idea of her trying to hide me. Us.

Even though I'd fucked a lot of women, I'd never felt so intimate with a woman. Darcy and I had fallen into an early-morning habit of starting our days together. Things had developed when I wasn't paying attention. I'd been deliberately looking away, but now I needed clarity. I wanted to know whether we were on the same page, except I wasn't sure what page that was.

"What?" she snapped. "My brother and Scarlett are downstairs. They have toddlers and an American mother. There are no boundaries. They are probably about to burst into my bedroom and we're both naked. Can we talk later?"

She was right. We didn't have time and I didn't know what I wanted to say. I rarely went into conversations without knowing the outcome I wanted, but like with most things, I found Darcy was the exception.

"I'm not sleeping with anyone else," I said as if that solved everything. "I just want you to know that."

She frantically covered herself with shower gel. "Can we talk about this later?"

Wait, wasn't it customary for her to tell me she wasn't sleeping with anyone else either? Granted, I was in unfamiliar territory, but I was pretty sure that was how these things were meant to go. Unless she *was* sleeping with someone else. "Are you?" I stepped into the walk-in shower, wanting to hear her answer clearly.

She tipped her head to the side. "Not unless you count Lane."

It took a second longer than it should have to realize she was joking. "Funny," I said, and she just shrugged as if we were talking about the fucking weather.

I'd spent my life avoiding conversations like this, dodging questions from women by being clear upfront that there would be no second time, no emotions and definitely no commitment. But here I was, with a woman I actually wanted to have this conversation with, and *she* was the one avoiding it.

"So you don't want to talk about this?" Was she being cold or distracted or both?

"Not now. We haven't discussed anything about anything and we don't have time to start."

Perhaps we'd both been avoiding having a conversation about where we were, how we felt and where we were headed. I had no road map, I'd never been here, felt like this. But we were at a crossroads and I wanted to know which road she saw us taking.

TWENTY-SEVEN

Darcy

What was it about Logan *freaking* Steele that had me losing my mind? I'd been planning for Ryder and Scarlett's arrival all week, but a kiss from Logan and I'd forgotten what day of the week it was.

I pulled on my jeans, watching out of my bedroom window at my brother, Scarlett and their children as they pulled things out of the car, dropped them, Gwendoline sat on them, Toby tried to climb onto the roof of the car and everyone generally messed about. It was Lane's day off and the children were distracting my brother and Scarlett, and I'd never been so grateful. I pulled on a shirt and wrapped my still-wet hair up in a clip. At least I was clean and had clothes on.

"I'm not hiding in the bathroom, Darcy," Logan said as he tied his shoes.

Had I really suggested that? "Yeah. That was a stupid idea, sorry. I'm just not ready to answer a thousand questions from my brother and sister-in-law. Not when we haven't even talked."

He turned to look at me, disappointment heavy on his face.

I stepped toward him and stroked my palm against his cheek. "I'm sorry. I lost track of my days—you're very distracting."

I shivered as he kissed the inside of my wrist. Shouldn't I be pleased that he didn't want to hide our relationship? I'd never really thought about what we were outside the bedroom. I'd spent so long determined to hate Logan that I hadn't allowed myself to think about what was growing between us.

"I'm warning you—Ryder is likely to give you a hard time, and Scarlett's going to demand to know when you plan to propose."

"Does that mean I don't have to hide in the bathroom?" He pulled me on to his lap.

"It doesn't bother you that—"

"We like each other, Darcy. Right?" He dipped his head, trying to catch my gaze.

"Kind of, I guess. I mean, I like sleeping with you. And you can be funny sometimes. And you don't bore me."

"Steady, or my ego is going to get overinflated."

I giggled. "I'm not sure a lack of ego is a problem for you."

"Well, I think all those things about you, too."

"I spend a lot of time around you trying not to smile," I confessed.

"Never boring," he muttered. "So, we're friends who are enjoying each other's company. Right?"

"Right," I said. Were we friends? Just a few weeks ago,

I'd hated this guy. And now he spent almost as much time in my bed as I did. "I guess we are."

Logan looped his arms around my waist and helped me up. "Then I suggest we go downstairs, say hi to your family and then I get back to my grandmother and the nine thousand emails that came in overnight."

Just like that? I wasn't sure why this was such a big deal for me, but it was. It might have been because I'd not introduced a boyfriend to my brother for so long or because Logan and I hadn't defined whatever it was between us. And it might have been because I was frightened. Vulnerable. My feelings for Logan were growing stronger with each day and I didn't feel prepared.

He stood, pulled open my bedroom door and waited for me to go first.

"I guess," I said. What choice did I have? I'd have to accept that I'd spend my brother's entire visit being questioned like a murder suspect.

We got to the top of the last leg of the stairs just as Scarlett burst through the door, her arms laden with a toddler and a bag of what looked like fake fur spilling out of the top of it—stuffed animals most probably.

"Hey," she called as we started down the stairs. She froze when she spotted Logan behind me. "Oh, hi. I didn't realize...Hi." Her grin was so wide I thought her head might fall off.

Ryder stumbled inside, bags draped over his shoulders and his son in his arms.

"Ryder," Scarlett said. "Say hello to your sister and..."

"Logan," he said as we got to the bottom of the stairs and he held out his hand. "Scarlett, I presume. I've heard so much about you."

"You have?" Scarlett glanced at me. "Well, I wish I could say the same. Very nice to meet you, Logan."

I tried to avoid Scarlett's wide-eyed stare and my brother's confused look.

"Logan?" Ryder glanced up the stairs as if trying to piece together everything that wasn't making sense to him in that moment.

"You know each other?" Scarlett asked.

"Yeah, we've done some business together. I didn't realize you and Darcy…"

"We're friends," I interrupted. "We're hanging out."

Logan began to chuckle. Hadn't that been what we'd agreed on? Perhaps he hadn't expected me to repeat him word for word.

"In a naked way?" Scarlett asked, her daughter slipping from her arms and racing down the corridor.

Gwendoline started chanting. "Naked! Naked! Naked!"

"How was your flight?" I replied, trying to dampen down the mortification.

"It was just fine, Darcy, but I'm far more interested in Logan. You're not leaving, are you?"

"As much as I would love to stay and chat, I have to get back to check on my grandmother before work."

"Your grandmother?" Scarlett asked.

"Logan spends his weekends with his grandmother at Badsley House," I said.

"Oh, just across the way. Well you must come back for dinner this evening."

Dinner? If I hadn't been ready for Ryder and Scarlett to see Logan for a fleeting moment, I was definitely not prepared to have us all spend the evening together.

"I'd love to," Logan said before kissing the top of my

head and heading out the front door. "I'm sorry to rush off, but I'll see you later."

Jesus, dinner with my family? What was he thinking? Weren't we trying to make this *less* complicated?

Scarlett watched him leave. "Darcy, Darcy, Darcy. Where did you find him?" She turned back to look at me. "And why on Earth didn't you tell me you were dating? This is so exciting and he's soooo handsome. Like *take-me-now* good-looking."

"You do know I'm right here?" Ryder said.

"Tell me everything," Scarlett said, ignoring my brother. "How long has it been going on? Is it serious?"

"So, you're dating him?" Ryder asked.

Overwhelmed, I turned around and followed the children into the library and tried to block out the questions as Scarlett and Ryder followed me.

"Are you okay?" Scarlett asked.

"Yes." Was I? Why had Logan agreed to dinner? We needed to talk, just the two of us before we had other people asking questions we didn't know the answers to. "We're just friends," I said with a sigh, concentrating on the children as they pulled toys out of an old trunk under the window.

"Friends?" Scarlett asked. "Friends who like to have sleepovers and kiss each other?"

"Don't give me a hard time," I pleaded.

Scarlett slid her arm around my shoulder. "I'm just happy for you. We worry about you being lonely here in this big old house, don't we, Ryder?"

"No, I don't worry my sister's not sleeping with enough men, funnily enough," Ryder bellowed from behind us. "She's perfectly happy here at Woolton."

Ryder was right, of course. I was happy at Woolton, but that didn't mean that I didn't want a future with a man I loved and a family of my own, but that wasn't who Logan was.

What we had was convenient. And uncomplicated.

"What do you want for dinner?" I asked. Shit, Cook would insist on doing something special when she heard Logan would be joining us.

"What's this Logan like, Ryder? Is he suitable for Darcy?"

Ryder slumped into one of the buttoned-leather chairs, keeping a watchful eye over the children playing happily with their newfound treasures. "I don't know him well. He's a tough opponent in business, but I've not heard that he's underhanded or into anything suspicious."

"Of course, he's not," I scoffed. "He's not like that." I turned to Scarlett to see her wide grin.

"You like him," she said.

"I'm saying he's not a dirty dealer."

"But you like him."

I shrugged. "Sometimes," I replied. "I don't like the fact that he still might be developing Badsley." I'd given him several alternative options to Badsley and he'd seemed enthusiastic about the Planton site, but until the appeal, there was nothing more I could do but enjoy our time together.

And Scarlett was right. I did like Logan, at least when we didn't talk about his business in the village. When things were just personal, I could put it out of my mind and concentrate on the way he made me feel.

"Wait," Ryder said. "When we ran into him at dinner the night before I left for Beijing, were you dating him then?"

"No! And we're not *dating* now."

"So it's just sex?" Scarlett asked as Ryder groaned. "Do you think it will turn into anything more?"

"Look, Scarlett," I said, gathering up some courage. "I used to like you up until ten minutes ago, when you invited someone you'd never met before to dinner and started interrogating me like I was on Interpol's most-wanted list. We're friends. We're hanging out. Yes, I like him—I don't hang out with people I don't like now that Frederick and Victoria spend most of their time in France. So can we leave the overanalyzing for now and just enjoy our day?"

She pressed her lips together, clearly holding back what she really wanted to say, and nodded. "Yes, of course. I got overexcited. You know how I am. I'm American and just can't help myself sometimes."

I rolled my eyes but grinned. "Come on. Cook said we could make apple pie in her kitchen with the children, but we need to pick the apples from the orchard."

"And afterward we can pick something for you to wear tonight."

Anxiety roiled in my stomach. Tonight felt like a big deal. Up until now I'd been able to live in the moment and not think about what was happening between Logan and me. But involving my family shifted things, and I wasn't sure I was ready. I knew Logan wasn't a man who did committed relationships, and looking at my history, I'd never been serious about anyone. With no experience and such a tumultuous short history, what hope did we have that we'd survive?

TWENTY-EIGHT

Logan

I rarely got nervous, but my stomach churned as I pulled up outside the front of Woolton Hall. I'd never met a woman's family before, and although I knew Ryder through business, there was no denying it was my personal relationship with Darcy that had led me to accept the invitation to dinner.

I'd worn a light-gray suit with an open collar. It might be Friday night in the country, but a place like Woolton Hall had decades of formality keeping the walls up.

Clearing my throat, I knocked on the huge oak door.

"Good evening, Mr. Steele," Mrs. MacBee said as she opened the door.

"Good evening."

"Everyone's in the library. I'll show you the way."

"That's okay, I can find them," I said. Although most of my time at Woolton had been spent in Darcy's bedroom, I did know where to find Darcy's favorite room in the house.

Laughter pulled me down the corridor and toward dinner with a girl I was sleeping with, a man I'd done business with, and an American I'd only met this morning. Although I'd been clear with Darcy that we didn't have to explain anything to anyone, I'd spent my day wondering what exactly it was we were doing.

I'd never dated someone exclusively, but looking back over the last few weeks, that was exactly what I'd been doing. And it wasn't scary or weird. Darcy was fun to be with—warm like sunshine and as honest as the dirt so often smeared across her face. I couldn't help but smile when I laid eyes on her and I never tired of her clever conversation and devotion to the people in her life.

"Logan," Darcy said as I stood at the entrance to the library. She lifted up on tiptoes and came over to meet me. She seemed much more relaxed than when I'd left her this morning. "Hey," she said, smiling up at me.

Sometimes, when I first set eyes on her, my breath left my throat. She had a glow about her that lit up her face and pulled me toward her. She was fucking beautiful and sweet and charming, as well as feisty and an occasional pain in my arse.

"Hey," I replied, bending to kiss her on the cheek and then handed her the posy of spring flowers I'd picked up at the farm shop.

"Flowers?" She looked as shocked as if I'd brought her a million pounds' worth of diamonds.

"Well, since your cook is preparing dinner, I thought you deserved flowers." Darcy knew I thought she was immensely practical and more than capable of handling just about anything life could throw at her, but that didn't mean I didn't like to tease her about having a staff.

"We baked the apple pie ourselves, I'll have you know." Darcy narrowed her eyes.

"Wow. Careful, you don't want to split a nail," I replied.

"Darcy is actually very practical," Ryder said, defending his sister.

"He's just kidding," Darcy said, taking my arm and pulling me over to join them.

The churning in my belly dissolved into warmth as I realized we knew each other a little better than I'd known any woman other than my grandmother. I liked that we had shared experiences and understood each other. I hadn't realized being so connected with someone could feel so right.

"Ryder's opened some ridiculously expensive red wine, so we're all drinking that...unless I can get you something else?" Darcy asked. Scarlett was perched on the old desk by the window and after we shook hands, Ryder retook his seat in one of the buttoned leather chairs.

"Whatever everyone else is drinking is fine with me."

"So how are you enjoying Woolton Village?" Scarlett asked.

"Very much," I replied. "I like being able to escape from London more than I thought I would."

"Such a shame you're hoping to ruin it with your plans for Manor House Club," Darcy said, sighing dramatically as she handed me a glass of red wine.

"I actually had some news on that front today." I took a sip of the dark-red liquid, pretending I wasn't acutely aware of Darcy's focused attention.

"Go on," she said, fixing me with a suspicious stare.

"I signed the paperwork this afternoon for the Planton site this afternoon," I said.

"Wait, the one I took you to? With Ivy?"

I nodded, as if I didn't know this would be a huge deal for her.

"You didn't tell me you'd made an offer. When did that happen?"

I hadn't said anything because I hadn't wanted to disappoint her if the deal fell through. But the truth was, developing the Planton site made much more sense than Badsley. "You knew I was interested. I said so when we saw the site together."

"I didn't know you put in an offer though. What does that mean for Badsley and your appeal?"

I shrugged. "Nothing. I'm going to develop the Planton site." Darcy's face broke into a huge grin.

"So you're not going to be developing Badsley? At all? You're abandoning the appeal?"

"I instructed my team to withdraw the appeal."

Darcy looked at me as if she was trying to make sense of what I was saying, then linked her arms around my neck and pressed her lips against mine as if no one was watching.

"You've never been so hot to me as you are right now. If Ryder and Scarlett weren't here and I hadn't made that apple pie, I'd be climbing you like a tree."

I chuckled. "You think I'm hot?"

"Always, but right now? You're white-hot." She grinned up at me. "I knew I could count on you."

Count on me? Sirens began to screech in my brain. I hadn't done this for her. This made sense from a business perspective. "It was the best option financially." The only person who relied on me was my grandmother. Why did Darcy think she could count on me? Expect things from me?

"Whatever you say," she replied, squeezing my arm. She clearly didn't believe me. But I was deadly serious. The last thing I wanted was to encourage Darcy to count on me. I didn't want the responsibility or the expectation.

Darcy and I had wandered into no-man's-land, where the rules and boundaries weren't clear, and I was paying the price. I didn't want anyone putting their faith in me. It was too risky, too easy to let people down. I worked hard to ensure people in my world had no expectations of me. That way I couldn't disappoint anyone.

I didn't want to be a man who broke promises, who left a trail of destruction and unhappiness behind me. That was my father's legacy, not mine.

The only way I could let people down was if they counted on me. Darcy had apparently done that once. She wouldn't do it a second time. I would make sure of it.

ALTHOUGH THE SURROUNDINGS were more formal than I was used to for a family meal, dinner with Scarlett, Ryder and Darcy had been relaxed—fun, even. And I'd managed to put her comment about counting on me to the back of my mind. I'd pressed pause. I would decide what to do about that later.

Darcy had a lot of responsibility, which she took very seriously, but the sweet, happy side of her that I got to see more and more often had shone through tonight.

"I'm going to go sort out the pie." Darcy had insisted on sending all the staff home as soon as our main courses were served.

"You want me to help?" I asked.

"I'll go," Scarlett said, setting her napkin on the table and following Darcy out of the dining room.

"So what made you move to the country?" Ryder asked as the girls left.

"My grandmother and Badsley. She grew up in the

house and I've always wanted to buy it back for her. And I enjoy spending time with her. She's my only family."

"And you're back here a lot?"

"Yeah. At the moment I come back on Thursday night, work from home on Friday and I'm here until Monday morning."

"The journey's not too bad, is it? I can normally do it in less than an hour and a half."

I nodded, but didn't confess that I used a helicopter. I knew that Darcy had banned her brother from landing one at Woolton and I wasn't going to start anything up between them.

"And you don't miss London at the weekends? I always thought you enjoyed the nightlife."

I couldn't remember Ryder and I ever having a conversation about anything personal but I had no doubt that my reputation wasn't one of a committed family man. "I like London and the country," I said honestly. And I liked Darcy. Seriously liked her. For the first time in my life, I thought about something other than work throughout the day, wondered what Darcy was doing and whether she was as distracted as I was.

But we hadn't known each other long, and I'd never been in this position before. I had no idea what happened after this. When it was just Darcy and me, I didn't think about the future because we were there, together in the moment, enjoying ourselves. But now I knew she had been expecting me to drop the plans for Manor House Club—for her. That she was counting on me...I couldn't just think about the here and now.

"I expect you to look after her. I know she's feisty and tough, but she's been through a lot. She's breakable."

What did "look after her" mean? I nodded, but didn't

know what to say. The last thing I wanted to do was hurt Darcy, but part of my attraction to her was that she didn't need looking after. "She's a wonderful woman."

I didn't know what would hurt Darcy. I didn't know how to take someone else into account when living my life. Ryder had told me to take care of her, but how? I had no idea how that translated into my day-to-day actions, or even if I wanted to be that man. If I took care of her, wouldn't she just rely on me more?

Tonight had meant to be casual and relaxed, but alarm bells kept sounding. First Darcy counting on me and now Ryder expecting me to look after her. Pressure built in my chest and my mind began to flip through possible solutions.

"Pie!" Darcy announced as she and Scarlett burst through the door.

"Excellent—I've never tasted your cooking," I said as Darcy placed the pie between us.

"You haven't missed anything," Ryder said.

"It's better than your cooking, Ryder," Scarlett said. "You could burn a boiled egg."

"I have other skills," Ryder replied. "Like earning enough money so that I don't have to boil an egg."

Darcy started to laugh. It was nice to see her enjoying her family. She clearly worshipped Ryder and the fact that I understood why made me like her even more, but it felt as if I were in quicksand, and I was sinking faster and faster. I just needed to put it to the back of my mind, get through tonight and get back to how Darcy and I were together when it was just her and me. If that was even possible.

As she sat down next to me, she placed her hand on my thigh.

"You okay?" Darcy whispered as she handed me my bowl of apple pie.

I nodded. "Sure. Looking forward to this," I said, glancing down at the pudding. Other than my mother and grandmother, I'd never had a woman cook for me. Not that Darcy had done this just for me. But it felt nice. Caring. Like she was looking after me—but I couldn't block out the sirens in my head.

I just needed to figure out if I should put out the fire or run for safety.

TWENTY-NINE

Darcy

The sky was dark like it was midnight, even though it was hours before and the rain echoed off the windows and roof as if it were trying to find a way in. Woolton Hall always seemed quieter and emptier when Ryder and Scarlett left, compared to how it had been before they arrived. I stood in the doorway, sheltering from the rain, warmed by the half hour of hugs and goodbyes I'd managed to squeeze out. I continued to wave long after the car disappeared down the drive and out of sight.

The sense that something had been missing grew in me as I closed and bolted the door. I hadn't seen Logan since dinner on Friday night, and although I appreciated that he knew I was spending time with my family, things didn't feel quite right without him with me.

I missed him. I missed him, and that was a problem, because I'd never missed any man before and I didn't know what to do with it.

I pulled my phone from my jeans to see if Logan had

messaged. I hadn't heard from him since he left after dinner on Friday, and something seemed off.

There was a distance between us. Perhaps I was creating it. The desire for him was unnerving. I'd always had to make an effort to find time for people I dated, but with Logan, space for him just appeared. I didn't need to try. Maybe I was holding back. And perhaps I'd created too much space for him.

I shouldn't read anything into it—we were both busy. Independent. We didn't owe each other anything. If I wanted to hear from him, I should message him. I brought up our last exchange and began to type different ways of telling him I missed him, then deleting them. I wandered into the library and collapsed near the unlit fire.

My phone buzzed.

"Hello," I answered.

"Hey," Logan replied. "Are your family still there?" His voice was like a warm blanket I wanted to sink into.

"They just left. I was thinking about lighting a fire—it's so dark and miserable out."

"Sounds nice. You going to toast some marshmallows?"

I laughed. "Maybe. You want to come over and join in the fun?" A knock on the door interrupted my grin. "Hang on, there's someone at the door and Lane left for the day."

I sped down the hallway and unbolted the door. Whoever was outside would be getting soaked to the skin.

As I swung the door open I came face to face with Logan. He held up a bag of marshmallows. "I missed you."

I wasn't sure if it was relief or excitement that meant I jumped into his arms and tangled my legs around his waist. "I missed you," I said as I kissed his damp nose.

"Can I come in? It's pretty wet out here."

"Yes, but I'm not getting down."

He chuckled and carried me through the doorway, closing it behind him.

It was so good to be in his arms, to feel his warmth and breathe in the clean, fresh smell of him. Maybe a little too good, but right then I didn't care. I didn't want to analyze or worry I was feeling too much. "I wasn't expecting to see you, but I'm so pleased you're here."

"You're just using me for my marshmallows."

"And the sex—don't forget about the sex." I pressed a kiss to his neck.

He laughed as he carried me down the hallway toward the library.

"Wait. You brought marshmallows—how did you know I'd want a fire?"

"I didn't. I just thought it was the weather for it."

I pulled back to look at him. "You, Mr. Steele, are a mind reader."

He opened his mouth as if he were going to say something, then thought better of it and continued into the library. "I have no idea how to light a fire," he said.

"City boys." I slid out of his arms. "I'll show you—I'm going to cheat anyway and use firelighters."

I tried not to stare as Logan unbuttoned his cuffs and rolled up his sleeves before kneeling with me before the empty fireplace. I handed him the kindling and wood in the order he needed it and coaxed him to shift things so they were set up for a perfect fire. Finally, I handed him the matches.

"Just light the firelighters and they'll do the rest."

"Whoa," he said as the flames took hold, poking at the logs.

"I'm going to get marshmallow stuff," I said as I got to my feet and headed to the kitchen, unable to wipe the smile from my face. The distance between us had fallen away and we were back to how we were together. Here he was, his hair a little damp, a day's worth of stubble on his chin, every bit as sexy and good company as I knew him to be.

When I returned to the library, he was still sitting in front of the fire, watching the flames.

As I closed the door, he turned and held out his arm for me to join him.

"I'm glad you're here," I said as he concentrated on opening the bag of marshmallows he'd brought with him. "I thought maybe Friday was a little..."

"I like it when it's just us," he said. "In the here and now."

Perhaps dinner with Ryder and Scarlett *had* freaked him out a little—even though he'd seemed relaxed and happy at the time, perhaps it had been too much. "You didn't like Ryder and Scarlett?"

"I liked them a lot," he replied, offering me the open bag of marshmallows.

"But you prefer when it's just us? It was you who didn't want to hide in the bathroom."

He rolled his eyes at me. "I don't like lying or misleading people."

"I understand that. But you said yes to dinner."

"I know, and I genuinely wanted to come. And I enjoyed it."

"But?" There had to be a *but*, a reason for the distance.

He sucked in a breath. "I'm new to this. Navigating it the best I can. All I have for you is that I like spending time with you. It's easy. When you introduce external factors... it's less...it's more comfortable when it's just us."

His answer provoked a thousand questions to burst from my brain. What was this between us? Was he looking for forever? Was I? Could I ever be with someone like Logan who was the opposite of the men I'd dated before him? I knew that if he wanted comfortable, then the kind of adjustment it took to build that kind of life together wasn't going to be what he was aiming for.

"I've been thinking." He took a marshmallow and spiked it with the end of his skewer. "What are you doing next weekend?"

"I don't think I have any plans. Why?"

"I thought we'd go away. There's a place in Scotland." He concentrated on getting another marshmallow on his skewer, then he looked up and found me watching him. "What do you think?"

Scotland would be just the two of us. He wanted to spend time with me, but wanted it to be easy. I wanted to go, and I wanted it easy and comfortable, didn't I? He wanted us to go away together. And I wanted exactly the same thing. As long as our expectations matched, that was all that mattered. "I think that sounds like a great idea."

He nodded and if it hadn't been dark and if the flames hadn't been casting strange shapes across the room, I could have sworn a slight blush crossed his cheeks. "Come and sit here." He pulled me between his legs so we both sat facing the fire.

So far, it was good between us when it was just us—easy and comfortable. Maybe it would stay that way. But if time with Ryder and Scarlett was a bump in the road, I knew from experience that life created far bigger obstacles that would be far from comfortable.

THIRTY

Logan

Every time I was away from Darcy, when I saw her again, it hit me in my chest like a sucker punch how beautiful she was.

"You have freckles across your nose. More than before. How come?" I asked as I took her hand to help her out of the helicopter and onto the grounds of the hotel. I'd spent the weekend her brother was over thinking about her and the alarm bells and decided to ignore them the best I could and try and take one step at a time.

"They only come out in the summer. I used to try and cover them up but—"

"You shouldn't. They make you even more beautiful."

"Logan..." she said, as if she was confused.

"What?"

"You can't say that stuff to me," she replied, shaking her head.

We made our way across the lawns toward the hotel. "Why? It's true." I hadn't wanted to put a label on what we were to each other, and Ryder's warning to me, and Darcy saying she knew she could count on me had freaked me out. But when it was just the two of us, I could feel myself falling for this amazing woman. The more time I spent with her, the more I wanted with her. The more I got to know her, the more I respected her...and wanted her to respect me.

"Have you been to this place before?" she asked, not-so-subtly changing the subject.

"No, actually, but I've always wanted to. My ancestors used to own the place."

"This was your ancestral home?"

"Our Scottish one. My father lost it in a game of poker before I was born."

"Wow. You didn't want to bring your grandmother?"

"I don't think she's got any interest in reliving history. But I've never seen it before, and sometimes it's good to remember the mistakes of the past." I'd been curious about this place for a while, and coming here with Darcy seemed like the right thing to do. She loved the countryside and you couldn't get more rural in Britain than the highlands of Scotland.

"Is it odd for you?" She slid her free hand up my arm, instinctively comforting me. Outside of my grandmother, I didn't know anyone who cared about my happiness.

"No. I mean, it's beautiful," I said, staring up at the dove-gray stone set against the bright-blue sky. "But I don't have any memories of growing up here."

"I'm surprised we're here. I always assume men will choose denial over anything else."

"Denial?"

"Yes, or compartmentalize. Men seem to be able to just pull down the shutter and move on to the next thing when they face disappointment. Ryder is the best at that. I've always envied him for it."

"I can do that when the need arises." I placed a kiss on the top of her head. "I want this weekend to be fun, though, and not all about my family's past."

"Fun?" She stopped stock-still and held my upper arms. "But you're Logan Steele—you don't have fun."

I rolled my eyes and hoisted her over my shoulder, like I had to get her into the helicopter during the "kidnapping."

Just like the first time, she squealed and squirmed, trying to break free, but I held her tight and marched toward the entrance to the hotel.

"Logan, you're in big trouble," she said.

"Lighten up and have some fun, Darcy," I replied setting her down on the slate-slabbed floor. "Anyone would think you don't know how."

"Mr. Steele," the receptionist said, interrupting our faux fight. "We have your suite ready for you. It's a beautiful room—the last earl had it as his bedroom suite."

Darcy squeezed my hand and pressed a kiss to my upper arm.

"Thank you," I replied.

"Is this weird?" Darcy asked as we climbed the stairs. "We could ask for a change of room."

"No, it's not weird. It's probably bullshit anyway. And it's likely to be the nicest room."

"I don't care about having the nicest room—I'm here to spend time with you."

"But *I* care about you having the nicest room." I'd never taken a woman away before, never shared stuff about my family. I wanted Darcy to enjoy herself, but it was good to remember that Darcy didn't care about the trappings.

"When did you get so cute?"

"Cute?"

She shrugged as we got to the top of the stairs. "Yeah. Cute."

I shook my head. "Oh no, Miss Westbury. Now I'm going to have to prove how very *not* cute I am."

A blush spread across her cheeks. "I've been counting on it," she whispered as I unlocked the bedroom door.

Somehow, our bags had made it up here before we had, so there was no reason for us to be interrupted. "Put the *do not disturb* sign on the door," I said, my cock hardening at the thought of her bent over the four-poster bed in the middle of the room.

I stood between the big bay window and the end of the bed, looking out onto the manicured lawns. Without asking, once she had closed and locked the door, she came over and began unbuttoning my shirt.

She pressed her lips against my skin as it was revealed. Such an intimate and welcome addition to what was now a pre-sex routine. She moved quickly, her fingers so used to my shape and movements that I couldn't tell where I ended and she began. Things were so perfect between us that sometimes it was difficult to remember a time before we were together. A time when I had to direct her more. When I was naked, she stripped down to her underwear and stood before me, coyly awaiting further instruction.

For the first time, I understood the appeal of monogamy. Why would I want anyone else when I could have Darcy?

I circled my arms around her, just wanting to hold her close for a few moments.

She pressed her cheek to my chest and relaxed against me, our bodies molding together. She sighed, and nuzzled closer. God, I loved when she was feisty and clever, but soft and vulnerable Darcy nearly ended me each time I saw her.

"Thank you for bringing me here," she whispered.

"Don't say I'm cute," I warned.

She giggled, the sound reverberating in my rib cage.

I slapped my palm against her ass. "Turn around and hold on." I tipped my head toward one of the four wooden posts of the bed.

She bent forward, giving me a fantastic view of her bottom and I followed her, standing close, my thighs brushing against hers as I dug my hand into the front of her underwear. She shivered against me. "Hold tight," I said. "We're just getting started...and you're already so wet."

Hooking my thumbs into the sides of her knickers, I pulled them down, allowing me free access to her pussy. She needed to come, fast, then I could take my time, finding new ways to pull pleasure from her incredible body.

"I'm always like that when I'm with you," she said as if it were the most obvious thing in the world.

"And it's all for me. You hear me?" I hated the idea of another man touching her. It had never occurred to me with other women I'd been with, but I hated the thought of any man seeing Darcy how I saw her, having the privilege of fucking her or making her come.

"Yes," she panted. "Just for you."

I rolled a condom on my straining cock and pushed into her. She gasped, one hand flying behind her as if determined to stop me from going any further.

"Too much?"

"I don't know if I can keep quiet. It's too good." She tried to catch the breath I'd chased from her.

"So don't," I said, pulling out and thrusting in harder this time.

She let out a muffled moan. "Logan," she said. "Everyone will hear."

"Yes," I said, beginning my rhythm, racing after her orgasm. "Anyone passing our door will hear me fucking you, will hear how good it is—they'll know what I can do to you. How crazy it makes you."

Her groans came regularly, echoing around the room. There was no holding back. Why she thought she could, I'd never understand. It wasn't who we were when we were together. We were open and honest and completely ourselves—it didn't matter if we were talking or fucking or toasting marshmallows.

Desire for her intensified with each thrust, and the effort it took to hold myself back created a sheen of sweat over my skin. I grunted and reached around for her engorged and throbbing clit.

"Logan," she screamed and with just a gentle stroke, her legs began to shake and her body arched. The thought that I had such power over her set my orgasm free, and I covered her back with my front and pushed into her, unable to stop, wanting to be as close to her as I possibly could be.

Panting and breathless, I guided her to the bed and pulled her into my arms. "Sometimes I worry I like you too much," she said, her tiny voice aimed toward my chest.

"Don't worry about that." I understood what she meant. I'd wondered what it meant and where it would lead, but I had to push it to the back of my mind or those alarm bells got too loud. "I think we just stay in the here and now. Just the two of us."

Her rib cage rose and fell, her breasts expanding against my chest and causing my cock to twitch. I'd have to have her again soon.

"Here and now?"

"Yeah," I said, tipping her onto her back, rolling on a

condom and positioning myself between her legs, my dick laying gently against her wet pussy.

"I think I need more than that. What are we aiming for?" she asked. "How do you feel?"

Her questions were getting more difficult and would require me to think about things that I wasn't used to considering. I'd been waiting, almost daring my feelings for Darcy to fade or disappear, but instead with every moment I spent with her, they strengthened, pulling me into a place I'd never been before.

She wanted to know who we were to each other, if this would last forever, if I loved her. "I don't know," I whispered in response to all of them. It was the only answer I had, but it was an honest one. I had no idea of how to navigate a relationship, no skills at having anyone other than my grandmother counting on me.

I plunged into her slowly, getting as deep as I could, relishing the pressure of her around my erection, the way her eyes watered, and her mouth opened as if she were readying herself for her sounds that would rip, unconstrained, from her throat.

She exhaled as I withdrew and slid her hands up over her head, readying herself for more. I kissed her collarbone in a thank you. We didn't need to ask each other anymore, we knew what the other liked, responded to, what would make each other wild. And in that moment, one thing became obvious.

She was everything to me. I wanted this to last forever.

Was that love?

I couldn't take my eyes off her as our bodies moved together. A low hum dragged across my skin—half my pleasure, half hers. She fascinated me. Everything about her was interesting, and I wanted to know more every time I found out something new. Like how long into the autumn would her freckles last? Why had she never had her ears pierced? Had she ever been in love before?

I grabbed one of her hands in mine. This wasn't just fucking anymore. What we had together was so much more than that. Emotion coated every physical move we made. I dipped my head and kissed her, our tongues melting together, through our pants, groans and declarations of pleasure.

Her body tightened underneath me and I could tell she was just seconds away from coming. I wanted to share it with her. I tightened my fingers in hers, deepened our kiss and pushed in, in urgent, desperate strokes. Fuck, she felt too good.

"Logan," she cried, her orgasm washing over her as mine unraveled, shooting up my spine and spilling out of every pore.

"Fuck," I spat and collapsed on top of her. Her fingers stroked delicately up my back as we descended from the airless atmosphere we'd travelled to.

"Logan," she whispered again. "I love you."

The words boomed in my ears. She didn't have to say it. I felt it in every look, every touch. But she *had* said it. And the alarm bells rang through my thoughts.

I rolled off her and pulled her into the crook of my arm, wanting to keep her wrapped up in me until it was dark and hunger made us move.

"I need you to be patient with me." I'd never believed in love. Not really. Not for me anyway. The idea of it was always too ephemeral for me to take seriously.

I was always so focused on the goals I could measure, on the things I could see. The deals, balance sheets and profit margins. Love had never been a focus. Deliberately so.

I'd mapped my life out years before and I'd stuck to my path ruthlessly and without compromise. My plan hadn't included love or a family—anyone or anything that I could let down or disappoint I'd erased as a possibility.

My father had let his heart rule his head at every turn, which had caused everyone in my family pain. I'd spent my life trying to be everything he wasn't. He'd had a wife and a family—was that what had caused his spiral of decline? Is that what commitment, promises, duty did? I was avoiding being like him at every turn.

And now, faced with Darcy, my plans didn't seem enough anymore. I wanted more. I wanted her.

"I know," she said, smoothing her hand across my chest.

She knew me better than to push and demand. More than that, she didn't want a response on those terms. We weren't playing quid pro quo—we weren't playing at all. This was real life, and I couldn't imagine my world without Darcy in it. I just didn't know whether abandoning my plans for her was worth the risk.

THIRTY-ONE

Darcy

I was trying to stay calm and not worry about how a million people were about to descend on Woolton Hall tomorrow for the summer party. How my list of things to do was growing, not shrinking, and what the consequences might be of my next trip to the bathroom.

There was no need to freak out.

"It's going to be fine," Aurora said.

"Can you promise that?" I asked, taking the paper bag from her.

"It's probably all the stress from the summer party—you know how you can get."

I nodded. That had to be it. Disrupted periods and headaches were always how I could tell I was stressed out. Except I hadn't had a single headache in the run up to the summer party, but my period was nearly two weeks late.

"I don't know how you could have left it this long to test. I freak out if I'm a day late."

"I've had a lot going on. I only checked the calendar yesterday, and anyway, we've always used condoms." And of course, I hadn't wanted to consider the possibility of being pregnant. But the longer I'd waited to test, the more the anxiety had grown in my chest until it was threatening to overwhelm my entire body.

"Should I have told Logan?" I asked, picking at the cellophaned box.

"That your period is late?"

"Yeah, and that I'm taking a pregnancy test." Things had evened out a little since Scotland and we'd gone back to our routine of spending much of every weekend together without interruption from family. The questions I had about our future had faded as his warm smiles and strong body had taken over. He was with me, and that was all that mattered.

"I don't know. I've not spent much time with you two together, so I don't know what your relationship is like."

Logan and I still didn't spend much time together with anyone—I wasn't even sure if his grandmother knew about us. I didn't know if he considered me his girlfriend.

He'd asked me to be patient. And so long as we remained cocooned from the world, it didn't seem like a big deal. And it allowed me to get comfortable with loving him. To settle with the knowledge that it was the first time I'd ever been in love. It was less scary for me now.

"We're taking things slowly." I knew he cared for me. I believed him when he said he wasn't sleeping with anyone else. His face lit up when he saw me, he tried to steal moments from his life in London to be with me. All the evidence was positive. That was enough.

For now.

Aurora winced. "I don't get it. He's coming tomorrow, right?"

"Yeah. Of course."

"And how will he be introduced? As your friend who you hang out with?"

"Don't."

Aurora had liked the fact that he'd had dinner with Scarlett and Ryder, but suspicious that nothing had moved on from there. But when I was with Logan, everything was perfect. But when I saw us from a distance, I understood where Aurora was coming from.

"You'll have to tell him if the test is positive, and there's only one way to find out." She tipped her head toward my bathroom.

I blew out a breath and headed through the door. "There's no need to freak out," I told myself.

Peeing on a stick sounded simpler than it actually was, but eventually I managed to catch enough pee for the test.

"Are you done?" Aurora asked through the bathroom door.

I set the stick on the counter and stared at it. "Yeah. I think so."

Aurora opened the door and we both continued to stare. "How long does it take?"

"I'm not sure."

"Let's find out, Miss Practical." She took the instructions from the box. "Three minutes. And we're looking for a blue cross."

"A blue cross is negative?" I asked.

"Positive."

"So a blue cross is *not* what we're looking for." I didn't want to be pregnant, did I? Logan and I hadn't discussed next week, let alone a life together. But I couldn't deny that there was part of me that was hoping to see two lines and not one.

"Right."

We both stared at the stick, waiting for something to happen.

"Okay, that's four minutes, according to my phone," Aurora said. "And that's just one blue line. No cross."

"Give me that." I pulled the instructions from her and re-read them. A blue line meant negative. A blue cross was positive.

And I was staring at just one line.

That was good. Right? "So I'm not pregnant."

"How do you feel?" Aurora leaned on the counter.

"Relieved, of course." It was the quickest, cleanest, easiest outcome for everyone involved. But a baby? A family of my own? Gurgles and giggles echoing through Woolton Hall? That could have been wonderful.

"Did you play out in your head what would have happened if it had been positive?"

"No!" I paused. "Well, maybe a little. I mean, I love being an aunt and everything, I really do, but I want my own children at some point."

She pulled me into a hug.

"If I'd been pregnant, even if Logan hadn't been interested, I would have handled it, you know?" I tried to keep my voice from faltering. I'd gotten the result that I'd wanted, but at the same time, an alternate reality had been snatched from me. Having seen that single blue line appear, I was clearer than ever that a family was what I wanted. That was what I was aiming for. I just wasn't sure it was what Logan wanted.

"This way, you have more control. You have a chance to

figure out if Logan is the one—find out if he really wants a family."

I nodded against her shoulder. "I know. I know. This is good. I'm not ready. Logan and I certainly aren't ready. It's all good." I pulled back and leaned toward the mirror, wiping under my eyes, and removing the escaped mascara. But I would have gotten myself ready. And next time I wanted to *be* ready.

When I took my next pregnancy test, I wanted Logan to be with me and I wanted us *both* to be hoping for a blue cross.

"And it means you can get drunk at the party tomorrow."

"Double win," I said, grinning a little more widely than was necessary.

"Is everything ready?" she asked.

"Yeah. Scarlett, Ryder and the kids are coming up from London this afternoon. They've been doing museums. Caterers arrive tomorrow."

"Caterers? How do Cook and Mrs. MacBee feel about that?"

I sighed. "Well, Cook's doing puddings and the caterers will do everything else. I've even had them do the drinks. Lane wasn't happy at first, but I want the staff to enjoy the day. Lane will still have to organize and supervise, but someone else will be doing most of the work."

"They're both getting older."

"I know. We all are."

Being with Logan had brought into focus for me how our lives were made up of chunks of time. For my grandparents, their twenties were about finding themselves and their thirties had been about family. I was coming to the end of my twenties and I was with a man who made my skin tingle when he looked at me, a man who knew how far he could push me. Someone I knew how hard I could push. Logan who made me laugh, made me feel adored.

I loved him.

The problem was, now more than ever, I knew what direction I wanted my future to head in. And I needed to know if Logan was going to be by my side on the journey.

THIRTY-TWO

Logan

I always enjoyed spending time with Darcy, but I wasn't looking forward to the summer ball. Part of it was because I would have to share her—she'd be busy all day with her guests, her brother, friends, nieces and nephews. And it was also because I knew how to navigate my relationship with her when it was just the two of us, not when we were surrounded by strangers.

I pulled up in front of the house and turned off the engine.

"She didn't want you to help her set it all up?" my grandmother asked from the passenger seat.

"She's got help. I would only get under her feet."

I got out, rounded the boot and opened the door for my grandmother. "At least they've got nice weather for it."

"Mrs. Steele." One of the ladies I recognized from the village came over. "How wonderful to see you."

"Grandmother, I'm going to park the car. I'll come and find you."

"Yes, yes. No fussing. Find Darcy and see if she needs anything."

I wasn't sure what my grandmother thought was going on—she'd never asked, probably not wanting to put any pressure on me. But she knew Darcy and I spent time together—and she did everything to encourage it.

I parked in the field allocated for cars and headed back up the gravel drive to the house. Looking for Darcy, I tapped on the partially open front door. "Hello?" The only response was a clatter of pans and muffled voices.

I grinned and headed down the corridor. The nearer I got, the more people seemed to appear out of nowhere, rushing by me with plates and trays. Today must have taken more preparation than I'd assumed. As I got to the kitchen, I scanned the people darting about but couldn't spot Darcy.

"Mrs. MacBee, have you seen Darcy?"

She looked up from arranging food on a silver platter and frowned. "I think she went upstairs to change her shoes."

"Thank you." She always seemed to kick off footwear at the first opportunity so she was probably trying to find something more comfortable.

I turned and headed for her bedroom, where I was sure to find her in her dressing room, in a pile of shoes.

I hadn't seen her all week, so catching Darcy on her own and stealing just a few minutes to hold her had the pulse in my neck beating a little faster than usual. I couldn't wait to tell her how beautiful she looked, how perfect everything was going to be today. And then I could sink into the background and spend the afternoon with my grandmother.

"Darcy," I called as I knocked on her bedroom door.

No answer. But if she were in her bathroom or dressing

room, she wouldn't hear me. I opened the door and called again. "Darcy?"

I stepped inside and found her bedroom empty, so stalked toward the dressing room. "Have you found some shoes?" I grinned, expecting to see her sitting on the floor trying to figure out if she could get away with wearing trainers, but there was nothing but a thousand dresses piled on the back of the pink velvet love seat.

I knocked on the bathroom door. "Darcy?" Twisting the brass handle open, I poked my head in, but that was empty, too. Where was she?

I caught my reflection in the mirror. My tie was a little skewed. I would probably be one of the few wearing a tie today, but Darcy liked me in a suit. And who was I to deny her? I stepped into the bathroom and faced the mirror properly, adjusting my tie so it was perfectly straight, then noticed a white stick behind the tap.

The pulse in my neck ramped up to a throb as I realized what I was looking at.

A pregnancy test. An *open* pregnancy test.

What the hell?

Grabbing the stick, there was a clear blue line in the results window. Fuck. Did that mean it was positive? Shit. I needed to find the instructions. I glanced around the room, peered into the bin, but there was nothing.

Shit, I had no idea if it was positive or negative. I pulled out my phone and began to Google how to read a pregnancy test.

My pulse raced in my neck as I found thousands of sites and pictures, each one with conflicting advice.

There was only one thing that was clear. She'd kept the test. Why would she do that if it was negative?

I grabbed on to the side of the sink.

I never wanted to be a father. I'd always been very clear about that. I couldn't have anyone relying on me. Not a wife, and certainly not a child. I'd spent my life cleaning up after a man who didn't deserve a family. I wasn't about to start the cycle again.

I exhaled and stumbled back, my arse landing on the side of the bath.

My heart pounded against my rib cage like an incarcerated wolf and questions ran through my head at a mile a minute. Why hadn't Darcy told me? How long had she known? She'd told me she was on birth control. Had she been lying? Had she been planning this?

I loosened my tie and undid the top button of my shirt, but I still couldn't get enough oxygen in my lungs. I slung the test back where I found it and stared at myself in the mirror.

I needed air, space. I had to be by myself and think all this through. A cacophony of thoughts competed in my head and I wanted to pull each one out, examine and make sense of it. The last place I wanted to be was at a summer garden party where I was expected to be all charm and smiles.

One thing was for sure—I didn't want to be a father.

THIRTY-THREE

Darcy

I watched for a few minutes to see if Logan would spot me. I'd been running from one set of people to another all afternoon, and every time I decided to seek Logan out, pull him behind the stables for a kiss, someone else decided they needed to tell me what a wonderful party it was and how they were sorry my grandfather wasn't here to see it.

"Excuse me, will you?" I said to Freida, who I'd been talking to about the caterers. "I've just spotted someone I must go and thank before the crowd swallows them up and they think I'm untenably rude."

"Of course, my dear." She patted my hand and headed back toward the other ladies of the Woolton W.I.

I tried to bite back a grin as I headed toward Logan. I rarely had the chance to see him like this from a distance, so handsome in his light-gray suit—even if he wasn't wearing a tie—so tall and commanding.

"Darcy." A tipsy Mrs. Lonsdale grabbed my hand.

"What a wonderful party. I'm so pleased the weather held for you."

I smiled but didn't stop. "Thank you so much, Mrs. Lonsdale. I'll catch up with you later. I must check something."

She waved me off. "Yes, yes. A hostess's job is never done."

I kept my gaze fixed on Logan, determined to avoid anyone else's eye. As if he sensed me, he looked up. I couldn't hold back my grin any longer, but he didn't smile in return.

If I hadn't known better, I'd have thought apprehension crossed his face.

Or perhaps he was reacting to something his grand-mother had just said. Or maybe something had happened at work this week. We'd spoken less than usual because I'd been so wrapped up in the party preparations.

"Hello." I bent to kiss Mrs. Steele on both cheeks and Logan rose from his seat and greeted me stiffly in the same way. His hands didn't linger over me like they normally did, his eyes didn't lock with mine in the way I was used to.

"I hope you're enjoying the match." I glanced at Ryder, Scarlett, Violet and Alexander on the croquet field.

"Take a seat and I'll go and fetch some drinks," Logan said, glancing over at the nearest drinks station as if he couldn't wait to escape.

"I'll come with you to help," I offered.

"No, stay and enjoy yourself. I'm sure you've been running around all day." Why wouldn't he want a few minutes with me, even if it was while we got drinks?

Confused, I took a seat and watched as Logan started in the direction of the Pimm's.

"How are you my dear?" Mrs. Steele asked. "Are you managing to enjoy your day at all?"

Still staring at Logan's suit covered back, I replied, "Yes, of course, but would you excuse me one second? I want to ask Logan to get me a soft drink. I've got such a lot still to do today."

I jumped up and weaved my way through the clusters of people until I reached him. "Hey," I said, grasping his arm.

"Hi," he replied as he came to a standstill. "I was just getting some drinks."

"Are you okay?"

He frowned at me. "Yes. Shouldn't I be?"

I scanned his face for clues, trying to figure out if I was just making up things in my head. "You seem a little..." I shrugged. "I don't know. A little off."

"I'm just getting drinks, Darcy."

"Okay. Well, can you stay tonight?" I pushed him. We'd made no plans for him to stay, and for whatever reason, he'd never stayed when Ryder and Scarlett were over.

"You enjoy your time with Ryder and Scarlett. I'll see you when they leave." He was colder than I'd ever known him. Even for a public setting, he was distant.

"Logan?" I asked, needing some kind of reassurance from him.

"What do you want to drink? Pimm's?"

"I don't want anything to drink. I want you to drag me around the back of the stables and kiss me into next week. I want you to look at me like you normally do. I don't understand what's up with you."

He forced a smile which did the opposite of reassure me. "We'll talk when the weekend is over," he said. "Ryder and Scarlett leave Monday morning, right?"

"If you've got something to say, I want to hear it."

He glanced over my head. "I don't have anything to say specifically—it's just a busy weekend, and you have house-guests." He would normally place his hand at the small of my back, but he didn't. He just started to walk. "Now, let's get you a drink."

"I just want lemonade or something," I mumbled under my breath.

"You're not drinking?" he asked.

"I have too much to do."

"Right," he said, and we joined the queue.

Once, not so long ago, Logan Steele had told me he never lied, but now I knew that wasn't true. This wasn't just a busy weekend. It wasn't that I had houseguests. He had something to say, but he was going to make me wait.

My head said that he could be stressed at work or worried about a million things but in my heart, I knew it was about me. It was about us. Maybe he was bored, or he'd gotten what he wanted from me and now was moving on. Whatever it was, it wasn't good news.

THIRTY-FOUR

Darcy

Just like before anyone can hear the rumble of thunder or see the rain, it's possible to tell a storm is coming, I knew that the next time I saw Logan, he would be bringing bad news. As I stood in the doorway, waving Scarlett, Ryder and the children off, I remembered the last time I'd been here. In the rain. Logan had arrived with marshmallows. But this evening was hot and humid. There was no need for fires. No reason for marshmallows.

I closed the door, took a mug of steaming-hot tea and sat in the library, waiting for him. Usually, I'd hear his helicopter over Woolton as he made his way into London on a Monday morning, but I hadn't heard it today and didn't expect to.

He'd said we'd speak when Scarlett and Ryder had left and I knew he'd turn up.

Normally, if I had been expecting Logan, I would have told Lane that I'd answer the door, but not today. If I was going to be disappointed, I wanted it to happen in here, where I felt safe and protected from the world. Bad news was threatening on the horizon and the library was my shelter.

I closed my eyes as I heard the expected knock, then the mumble of voices.

I took a deep breath when Logan came straight in.

"Hi," he said. "Is now a good time?"

I shrugged as I sat back in the green leather chair, clutching my tea. He closed the door behind him and slid his hands into his pockets as I watched him out of the corner of my eye. I didn't want to talk about the weather or his weekend or Ryder and Scarlett. Whatever was coming, I wanted it over with.

He pulled the chair nearest mine slightly closer and perched on the edge of the seat. Seconds ticked by, but I didn't say anything, didn't try to make either of us more comfortable by talking about something and nothing. I didn't want to make this easy for him. I wouldn't ask him what was wrong or give him any kind of in.

"Do you have something to tell me?" he asked.

My heart lifted in my chest and I met his eyes for the first time. Had I read him wrong? If he was here to ask me something, then perhaps he wasn't about to deliver bad news. "No. Nothing in particular."

"Darcy," he said, as if he knew I was hiding something.

I searched his face, trying to figure out what I was missing. "What? You seem to have something to say to me."

"I found the test," he said.

I could pretend I didn't know what he was talking about but the image of Aurora and me peering at the white stick flashed into my head. How had he seen the test? Had he been snooping? "Oh, right. I was going to tell you, I just—"

"I'll support you in whatever decision you make. Financially. But I can't be a father. It's not who I am."

I tried to make sense of what he was saying. "I'm not sure I know what you're talking about. The test was negative."

He pulled back as if someone had punched him. "But I saw the test."

"I don't know which test you saw, but the one I took—the two, in fact—they were both negative."

He blew out a breath and pushed his hands through his hair. "I see."

I scooted forward on my chair and placed my cup next to me on the side table. "Is that why you were so weird with me at the party? You thought I was pregnant?" This was all some terrible misunderstanding. Now that he knew, this weirdness between us could disappear and we could get back to normal.

"You should have told me you were concerned. That you thought you might be," he said.

"I was just triple-checking. We're always careful, and it's not unusual for me to be late if I'm stressed. It was no big deal. I would have told you eventually."

He'd been really worried about this. For no reason. He should have just said something and I could have put his mind to rest days ago. I leaned over and placed my hand on his leg. "I'm sorry you got a scare."

Abruptly he stood, moving away from my hand. "Darcy, I can't do this anymore."

"Do what? I'm not pregnant. Nothing's changed."

He reached around his head and scratched his neck. "Everything's changed. I'm sorry. I'm not the right man for you. You deserve someone who wants to get married and have children, and I can't give you those things."

Even though I'd been prepared for something, I hadn't been expecting this—or maybe I had, but I hadn't thought it would feel this heavy, this hurtful.

I took a few steadying breaths. We just had to be logical. Practical. I would talk him around. "And when did you decide this?"

"You've always known that's not me. We both got into this knowing it was temporary. I let it go on too long."

Each word was like a blade slicing through my skin. "And now temporary is over? Just like that?"

"It had to end sometime."

"Says who?" Could it really be that easy for him? "So, you don't feel anything?"

"It's not that I don't care about you, but we want different things. It's senseless to carry on when—"

"When we're so happy? Because I know you are. And I know I am. So why give that up?"

He closed his eyes as if trying to block out the truth of my words. "We want different things. We deserve different things."

I'd never felt so connected to someone, so completely in tune with a man. I wanted *him*. I wanted *everything* with him. "I don't think that's true. How can we want different things if we're so happy when we're together?"

"I can't give you what you need." He wasn't answering my questions. As if he didn't want to reveal any chink in his armor. The more I pushed, the more he retreated, and I could feel the growing distance between us as if he were in a jet, taking off, and he'd left me on the ground, watching him go. I was helpless, powerless.

Panic ran through my veins. I wanted him to come back to me, change his mind. Remember what we were to each other just a few days ago. "I want to spend every night with you, want to tell you everything that's going on in my head. I love you."

He closed his eyes. "Don't."

"Don't? Don't be truthful? We might have started off temporary, but that's not what it feels like to me." We'd spent so much time together, been so happy. Had it all been a lie?

"I let things extend...I..." I wanted him to finish his thought, tell me that he'd let things go on because he'd enjoyed our time together, loved me. But he didn't. "And better now than..."

"Than when?" But I knew the answer. When next time, the test wasn't negative.

He sighed and bowed his head. "This has clarified things for me. I've never wanted to be a father and that's not going to change. You deserve someone who wants the same things you do. Someone who..."

"Isn't afraid to love me?" I finished for him.

"It's not about being afraid—I just can't give you what you want," he said, staring into the empty hearth where just a few weeks ago we'd toasted marshmallows and kissed so much that my face had been raw from the heat and his stubble.

Had I always known it had been temporary? I had grown to love the man who was pulling my heart apart, and love wasn't temporary. Not for me.

At first, Logan was the most unsuitable man I could ever have dreamt up. He was born for the city, insisted on travelling by helicopter and wanted to destroy Woolton Village. He was far too handsome, too confident, too charming. But somewhere along the road, all the reasons I had not to fall for Logan Steele had drifted away. I couldn't think of a man more perfect for me.

"But surely what people want can change over time. You don't fix in stone your ambitions and plans for your life and then never veer off course, no matter the consequences."

"Perhaps some people don't. But for me, I don't commit to anything unless I know I can see it through. That's not a bad thing. This isn't selfish, Darcy. I'm protecting you. It's easier for you this way."

"I don't need protecting from you. There is no certainty in the world. I of all people know that. And I've never asked for any guarantees from you."

"I can't half-arse things. And if whatever was between us was to continue, I couldn't predict what was down the line, that I wouldn't let you down or disappoint you."

"But that's life, Logan."

"It's not a life I want to live."

He'd stolen any response I had and my hands began to shake. My body weakened. There was no comeback if he didn't want me. If he didn't want to try. Whatever we had wasn't enough for him. Or maybe it was too much.

"So that's it. Game over. We shake hands and move on?" It was a stupid question—that was exactly what he was saying. It just felt so hopeless. So heartless. Such a waste.

"I'm sorry."

"Well, that's okay then," I snipped. I couldn't make him love me or want a life with me. And I could tell from the way he couldn't look at me that his mind was set and I wasn't going to change it.

I'd never been in love before Logan, but I'd spent the last few months wanting to share every thought, every moment with him, and now I wasn't sure if I'd ever see him again. I was going to have to find my strength.

One step at a time. I just needed to get out of the library

without breaking down. Without collapsing at the thought that he'd never hold me again, that I'd never watch his muscles flex as he showered, that I'd never hear him talk about the students from his old school.

He was the first man other than my brother and grandfather that I'd ever felt was on my side and in my corner like he could become part of my family, and now he was walking away. Abandoning me. And I was left on my own. My chest felt hollow and the taste of metal lingered on my tongue. I needed to leave. It was too painful to sit here and watch him go.

"I'll see you around," I said as I stood.

"I'm sorry."

I ignored him. An apology was the last thing I wanted from him. And I'd lost my voice as he'd ripped my heart into pieces.

I swept past him and through the door. All I could do now was wait for time to pass and for my feelings to fade. Because that was what people did, right? They got over heartbreak. I was sure it was possible in the abstract, but right then and there I couldn't see how it could be true.

I walked as fast as I could without running and straight up the stairs. I wanted to dive into my bed and not come out until this pain had relented.

Until I'd stopped loving Logan Steele.

THIRTY-FIVE

Logan

I had to remind myself who I was. I stepped out of the car and tipped my head up to take in the tower of offices in front of me, trying to breathe in the sense of power I normally got from business. My usual view of my workplace on a Monday morning was from the top of the tower as I arrived by helicopter. It had seemed distasteful to break things off with Darcy then fly out of the village, so I'd arranged a car.

Today was the last time Darcy would knock me off course.

Her reaction had played through my mind on the journey in. I hadn't been expecting her to be so calm. When I'd brought up the pregnancy tests, she'd acted like it was no big deal. She had me questioning myself. Did women worry about getting pregnant a lot? I had no experience with a pregnancy scare. I wore condoms whenever I was with a woman. And I was pretty sure that with my money, if anything had gone wrong, I'd have heard about it.

Was it as easy as she'd said it was—she was late, she tested, it was negative? Maybe so, but it couldn't undo the train of thought that it had unlocked.

For months, I'd insisted on living in the moment, not thinking about the future, not remembering about how I wasn't built to be part of a couple or to be someone's husband. Seeing those pregnancy tests meant I was forced back into reality. Darcy and I *were* a couple and even the smallest habits and expectations couldn't be ignored. The way I'd been staying over at Woolton Hall each weekend, the way I wanted to hear her thoughts about everything that happened when I wasn't with her, the way I couldn't wait to see her whenever we were apart.

We weren't friends who hung out. And that wasn't ever part of my plan.

"Good morning, Mr. Steele," a receptionist greeted me as I swept past. Her smile and the way she cocked her head was a little familiar. Did I know her? As I waited for a lift, she looked back at me over her shoulder. Her black hair was swept up into a bun, her lips bright red, her tanned skin glowed—physically, she was Darcy's complete opposite and exactly the type of woman I used to fuck.

I hadn't noticed her on reception before. Was the fact that I had now a sign? Proof that I'd moved on, that life would get back to normal now?

I took the lift up to the top floor to find my assistant waiting for me as the doors opened. "Malcolm is in your office."

I glanced at my watch. "I've been tied up this morning."

"You want the helicopter on Thursday or shall I stand them down again?"

I sucked in a breath. I'd only been going back to Badsley on a Thursday because of my grandmother's fall, then because I'd wanted to spend more time with Darcy. "No, not Thursday. I'll be in the office on Friday. And I'll take a car back to Badsley in the evening."

I'd been right to call things off with Darcy, but I knew how much the helicopter irritated her, and I didn't need to torture her by flying over Woolton Hall.

"I hope you have good news for me," I told Malcolm as I rounded my desk and took off my jacket, placing it on the back of my chair.

"I do. We're all on schedule. The plans have been approved and construction is due to start at the beginning of next week."

"And do you have the operational plans?"

"I'm still working on those. I know you want to be heavily involved, so I'm trying to work the timetable around that."

He was right. I'd wanted to oversee every detail of Manor House Club when I'd first arrived at the concept. This would be the first business that I'd ever built from the ground up and I wanted to ensure everything was being done as I planned. But things had changed. I needed some distance from anything that reminded me of Darcy.

"I've got a number of things that have come up that are going to be pulling my focus for the next few months, so I'm going to ask you to take the lead on most of the Manor House Club development, including the operational plans."

I needed to be in the city. It was where I belonged. Where Darcy wasn't. I was never suited to the country. And I'd made my fortune by having good people around me that I trusted. I wasn't a micromanager and I wouldn't change that just because this was my first organically grown business. I needed to stick to my plan, get back to what I was good at.

"Whatever works for you. Do you want to come down in a week or so to see progress?"

I brought up my emails. "No, you can brief me with reports and any necessary photographs. I do want to see the operation plans, but don't build me into them. If you need additional resources, then bring me the rationale and we'll discuss it. Is there anything else?"

Malcolm rose from his seat. "Not at all. I'll get right on that."

I'd just moved out of his way and given him additional responsibility. I'd say I was Malcolm's favorite person right now.

I was used to making decisions that involved a lot of money, time, people, and resources, and I always knew I'd made the right one by how I felt a couple of hours after the hammer came down. Being back in London now, everything felt great. I was cleaning house. Getting back to normal.

Back to life before Darcy Westbury.

The day passed quickly in a whirr of meetings and conference calls. A couple of times I found myself checking my phone for messages from Darcy. Another habit, another routine that I'd acquired without realizing it. I'd soon get over it. Thank God I'd ended things before I'd gotten in any deeper. Although she'd told me she loved me, I knew how resilient she was. She'd soon realize this was best for both of us. We'd just have made each other unhappy if we'd dragged things out.

I just needed to make sure I kept busy and distracted for a while so my mind didn't wander to her. I'd double my efforts at the gym, perhaps kick off a strategy overhaul for our overseas businesses.

I made my way out of lifts and across the lobby and glanced across at the reception desk.

"Working late, Mr. Steele?" the same sleek-haired brunette asked as we locked eyes.

I slowed my pace. After eight, most of the office staff had already gone home. "You too, I see." The way she singled me out suggested I knew her, but I was sure I'd never spoken to her before.

"I've got ten minutes until I finish for the day. Thought I might grab a drink if you know anywhere?" Her eyes danced brightly as she spoke.

"Excuse me if I'm being rude, but do I know you?"

"I see you come into the office each day, though not usually on a Monday. Rumor has it that you fly in by helicopter to start the week—but I guess it's in for scheduled maintenance today."

I smiled, finally understanding what was going on. "Something like that." I'd forgotten that this was how I picked up women. Meeting a backward glance, noticing a smile across a lobby. This was me getting back to normal.

"I'm having dinner at the French brasserie on Threadneedle Street," I said.

"I love that place." Her tongue dipped out of her lips.

"Well, you'd be very welcome to join me when your day is over."

"Then I'll see you then," she said.

I nodded and headed out.

Yes, this felt right. This was the old Logan Steele. I was back.

The air was warm and thick as I stepped out of the air-conditioned offices and I realized I'd not been outside all day.

"Mr. Steele," the restaurant owner greeted me as I arrived. "So good to see you again. Can I get you a table at the bar?"

"That would be great." I was just planning to enjoy her flirting, see if I wanted to fuck her, and then we'd leave. We'd eat something light at the bar—there was no point in clogging up a table. We wouldn't be here long.

I'd taken my second sip of whiskey when she walked in. Several heads turned as she paused at the top of the steps. She was striking rather than pretty. Tall—a good four or five inches taller than Darcy and had the tanned skin and kind of athletic shape that I'd always gone for.

"Is this seat taken?" she asked as she came up behind me.

"I believe I've kept it free for you," I said. With her huge saucer-like brown eyes and perfect skin, she was even more attractive up close.

She slid onto the stool next to mine with an easy grace.

"What would you like to drink? And eat?"

"A glass of white wine would be great," she said. "But I'll pass on the food."

"Can I get a glass of—" I turned to her. "What kind would you like?"

"I really don't mind."

I nearly asked for sauvignon blanc—Darcy's favorite. "Can we get a glass of white wine here please?" I asked the waiter, then turned back to the woman next to me. "You do seem to know more about me than I know about you—let's start with your name."

"Abigail," she said.

It didn't suit her. Abigail was a name I'd expect someone in Woolton Village to have, rather than someone working in the City of London. "How long have you worked in the building?"

"About three months," she said. "You've never come in

the front door on a Monday morning—what was different about today?"

Three months. Three months ago, I'd moved to Badsley. Three months ago, I'd met Darcy. Apparently, three months ago I'd stopped noticing other women. Was that what monogamy was like? Had I stopped noticing beautiful women because I'd been happy with Darcy?

"Nothing different," I replied. I wasn't about to confess that I'd ended whatever had been between me and the first woman I'd ever cared for. I didn't want to think about it, let alone talk about it. I'd done the right thing. Now I needed to get back to normal. Get back to the life I knew.

"Where does your helicopter normally fly in from?"

The waiter placed a glass of white wine in front of her and blushed when she smiled at him. There was no doubt Abigail was beautiful. Three months ago, we'd have skipped the drinks and I'd have made her come by now. But I was rusty.

"I have a place in the country."

She took a sip of her wine and tilted her head before swallowing. "How nice, but do you have a place nearby as well?"

She traced her finger across my wrist. I liked a woman who knew what she wanted, especially when she only wanted something physical. Abigail was exactly what I needed. "Yeah, I have a place. And even better, there's a hotel just around the corner."

"Sounds good. I'm not a girl with much patience. When I see what I want, I tend to go for it."

She was perfect to get me back on track. Assertive, beautiful, and most importantly, right in front of me. "Do you know how to do as you're told?" I asked. I didn't want to waste my time.

She paused. "I prefer to be told rather than asked."

I nodded. She ticked every box. But I hadn't asked for the bill yet. I needed to get the fuck out of my own head and focus on the here and now. I was usually so good at that. "Are you sure I can't get you something to eat?"

She fingered the rim of her glass and looked up at me through her eyelashes. "I don't like to exercise on a full stomach."

The ball was firmly in my court. I could ask for the bill, take her to the nearest hotel and fuck Darcy Westbury out of my system—or I could go home and spend the night tossing and turning, wondering exactly what Darcy was doing.

It should have been an easy choice.

Before Darcy, there wouldn't have been a decision to make. But whether or not I liked it, I was beginning to realize that the last three months had changed everything.

THIRTY-SIX

Darcy

I thought a different bed would be better, but I hadn't slept a wink for the third night in a row.

The noise of chaos got louder as I padded downstairs toward the open-plan living area. The television, the baby squealing, the crash of crockery and the unmistakable sound of my brother trying to keep his temper was why I'd come to Connecticut in the first place. Distraction. Back at Woolton, everywhere I looked, Logan was staring back at me. I needed a change of scenery. I needed to be in an environment where I could breathe again.

"Did you sleep well?" Scarlett asked. "The best part of this morning, like any morning in this house, is that we have an enormous pot of coffee. Can I get you a cup?"

"That would be great, thanks." I could have gone to stay with Violet and Alexander, and at least then I would have been in the city, but I'd needed the noise of being here, needed the chaos that only children, my brother and his wife created. There was something about family that made me feel safe.

"You look pretty," Scarlett said.

I'd managed to shower, wash my hair and shrug into jeans and a white shirt—Scarlett was clearly trying to make me feel better. "I've not slept in three days and I'm not wearing a scrap of makeup to try and hide it. I definitely don't look pretty."

She glanced up from the toast she was buttering. "You look absolutely wonderful—isn't that right, Ryder?"

Ryder scooped up Toby from the floor and slotted him into his high chair. "She has Westbury genes. What did you expect?"

Scarlett rolled her eyes and gave the slice of buttered toast to her son, who placed his palm flat on the bread as if he were trying to make a handprint.

"I thought we'd go shopping today, have some lunch. We'll take the driver so we can have a glass of champagne."

"Aren't you going to work?" I'd expected to spend the day messing around with the kids, getting under the nanny's feet, and maybe even taking a dip in the pool.

"Absolutely not. I want to spend some time with you. I don't get to see you often enough."

I didn't want to be mollycoddled. I wanted to get back to normal, I wanted my heart to feel less heavy. "You don't have to babysit me."

"I know. If I thought you did, I'd leave you with the nanny. I want to take advantage of you being here, skip work and have a girls' day."

Ryder came up to his wife, put his arm around her neck and pulled her into a friendly headlock. "I love you," he said and he kissed on the top of her head the way Logan used to do to me.

I turned and stared out the French doors over the water. I concentrated on keeping my breathing steady and tried to empty my mind of Logan. It would get better. It had to get better. But at the moment, all I could think about was being with him again.

"Are you ready?" Scarlett asked. "There's a great little boutique that I want to take you to that's only ten minutes away."

"If you have the day off, wouldn't you prefer to spend it with the kids?" I asked.

"Are you kidding me? I spend enough time with them already, and anyway, I think they prefer Jenny."

Ryder chuckled. "That's not true. I'm their favorite, and you just beat the nanny into second place."

"They only prefer you because you give them unlimited chocolate spread," Scarlett said.

"Whatever it takes."

"Seriously," Scarlett said turning back to me. "The kids have activities all day, so Jenny is really just chauffeuring them around. We can spend some time together, enjoy the sunshine and catch up."

At that moment, Jenny appeared, all smiles and cheer, and I couldn't help but notice the relief that passed over Ryder's face.

"Right, I'm off to work. Try not to burn the place down," he said to his children. "And you two," he said, glancing between Scarlett and me. "Have some fun and I'll see you for dinner tonight."

Scarlett grabbed some keys from a hook on the wall and her bag from underneath the highchair. "Come on, let's escape while we can. Bye, everyone," she called as she swept out, blowing kisses into the air.

I followed her—it was why I was here in the first place.

To keep myself busy. To enjoy some time with my family. To be surrounded by people who loved me.

The driver pulled out of the drive and made its way down the quiet road. I had no idea where we were going and frankly, didn't care. The sun was out and I was three thousand miles away from Logan Steele.

"Max and Harper are coming to dinner tonight," Scarlett said. "It's been so long since you came over—everyone's dying to see you."

"Oh, how lovely. I can't wait." More distraction. More noise. I *knew* coming here had been the right decision. "Do you mind if I open the window?"

Scarlett rolled her eyes. "Not at all. But I'll never understand why you Brits don't embrace air conditioning."

I smiled and opened the window just enough to feel the warm breeze on my face.

"Do you think you'll be able to spend some time in the city before you go home? I know Violet and Alex want to see you."

"I've not really thought about anything other than getting here."

"Stay as long as you like. Move in. I have a list of things you can fix for me. In fact, I bought some of those miniature screwdrivers you love so much."

I laughed, and it was the first time I felt it reverberate in my belly for days and the sides of my mouth strained at the unfamiliar position. "Well, you know how I like to be useful."

"Here we are," Scarlett said as the car pulled into a parking space. No matter how often I came to America, I was always a little shocked at how different it was. Everything from the architecture to the fire hydrants were distinctly U. S. of A. There was nothing of Woolton Village here. Nothing of Logan Steele. "There are some beautiful clothes in here, a shoe store across the street, and a bistro for lunch at the end of the block."

I wasn't really in the mood for shopping, but I wasn't really in the mood for anything.

Scarlett made a sharp left as she entered the shop and began to look through the racks of clothes in an organized and precise way, one item at a time. "Have you heard from him since...you know?"

It was the first time she'd mentioned Logan, and my stomach churned. I shook my head and began to follow her, pretending to check out the rails of clothing. "No. Nothing." A part of me had wondered whether he would have a change of heart and realize he'd made a terrible decision, but it was better if he didn't.

"I just don't get it." She paused and pulled out a sheer white blouse, inspecting it front and back before putting it back on the rail. "He came to dinner, met your family. He seemed so relaxed with everything."

True. The last thing I'd wanted to do was to introduce him to Ryder and Scarlett, and I'd certainly never expected him to accept a dinner invitation. "I know, but things were really casual between us at the time—it was only when he was forced to think about the future that he clearly decided it wasn't what he wanted."

"What about you? What did you want?"

"At the beginning, the same thing he did." I paused at a pair of jeans, but decided they were too similar to what I already had. If I was going to buy anything on this trip it was going to be something entirely different. "But then we drifted into something that seemed more than just physical. Still, he was the last person I expected to fall in love with. But the more we did, the more I realized that the list of attributes that I'd been looking for in a man were misguided."

"Yeah." Scarlett cocked her hip and held a white sundress against her body. "It's always the ones you weren't expecting who cause the most trouble. Look at Ryder and me."

"I never thought Ryder would get married. Not ever," I said. "I mean, I was grateful that he did—it saved Woolton. But he'd been firm for so long that he wasn't the type. Then he met the woman who changed his mind. I just wasn't the one for Logan. I have to accept that."

"Hey," Scarlett said, sliding the hanger back on the rail. "Don't look at it like that. See it as a warm-up. You haven't dated anybody for ages and Logan got you back on the horse. The next guy who comes along is going to realize how lucky he is."

Everything inside me groaned. The idea that there would be someone else? That was just crazy. I'd been on my own for so long because I rarely felt attracted to men I met— they weren't worth the effort or the compromise. Once, I'd thought the same of Logan, but in the end I'd thought he'd been worth falling in love with. I'd been wrong.

I glanced at Scarlett, who was looking back at me. "Are you still hoping he'll change his mind?"

"No. Not at all. It's way too painful. I didn't expect it to bring up so much stuff for me." The feeling of abandonment had laid dormant in me for years. Logan ending things had brought it to life.

"But you know, sometimes guys mess up and they put it right."

"Maybe. But the last person who's right for me is someone who can't handle commitment. It's the one thing I need from a man." I didn't want to live in fear that I'd have to relive the pain from my childhood again.

"You said he'd never wanted kids or marriage."

"Or even a relationship." I'd always known who he was.

"Did he just like women? Or was there some kind of reason behind that for him?"

"He has issues with his father. But what does it matter? The outcome's the same whatever the reason."

"That's the problem with these high-achieving men. They find a formula that works for them and they stick to it."

"I guess." The problem was, I knew he cared for me. I saw him make adjustments in his life to spend time with me. He had changed. But perhaps not at his core. Not enough.

"Well, they say that when someone tells you who they are, you should believe them."

There was no point in hoping that he might change. Logan had a lifetime of reasons to be who he always had been.

"You will get over this," Scarlett said.

"I know." We were never more than some transient affair.

He was gone. I just needed to get used to the idea.

I knew it was possible. I'd recovered from worse. I had to accept that there was no pill or cream that would take it away. I needed to exist long enough for the pain to begin to fade.

THIRTY-SEVEN

Logan

Everywhere I glanced around the farm shop, I saw elements of Darcy. The attention to detail, the way there were products representing all the different skills of the village even though many of them wouldn't sell—that was Darcy's kind heart, which so often ruled her head. The freshly cut flowers by the till would have been her idea, too. Even the general sense of happiness in the room embodied her. But she wasn't here. I'd been dreading this trip to the shop since my grandmother had suggested it, but I couldn't decide if it was because I wanted to run into Darcy. Or because I was afraid I wouldn't.

Both, maybe.

The week had been much more challenging than I'd anticipated. Even though I didn't see Darcy during the week, I'd still reached for her every morning. Still went to dial her number ten times a day to tell her something either funny or annoying. They were all signs I'd taken things too far, left things too long. I'd never given a woman a second thought once I'd left her, yet Darcy's memory clung to me. Her generous smile greeted me every time I closed my eyes, her sweet scent lingered on every item of clothing.

She was everywhere.

I just had to wait for it to pass—and never make the same mistake again.

I hovered by the door as my grandmother took various items to the till. It would be better if we managed to leave without seeing Darcy.

I hoped I was managing to cover up my discomfort at our parting, but I wasn't sure how Darcy would have taken things. She was probably mad at me and I didn't want a scene, though I'd prefer her angry rather than sad. I hated the thought that I'd hurt her, which was more proof that I'd done the right thing. Breaking up with Darcy wasn't personal—I didn't want to be with anyone.

I willed the assistant behind the counter to pack up the items my grandmother had chosen more quickly, but they were talking and laughing and it was good to see my grandmother so happy. I just wanted us to get back in the car, to escape and then we could go back to Badsley, where I knew Darcy wouldn't be.

I pushed my hands into my pockets grabbed my car keys as several people filed out of the shop. I tuned into my grandmother's conversation, to see if it was wrapping up.

"She's in Connecticut," the shop assistant said.

He must be talking about Darcy, right? Who else from Woolton Village would have a reason to go to Connecticut?

"Oh, that's right, her brother and his family live over there, don't they?" my grandmother asked.

Yes, it was definitely Darcy they were talking about.

I didn't know if her leaving the village was a good sign

or bad. The thought of her hating me was horrifying, but maybe it was better that way.

"Are you ready?"

Startled, I realized my grandmother had finished at the till and was right beside me. "Yes, you done?"

"Are you okay?"

"Sure, I was just thinking about some stuff at work." I pulled open the door, the bell above tinkling as I guided my grandmother out.

We were in the car less than fifteen seconds before the inevitable questions started.

"I don't remember Darcy saying she was going to Connecticut, do you?"

I should have planned for this. Although I'd never told my grandmother that Darcy and I had been...What had we been? Lovers? Partners? Dating? Or just friends who hung out? It didn't matter. My grandmother was smart enough to have seen the connection between us, and I knew that she'd been happy for me.

"No, I didn't realize she was going."

The few seconds of silence that followed were excruciating. I could hear my grandmother's brain whirring.

"She didn't tell you? When was the last time you two spoke?"

I focused on turning out of the car park, futilely hoping that she would drop it. "Umm, I'm not sure. Monday, I think."

"And she didn't let you know she was going?" My grandmother tapped her nails on the window frame. "What did you do, Logan?"

I changed gears and glanced over to find her mouth set in a serious, straight line.

"I didn't do anything."

My grandmother sighed. "Logan." My grandmother rarely admonished me, but when she did, she normally had good reason.

"Things got a little out of hand and I—I..."

"Out of hand?"

"You know that I like Darcy, but our expectations weren't the same."

"Good God, Logan. What are you talking about?"

I groaned. I didn't need Darcy to occupy my thoughts any more than she already did. "You know me. I'm not the sort of man to settle down. I don't want a family, and that's what Darcy needs. It's what she deserves."

"I've never understood this obsession you have with being on your own." She shook her head in dismay. "I thought you liked her?"

"I do. She's a lovely woman, but that doesn't mean I'm going to change who I am, what I want, or what I know is right."

We pulled into the drive at Badsley and I was determined to get inside as quickly as possible. Hopefully, the change of setting would encourage my grandmother to drop the conversation. I parked, turned off the engine and went to open the door, but my grandmother laid her hand on my arm.

"Just hang on—I want to hear about this."

"Can we please just drop it? The decision is made. It's best for both of us."

"My darling boy, most of the time I leave you alone to make your own decisions, but I can't stand by if I think you are hurting yourself and the people you love."

Love? I should never have gotten involved with Darcy in the first place and the last person I wanted to hurt was my grandmother. "I know she adores you, and just because she and I are...I'm sure you will still see her."

"This isn't about me, Logan. I'm concerned about you not knowing what's good for you. Darcy is a wonderful woman—she's kind, beautiful, clever and gives you a run for your money, which is the thing I like best about her. I've never seen you as happy as you've been with her—I could tell from the moment you met her that she was made for you."

Made for me? My grandmother didn't understand. No one was *made* for me. I couldn't have anyone counting on me.

"Did you have a fight?"

I tipped my head back on the headrest. "No, nothing like that. Things were escalating and we couldn't keep moving forward as we were. I've never..." How could I explain that I was used to a series of one-night stands? "I've never dated a woman before. Not really. Not since university."

"So being faithful was difficult for you?"

"No, I never wanted anyone else when I was with Darcy." I still didn't. Not even a woman like Abigail, who I'd put in a cab home after our drink on Monday night. "I never even looked at another woman." Darcy didn't leave room for anybody else.

"So why did you decide to end things?"

"Her feelings were growing and I couldn't give her what she wanted." I wasn't about to tell her about the pregnancy scare.

"So, she told you she loved you and, instead of admitting that you loved her too, you got scared and threw it all away? Is that about the size of it?"

I couldn't remember the last time my grandmother had

sounded so exasperated with me. It was the same voice she'd used when I used to come home covered head to foot in mud after playing with my friends.

"It's not about being scared. It's about me knowing what I want, what I'm capable of. I've always known that I'd never settle down or have a family. It just isn't what I want, and I had to end things before Darcy got in any deeper."

"You're acting as if you don't love her. As if you were just along for the ride. But I know differently, Logan. I saw how you were together. How much more relaxed you were. How she didn't let you take yourself too seriously."

"That might well be true, but it doesn't change anything."

"Just help me understand why you're so convinced that you don't want to share your life with anybody?"

"I put my work first, and that will never change. I don't have room in my life for a woman—any woman. And certainly no place for a family. All I would do is disappoint them, and I will not be that man. So, you see, although things look as if Darcy and I are suited now, it's just not the case. I can see further down the road—I'd let her down at some point."

I turned to my grandmother expecting understanding, but instead found pity.

"Of course you will let her down. That's what happens. She'll let you down and you'll disappoint her—that's just life. But when you're in love, you forgive each other."

"How you can say that after everything my father put you through?" I regretted mentioning my father as soon as the words left my mouth. We never spoke about him, and I knew that even now what had happened still hurt my grandmother.

"Oh, my dear boy. Is that what this is all about? You

don't want to make your father's mistakes?"

I didn't say anything. I didn't need to.

"I had no idea. We should have talked about this years ago. First, there is no genetic code that requires you to make the same silly mistakes and unwise choices your father did. Bad judgment doesn't pass down the generations, and you've more than proved you have more sense than your father ever did both in terms of business and in terms of family."

It wasn't that I thought that I have some genetic predisposition to let those around me down. More that I was learning from history, from someone else's mistakes.

"It's impossible to draw parallels between your life and his, Logan. He was a man who had his own issues. Everything had been given to him. He had nothing to work for, strive for. He just wasn't the man you are."

"He put himself before his family. Let people down who were relying on him. I can't be sure I wouldn't make the same mistake. And I won't take the risk."

"The fact that Darcy told you she loved you and you know it's true is something precious and something to cherish. You are not your father—you deserve a life filled with the love of your wife, of your children. Don't deny yourself that because of a man who's no longer in our lives. Learn from the past, but don't let that ruin your future."

A hard mixture of pain, guilt, loss and love lodged at the bottom of my throat. Had I been trying to avoid a future that was never my destiny? Had I already proven I was not my father?

Had I given up Darcy for nothing?

"Well, it's too late now. I don't want to make promises that I don't know if I can keep. The decision has been made."

My grandmother flung her car door open. "Then unmake it."

I scrambled out and around the boot to help her, but she slapped my hands away. "I'm perfectly capable. You've never let me down. You're loyal and honest and hardworking. That's the man you are. You seem to think that you don't make promises and commitments all the time. You do to me and in business. Why are you singling Darcy out?"

"I can't possibly have a wife and family without making mistakes, breaking commitments and letting people down."

"And as I said, if she loves you and you get it wrong, then she'll forgive you."

Could that be true? Could I allow myself to make mistakes in front of Darcy and have her forgive me them?

"Just like," my grandmother continued, "when *she* makes mistakes, you will forgive *her*. Because you love her." My grandmother turned to look at me. "And don't you dare deny it."

The evidence was there. The way I didn't notice other women when we were together, the fact that even now I couldn't follow through with another woman, the way I hated the fact that Darcy was so far away.

I loved Darcy Westbury...and I had no idea what to do about it.

"Make it right," my grandmother whispered. "Don't let this be the mistake that you regret for the rest of your life."

She patted me on the chest and headed to the kitchen, leaving me a different man from the one who had left the house just an hour before. She'd questioned my entire personal philosophy. But one thing was clear to me—I couldn't bear the thought of not loving Darcy Westbury for the rest of my life.

THIRTY-EIGHT

Logan

Determined to "make things right" with Darcy, I was three thousand miles away from Woolton and parked outside Ryder and Scarlett Westbury's Connecticut home. Darcy was the woman I wanted, and an ocean wasn't going to keep me away from her.

I couldn't rule out the possibility that she'd refuse to speak to me and I wouldn't blame her if she did. I had been callous and unfeeling and, worst of all, in denial about how important our relationship was to me.

I turned off the engine and stepped out of the car, carrying the documents I'd brought with me. The sky was strangely cloudless, and only the breeze kept the heat from being overwhelming. Children's shrieks and laughs snaked out of the house. I hadn't seen Darcy with her nieces and nephews, but I imagine they adored her. I knocked on the door and took a deep breath.

The look on Scarlett's face as she swung open the door

started off as welcoming and dissolved into awkward reserve. "Logan. What are you..."

"I was hoping to have a few words with Darcy, if she's here?"

Scarlett frowned and glanced over her shoulder. "She's here, but I'm not sure..."

"I understand she doesn't want to see me, but could you just tell her that I'm here?"

Scarlett nodded and I watched at the doorway as she went to find Darcy.

My heart lifted in my chest as soon as I heard her voice. "I fixed it," she announced, holding something the air, then froze when Scarlett whispered something.

Darcy glanced over at me and then quickly turned away. It was like a knife to my heart.

Was seeing me so painful? Should I not have come? I'd spent all these years avoiding caring about someone, and I didn't know what to do now that I did. My grandmother had said I'd inevitably let Darcy down. That was what people did, but that love allowed them to forgive. But perhaps it was too late for Darcy and me. Perhaps I'd hurt her too badly.

I could do nothing but stand and wait, wondering whether or not I should have given Darcy more time. I'd wanted to tell her how I felt as soon as possible, but perhaps I'd been selfish.

After a few more exchanges, Scarlett pulled Darcy into a hug, then let her go to negotiate with one of the children while Darcy headed toward me, her head bowed.

I steadied my breathing. Darcy could close the door in my face or refuse to speak to me, but I wasn't going to give up without a fight.

The closer she got, the less I could understand how I'd

ever let her go. She was beautiful in England or America, in jeans or a cocktail dress, covered in mud or five minutes after waking.

"Hey," I said as she stood opposite me. "I was hoping we could talk."

"They have phones in the United States, you know."

I couldn't help but smile. She never wasted an opportunity to put me right. "Some things are better explained in person."

"I don't need to hear any more explanations."

I nodded. "I understand. I'm not here to justify what I did, and I don't expect you to forgive me, but I owe you the truth."

"Have you been lying to me?"

"More to myself, I think." I'd been trying for too long to deny my love for Darcy. "I'd just like a chance to explain."

"Logan, I'm tired. I'm done. There's no point in rehashing things."

"Please, Darcy, just five minutes. And if you don't like what you hear, I'll disappear out of your life forever."

Her shoulders dropped as if in defeat as she stepped aside and invited me in. "Let's go to the back of the house. We can walk down to the river."

Just the thought that I would be with her for the next few minutes renewed my determination to win her back. I couldn't let her go. I had to find a way back to her.

Being so close but unable to feel the heat of her body or soothe her pain was harder than I'd expected, but still easier than not being near her at all.

She kept her gaze fixed firmly on the horizon as we headed down to the garden. I couldn't keep my eyes off her. It was as if I hadn't had water for weeks and was being given a chance to drink. I wanted to take in as much as I could.

"It's good to see you," I said.

"Why are you here, Logan?"

"To explain. To apologize." I didn't know where to start. "I've thought of nothing but you since our last conversation, and I've had a number of realizations that I need to share. I hope it will go some way to explaining my stupidity, my self-ishness and my complete lack of understanding of myself and how I felt about you."

Darcy paused. "I don't need any kind of explanation from you—I accept your decision and I'm trying to move on."

I closed my eyes to block out the thought that she might be over me. "But that's what I'm trying to say. I don't want you to move on. I'm in love with you and I want us to be together."

She stayed silent, her face full of confusion.

"I'm so sorry, Darcy. I was scared of the feelings I had, of the feelings you had for me. So, like a coward, I ran, I retreated. I went back to what I knew best." I took a long, deep breath. "My grandmother helped me see what I'd done."

"You talked to her about us?" Darcy glanced up, and it took everything I had not to sweep the escaped lock of hair back behind her ear.

"Yes. She's the wisest woman I know and she set me straight. She made me understand how loving you wasn't something to run from."

Sadness flickered across Darcy's face and she turned away from me, hiding her pain. But I deserved to see it. After all, I'd caused it. She crossed her arms and jutted her chin up, trying to regain her composure.

"I've always been so determined not to be my father that I've shut myself off from a lot of things. From you. I've been so focused on not making promises I can't keep and avoiding destroying everything around me that I haven't realized the damage I've done. What my father did affected me so fundamentally, I didn't fully understand. He scarred me forever and the easiest way to ensure I never inflicted the hurt he did, never let anyone down, was to make sure I loved as few people as possible and that no one loved me."

"Let's walk," Darcy said, hugging herself tightly as we made our way toward the river.

"I never expected what happened between us—it crept up on me. You burst into my life and from the moment I met you, I knew you were different, special. I just didn't realize what a profound effect you'd have on me. I wasn't prepared. I'd been living in a safe, cloistered world, trying to avoid anything that would suggest I was in any way related to my father. I was so focused on my past I completely missed my future when she arrived. And so I ran. From you, from how I felt about you, from the fear of disappointing you. Is this making any sense?"

"I guess. And I'm sorry for you, Logan. I knew your father's actions still haunted you, and I understand that you didn't want to repeat his mistakes."

My heart swelled. Beautiful, understanding, incredible Darcy. Of course she'd find it in her heart to see my point of view. It was more than I deserved. Encouraged, I reached for her, stroking my fingers over her cheek, but she stepped back and my hand fell away. She understood, maybe even forgave me, but she also bore the scars that I'd given her. And for that I only had myself to blame. "I'm so sorry."

"I believe you."

"Darcy," I whispered. "I want you. I want you to come back to me. I want you forever."

She pushed her hands into the pockets of her skirt and

shook her head. It was as if a hand had slipped inside my chest and was squeezing my heart tighter and tighter. I couldn't have lost her. Please God, I needed to be able to make this right. I couldn't have found the woman I was supposed to spend the rest of my life with only to have messed things up.

"I know this must be a shock. And I know you must hate me right now—"

"I don't hate you, but that doesn't mean what happened is okay. What you said makes sense, but it doesn't take away the pain. You have your ghosts, and I have mine. You left me when things got too much for you. I've had too much of that in my life, and I can't risk that happening again. I have to protect myself, Logan."

Of course she'd be cautious. It wasn't that I expected anything different. She wouldn't be my Darcy if she just capitulated. She was no pushover. "I understand. But do you think that in time you would be able to forgive me?"

"They say time heals all wounds and I'm sure that includes this one. But I can't go back. Being left by you. It brought back so much. It was too painful. It's *still* too painful."

"Just tell me what I can do. I'll give up Manor House Club. I'll get rid of the helicopter. How can I prove to you I'm serious?" I'd almost forgotten the folder I was carrying. "And this. I wanted to give you something." I offered her the buff-colored file.

"I don't need *things* from you, Logan."

"Then what? Anything. Tell me and I will give you anything within my power."

"All I wanted was for you to love me. And I understand why you can't. But you have to let me get on with my life."

"But I do. I love you so much it hurts to be away from you."

"Until the next time you struggle, push me away and leave. What happens if I actually got pregnant? I want to be with someone who will share my joy in that moment, not tell me he's in too deep and abandon me *and* our children."

I didn't know how to prove something in the future. How could I explain that I was on a one-way street and I could never not love her now?

I was out of ammo. "I'll always love you, Darcy. I've never been so certain about anything."

She worried her bottom lip, but didn't look up.

"I mean it, I love you. And just a few weeks ago you told me you loved me. Isn't that worth fighting for?"

"Maybe you love me in your way, but it's just not enough. What happens the next time you get spooked? What happens when you catch a glimpse of the life you had before me, or another woman catches your eye?"

"It won't happen. I love *you.*"

She shook her head. "I can't live with the uncertainty. I can't worry that you're going to turn around and leave me."

"Then I'll just have to prove to you that I'm going nowhere. I can't give up, Darcy. There's no one else for me. I want to marry you. Have kids with you. Write in the sky above Woolton Hall how much I love you."

"Please stop." She scrubbed her face with her hands. "I've been independent my entire life. And I'd come to expect things of you. And when you left, I'd never felt so vulnerable. So alone. That feeling brought back every bad memory I ever had. And I can't live worrying that I'll feel that again. Please, Logan. You need to go."

"Just one more thing," I said, holding out the file I was holding. "This is for you."

"I told you that I don't want things from you."

"I know, but I want you to have this. Whatever happens between you and me, you should have it."

Reluctantly she took the file and opened it, flicking through the papers inside. "I don't understand. What is this?"

"I've transferred some of Badsley's land to you. Not to Woolton, but to you."

She kept turning the page, back and forward. "But why?"

"It's just a piece of land from the edge of the estate. From your favorite spot in Woolton where we first met, down to the river where you used to play with Ryder."

She turned away from me. "I can't take this," she said over her shoulder.

I stepped closer to her. She didn't want me to see her upset, and the last thing I wanted to do was to make her cry, but she deserved this. "You're not taking anything. I'm giving this to you willingly. Now you can be assured that whatever happens, those special places will be preserved. I'm not asking for anything in return. I just want you to understand that I care about you, and whether or not you love me, I will do anything to make you happy."

Because I was an impatient, selfish man, I wanted to have won her over, to have changed her mind. But her silence told me I'd done neither. "Perhaps I shouldn't have come today. I just wanted you to know how I felt."

"No. I'm pleased you did. I'm sorry, I just wish I could forget—"

"You have nothing to apologize for. I'm the idiot. I'm the one who fucked this up. This is all me." Ending things with Darcy had been the worst decision I'd ever made. And I hated myself for it. "But I will put things right. I will prove to you that I won't get spooked again. I can't just give up on you. On us."

"Logan..." Darcy exhaled a shaky breath.

"I should go." I just needed one touch to keep me going. I kissed the top of her head. "I love you. Please don't be sad. I'm going to make this right." And I walked away from the only woman I'd ever loved. But I wasn't giving up on her.

THIRTY-NINE

Darcy

How had I let myself be talked into speed dating? I just wanted to be left alone at Woolton Hall, to bury myself in the estate and all its comings and goings. To get back to life before Logan.

Aurora...she'd had other ideas, which is why I'd just explained for the fourth time this evening where Woolton Village was to a complete stranger.

True to his word, Logan hadn't given up. I'd heard from him every day. First in Connecticut. And then he must have known I'd come home about ten days ago, because each day since, I'd received a card or flowers or handwritten notes about his day and how he missed me. I also hadn't heard the helicopter since I'd come back from Connecticut.

I was still trying to move on, but I wasn't sure speed dating was my thing.

In front of me, the man in the white pleather jumpsuit shifted uncomfortably. "Sorry, it just gets a little uncomfortable. I don't think I used enough baby powder. But you're the hottest thing in this room."

I tried to keep the smile on my face steady. "Thank you." The bell rang. Hallelujah.

"Just to let you know, you're going down on my sheet as 'hell-yeah'," he said with a wink.

"Good to meet you, Elvis." He wasn't going on my sheet at all. The next guy couldn't be worse, surely.

"I'm Andrew." A tall blond man stood in front of me, holding out his hand. Given he was wearing trousers and a shirt rather than fancy dress, it was a better start. "How old are you?" Okay, so maybe he'd skipped charm school. "I'm into older women."

"May I ask you the same question, Andrew?" I wasn't about to admit to this guy I was older than him, even if I was.

"Twenty-two. I reckon you're twenty-nine or thirty. Too bad—I'm into women in their forties. Not looking to get married. Fantastic in bed. Winners all around."

At least we were matched in that his age was an issue for me, too—I wasn't into twenty-two-year-olds. "Well, I hope you find her." I was officially out. I'd given this evening a chance, but if I stayed a moment longer I'd likely never want to see Aurora again. I caught her eye across the room and stifled a giggle at her yawn. I headed over to save her.

"What were you thinking?" I asked as we stumbled outside, desperate to leave before the next bell sounded. "You said tonight would be fun."

"I know. Desperate times call for desperate measures."

"These are *not* desperate times." I'd returned from Connecticut ten days ago and I'd barely left Woolton Hall. It was my safe space, and I knew as long as I stayed there, I'd survive. I might never be happy, but I would pull some kind of life together for myself.

A life without Logan.

I thought about him constantly. I replayed the conversation in Connecticut that we'd had on a loop. Even now, I wasn't sure I'd done the right thing.

"You're thinking about him again, aren't you?" Aurora asked.

I was always thinking about him. "That was a disaster."

"It wasn't one of the better events they've put on, but I have met a couple of nice guys that way."

"Not so nice that you're still dating them," I said.

Aurora linked her arm through mine as we made our way around the corner to pick up a cab. Right now I could happily have taken Logan's helicopter back to Woolton. Being in the city felt a little bit too close to him. But we were staying at the Hill Street house tonight and heading back to Woolton tomorrow.

"No, you're right, but you have to take a chance on these things or you might miss your perfect match."

I admired the way Aurora kept putting herself out there, kept searching for the love of her life. I just didn't know if I had it in me. I had never loved anyone the way I'd loved Logan and I knew I wouldn't have that again, so what was the point of looking?

"You know what I think?" Aurora asked. "I think you already found your perfect match."

My stomach swooped. "Sometimes, things just don't work out."

"And sometimes things that are meant to work out have a shaky start. Nothing is ever perfect. Don't you ever wonder if you should see if what you and Logan had would clear the bumps and get to the other side?"

I held my arm out for an approaching cab. "I just don't want to spend my whole life not knowing if Logan will change his mind and leave."

"But isn't that always the risk in any relationship?" she asked as we climbed into the cab. "People divorce because they change their minds."

"But I need to be sure."

"Impossible. Nothing is certain in this world. Woolton might burn down, there's a pretty good chance that I will turn to lesbianism, the W.I. might disband—anything is possible."

"How can you say such a thing? The W.I. will survive us both." I hadn't expected Aurora to suggest that Logan might still be the one.

Aurora giggled. "That's probably the biggest certainty in our lives. But things do change, and I think you've got to enjoy the good times when they're offered. I'm not saying that you should just live in the moment with Logan, like you were doing. But he's not saying that either. He wants more as well. And you love him and now you know he loves you. I don't think you should throw away a chance at happiness because it *might* not work out. The right guy doesn't happen along often, believe me."

I knew what Logan and I'd had, or at least what I had felt for him, was special. I'd never loved someone before and I fully accepted I never would again. "I just can't bear the pain of the people I love leaving me. I've had enough loss. And if I love him now, it will only be worse down the road. The pain would be unbearable."

"The only way to guarantee that you'll never hurt is to never love anyone, and I don't think that's who you are. You deserve a family, someone who adores you, someone you adore. You have so much to give, Darcy. Don't let fear be the thing that keeps you from being happy."

I *was* afraid. Afraid of being hurt, scared of being rejected again. My grandparents' death, my parents' abandonment—those had been awful, but I'd survived. Losing Logan was a sharper, more piercing pain, and now that it had begun to dull, I wanted to ensure I never felt it again.

"And you've seen what the dating scene is like. You're not going to find the love of your life at every speed dating event. You used to think you were destined to meet some landowner wedded to the country, but Logan showed you what you really need. That doesn't happen a lot."

"You're right. The picture of who I thought I'd end up with doesn't come close to Logan Steele." I'd thought I wanted the exact opposite of him.

"I think you were too concerned with checking boxes—you need someone as passionate, as feisty and single-minded as you are. And I think you owe it to yourself to get over your fears, get over this bump in the road and see what's on the other side. With Logan."

In so many ways, Logan wasn't what I'd wanted, but he was everything I needed. He was strong, funny, focused and hardworking. He was devoted to his family and would move mountains in order to do the right thing. "Do you think that's why it hurt so badly? Because I loved him so much?"

"Maybe. I'm not sure I've ever really been in love. Not even with your brother, even though I thought otherwise. But now that I've seen you and Logan together, I know what true love looks like. I know what I'm aiming for."

I cleared my throat, trying not to cry. "Do you really think that?"

Aurora nodded. "I really do. And I think it's special and

you need to grab onto it. From what you've told me, he gets that he made a huge mistake."

"But it was a mistake that broke my heart, Aurora."

"And one that he's trying to make up for. I've never seen so many flowers and letters. The guy is sorry. He's showing you he's not running, that he's serious about you. I don't think he'll make the same mistake again. Don't lose him because you're afraid to try."

I could change the washer of a tap, convince a planning committee to reject a new development, I could even re-shoe a horse. But perhaps I had been too scared to let myself love Logan Steele enough to forgive him.

FORTY

Logan

Nothing had been the same since I'd come back from Connecticut nearly two weeks earlier. I'd lost the woman I loved, and I just didn't know how to live with that. I wouldn't give up, but hope was fading. I'd not heard anything from her and I wanted to go home. Mope. Feel sorry for myself. Business was the last thing on my mind.

"Cancel everything this afternoon. If anything urgent comes in, you can call me," I told my assistant. There was plenty of urgent stuff sitting in my inbox, but nothing mattered anymore.

"No problem. I was about to come see you when you called me in. Apparently, there's someone in reception for you without an appointment, but I'll deal with them."

I nodded and began to log off my computer. "Do you know who it is?"

She glanced down at her notes. "A Darcy Westbury? I've never heard of her. Don't worry, I'll get rid of her." She reached for her phone.

Darcy? Darcy was here?

"No! Where is she?" My heart started to pound. Why would Darcy be here? Had something happened to my grandmother? Was she hurt? Or could I let myself hope that she was here to see me, that perhaps she'd changed her mind?

"In reception, I guess. You want me to see why she's here?"

I'd already started across the office. Sure enough, I saw Darcy talking animatedly to one of the receptionists, her beautiful chestnut-brown hair loose and swaying down her back. I yanked open the glass door and our eyes locked. Without saying anything, Darcy silently followed me back to my office. Whatever she'd come here for didn't need an audience.

My assistant said nothing as I led Darcy inside and closed the door behind us. "Is everything okay? Did something happen with my grandmother?"

She shook her head and frowned, two small ridges forming above the bridge of her nose. Had I never noticed that before, or was she wearing a facial expression I'd never experienced? Somehow, I felt cheated. There would be so much of Darcy that I would never know. I was such an idiot.

"What are you doing in London?"

She ignored my question and took a seat in one of the chairs in front of my desk. I wished she'd just tell me why she was here. My palms were sweating. I was fighting every instinct I had that told me to touch her, kiss her, hold her.

"Aurora and I went speed dating last night."

I banged my fist against the door, trying to contain my anger into that one single movement. Dating? Fuck. What had I expected? I blew out a breath, then took a seat behind my desk. "Go on."

"I stayed at the London house last night, not that I've slept," she mumbled. "I've been doing nothing but thinking and missing you—it seems that's all I do these days."

I tried to control my breathing and listen carefully. Had she just admitted to missing me? "What did you say?"

"I can't just turn these feelings off. I've tried, but I still love you."

Her words slid over me like a cool shower on a muggy August day. I closed my eyes and took a breath. When I opened them, she was looking right at me. "So, I decided to come here this morning and tell you."

"And what about the guy, or guys from last night?"

"From speed dating?" She shook her head. "Obviously, they were all awful. None of them were you."

Was she prepared to give me another chance? I didn't want to push her, but I needed to know more. "It's good to see you. I mean, it always is, but I've missed you so much. I wondered if I'd ever lay eyes on you again."

"You hurt me so badly. I've never known pain like that."

Her agony wound around me in a mixture of guilt and shame. How could I have been so selfish? "I know, and I'm so sorry. I want to make it up to you, to prove to you that I'm worthy of your love."

She trapped her bottom lip between her teeth. I rarely saw her look so unsure about anything. She was so capable and confident. Had I robbed her of that?

"What can I do? Please, Darcy. Anything. I'm miserable without you. I'm *nothing* without you."

"Don't say that. You're everything I never realized I wanted in a man."

My breath caught in my throat. The more she spoke, the

more hope filled up my chest, my heart, my soul. Hope for a future. "If you give me a second chance, you'll never regret it. I pledge to you right now that I will love you forever. My feelings took me by surprise, but I understand them now. I understand what you are to me. You're everything, and I won't make the same mistake twice. I love you, Darcy. I'll always love you."

"But you will make mistakes," she replied and the fist around my heart tightened. "And so will I. We need to get better at working through them. Because I can't lose you again."

I couldn't hold back any longer. I stood and rounded my desk. I had to be closer to her. "Do you mean..." I could barely form the words. "Have you come back to me?"

She stood and tipped her head back, her hand sliding over my chest. "I never left."

I'd missed her warmth, her touch, her scent so much that it was almost overwhelming me. "I'll never let you go again."

"I don't think I'd survive if you did."

I wanted to ask her to marry me right then—I wanted to bond us together, make this permanent, but I knew ever-practical Darcy would think it was too soon. For now, I would settle for having her in my arms. I had some work to do to prove that I would be a worthy husband. But I was confident that I understood my priorities now and it wouldn't be long before I made her my wife.

FORTY-ONE

Darcy

As soon as I saw Logan, the gray half-moons under his eyes, the way his jacket fit more loosely than it should, I knew he was hurting just as much I was. And now, in his arms, it was as if the world had been put back together. I reached up to cup his face, to check that it was all real.

"I love you so much," he said.

"We need to expect failure—one or both of us are going to freak out sometimes. You're just not allowed to give up," I said.

"I get it." He slid his hands over my arse and pulled me toward him.

"Logan, we're in your office."

"Right," he replied. "My totally private office."

"Never going to happen," I replied. "I'm not becoming the topic of office gossip. That's my brother, not me."

He walked backward toward his desk, pulling me with him. Without letting me go, he grabbed his wallet and phone and slid them into his pocket. "Then we'll leave. It's been far too long since I've kissed you. Even longer since you were naked in my arms. I can't wait any longer."

"You have work and we have a lot to talk about. A lot to figure out." We had to be sensible. But I wanted him too. "And a lot of naked time in our future."

"Don't you get it?" he asked. "Work doesn't matter to me when you're in the room. I've learned my lesson, Darcy. You're my priority now."

I knew Logan Steele well enough to know that he didn't say anything he didn't mean. To hear how he loved me and how he wanted to make things work—I knew those weren't easy things for him to say. He meant it. He was a man of honor. I knew our road ahead might be bumpy, but I was now convinced that he was committed to the journey.

"You can't just abandon your company for the day. Be practical," I said.

He sighed. "I absolutely can." He took my hand and pulled me out of the office. "Julie, I've left for the day. Oh, and this is Darcy. She never needs an appointment and can interrupt any call or meeting I have."

"Logan," I said, wanting him to stop.

"She's my...everything. And she comes first."

Julie's face lit up. I wasn't sure it was delight or shock. "Good to know, sir. Enjoy your day."

I didn't even have a chance to say hello to Julie before Logan was striding to the lifts. I just offered her a little wave and she gave me a thumbs-up.

I figured that Logan was on a mission to prove he'd changed. That he was no longer convinced that he didn't do relationships, that we were no longer friends who hung out. The determination in his grip, the resolve in his words...he meant business.

We stepped into the lift. "I know you wouldn't say yes if

I asked you right now," he said, pressing the button for the lobby, three or four times. "But make no mistake, we're together forever. I'm going to buy you a ring, take out an advert in *The Times*, and pledge to honor and cherish you in front of the entire universe. It's all going to happen."

It took me a moment for his words to sink in. Was Logan Steele talking about marriage? "You don't need to do any of those things. You're enough, Logan."

"I'll never be enough, but I'm going to spend my life trying to be the man you say yes to."

He was right. A proposal right now was too soon. But there would come a time when our road wouldn't be so bumpy, when things would have settled between us and we'd be looking forward to the rest of our lives.

I believed it. I believed in us. And I couldn't wait.

FORTY-TWO

Logan

The bird's-eye view of Woolton Village had never looked so perfect. It was possible to make out the farm shop, the community center and the pub, and of course, the estates of Woolton Hall and Badsley House, nestled right next to each other.

Next to me, Darcy said, "I can't believe I let you talk me into the helicopter."

"It was the fastest way home."

"You'd better land in the grounds of Woolton Hall then. I want you to myself for a while before we take tea with your grandmother."

"Yes, let's not think about my grandmother for a few hours. It's likely to kill my libido."

"And we don't want that," Darcy said, raising her eyebrows.

I clenched my jaw and ran through the time it would take to land, get to the house and strip us both naked. I reckoned we could do it in less than five minutes.

In the end, it took seven.

"God, you take my breath away," I gasped as Darcy came out of the bedroom in her underwear.

"You're already naked," she said. "I thought you'd want me to undress you."

"Not today. Not now. I just want to be with you." I reached for her.

She tilted her head as if she didn't yet believe how much I wanted her. "How can two people, so stubborn and single-minded about so much, work together so well in bed?" she asked, stepping toward me.

"I don't know," I said as I walked her back toward the bed. "But I'm not arguing."

I cupped her breasts, one in each hand, enjoying their delicious weight in my palms before I bent to take one in my mouth. I groaned as the soft flesh connected with my tongue. Fuck, I'd missed this. I'd missed *her*.

Now that I had her back, all I wanted to do was worship her.

Her hands trailing down my arms as I stepped away. I needed to look at her, study her curves, make sure I wasn't missing anything. No, the sweep of her neck into her shoulder was still the same, the way her breasts jutted out in need, familiar. The arc of her waist was how I remembered. The softness of her stomach, the smooth, milky skin. She was still my Darcy.

"Logan," she whispered, distracting me from the hypno-tizing pull of her body.

I glanced back up at her. "I've missed you so much. I'm so lucky you gave me another chance."

I lifted her up onto the mattress and crawled over her, caging her in. She was mine. Now and forever. I had the rest of my life to be with her, the rest of my life to discover every expression she had. "So beautiful," I whispered as I pressed my lips to the base of her throat.

She drew her legs up and the slide of her skin against mine set sparks off all over my body. How had I let this woman go? Even for a moment? I paused, wanting to remember it, to scorch the relief, the joy at having her back onto my brain. I wanted to treat her with honor and adoration. But I also needed to fuck her, make her mine again, push into her and prove that we were supposed to be together.

"Hey," she said, stroking her fingers over my jaw. "I'm not going anywhere. We can do it all."

"I know," I replied. "But it's different now." I'd always respected and admired Darcy, but I had a new level of reverence for her now. She was the woman I was going to spend the rest of my life with. The woman I was going to have children with. I would only make love to *her* for the rest of my life. And I wanted to do it right.

She shifted underneath me, teasing my cock with a circle of her hips. "I really hope the sex isn't different." She grinned. "Because that might be a game changer. Don't treat me like glass."

Christ, sometimes this woman knew me better than I knew myself, but she was right. The sex between us was always better than the best I'd ever had, and there was no reason that would change now. I thrust into her, rough and hard, erasing any doubt the sex would ever be something that was a problem for us. I wasn't sure if it were pressure or performance anxiety that had put me on pause, but whatever it was, Darcy had cut through it.

She always did.

"Using me for my body." I grunted.

She sucked in a breath and bit her lip as I pushed in

again. "You'd better believe it." She struggled to keep her voice level as I fucked her with deep, punishing strokes that turned her words to the desperate sounds that I loved to hear so much.

Our eyes met and her love for me, my devotion reflected back, was almost overwhelming.

This was what being in love was. Connection on every level. Being someone's world and them being yours. Knowing I'd do anything to make her happy.

My body clenched as I realized I wasn't going to be able to hold back for long. I liked making her come first, took satisfaction from that, but not today.

"I want us to come together, Logan." She trailed her fingernails down my back, tracing pleasure up and down my skin. It was too much.

I grabbed her hands and pushed them over her head. "You want me like I want you?" I knew I'd been the one to push her away, I'd fucked up but I'd more than learned my lesson. I'd never needed reassurance from a woman before. Never needed anything from anyone. But Darcy was so mixed up in who I was now, who I was becoming that I had no choice but to need her. She was a part of me.

She held my gaze. "Always."

It was what I needed to hear, and it released something in me, and in her, too.

"Logan." She tightened her grip. "Logan."

I dipped down to kiss her, wanting to swallow her sounds, experience her pleasure as she came. With just the sweep of her tongue over mine, my orgasm coursed through my body, meeting hers with a vengeance, binding us together.

EPILOGUE

Darcy

"I'm just not really a ring type of person." I took in the tray of huge diamonds in front of me, a little overwhelmed. They were all massive and showy and although I appreciated the thought, none of them seemed like me. I squeezed Logan's hand—I didn't want him to think that I was being ungrateful.

"I don't understand. Are you telling me you won't marry me or that you don't want to wear a ring?"

"I've already said I'll marry you." We were on the top floor of the Hilton Park Lane at the same restaurant we'd come to for our first date. He'd warned me the proposal was going to happen, he'd been warning me most days since we'd been reunited, but I'd known from the moment I'd gone to his office all those months ago that we'd be together forever. I'd never needed a proposal, but Logan had insisted.

"Just no ring?" he asked.

I glanced up at the Cartier jeweler who sat on the other side of the table. How Logan had convinced him to bring such an extensive collection of jewelry outside the safety of their store, I had no idea. The six-man security detail that had followed him in probably had something to do with it.

"They are all very beautiful," I reassured Logan. "I'm not sure it's practical. I'm up to my knees in mud most days and then with the horses or—"

"You don't always have to be practical, Darcy. Sometimes you can just buy something because it's pretty. And you can always take it off when you're out on the estate."

"What's the point in that? If I'm going to marry you, it's not a part-time gig."

A smile curled his lips and I cupped his face, smoothing my thumb over his mouth.

"What about just a simple band?" I suggested. "Just plain gold, if it comes off and gets lost, it wouldn't be the end of the world."

Logan chuckled as the jeweler closed the lid on the heavy leather box on the table and replaced it with an identical one. "What about something like this?" he asked. "Normally bigger is better, but personally, I like these simple bands that look like a row of diamonds. People wear them as wedding bands, but it might suit you as an engagement ring."

He opened the lid to reveal at least fifty rings, just as he'd described. Elegant and sophisticated, less likely to get caught in horse hair or torn off as I moved bales of hay. "Yeah, this is better."

"Only you would want the least expensive thing in the store," Logan said, shaking his head.

I glanced up at him, grabbed his tie and pulled him toward me for a kiss. "I love great jewelry. Just not for every day. I want an engagement ring that represents us—we don't need showy. I always figure a big diamond is making up for something that's missing."

"Do any in particular catch your eye?" the jeweler asked.

I studied the rows of bands. They were all pretty.

"What about this one?" Logan pointed.

The jeweler pulled it out of the leather and handed it to Logan.

"I like it," he said, showing it to me, taking my left hand. It was very simple, even though the diamonds were some of the biggest. It looked like a row of raindrops had been wound around a ring of platinum. It was simple and light and very pretty.

Logan slipped the ring on and my heartbeat scattered in my chest.

I bit down on my bottom lip. I'd known in theory that we were going to be together forever, but watching as he put that ring on my finger, it seemed more real somehow.

We both stared down at my hand. "I think it's perfect," he said. "It's completely you."

The ring fit exactly and I wondered whether every piece that was here today was in my size. "I love it."

Logan turned to the jeweler. "I think that's our decision made."

"It looks beautiful on you," he said and gathered up his boxes with the help of his burly security guards, then left the two of us alone.

"Now we just have a wedding to plan," Logan said as he slid me onto his lap so we were both facing the twinkling lights of the city, the countryside a dark blanket off in the distance.

"You want to get married here?" I asked. "You said it

summed us up, London and the countryside in one perfect view."

"I think this view is about who we were when we first met. Now, I'm not so sure." He nuzzled into my neck and pulled me closer. "I would have thought Woolton Hall was the most obvious place to hold the wedding."

"Maybe, but I think our wedding should be about us and our friends and family."

"But doesn't that include the entire village? You know, I think every woman in Woolton sees you as their daughter."

I sank back into him. He was right. The whole village had seen me grow up, helped raise me, given me my values, showed me what was important in life. It was only fitting that they should witness me move on to the next phase of my life.

"Perhaps you're right. The ceremony could be just a few of us and then we should just have a big party and invite everyone."

"Sounds like the perfect compromise," Logan said.

We'd been getting better at making those. He was moving into Woolton Hall and I'd promised to come to London two nights a week. We agreed that eventually Mrs. Steele would move in with us, but she wanted to keep her independence, and her garden, as long as possible.

"I think you're right. I've been looking for family every-where my whole life. And now I've found it." I turned my head and kissed his jaw. He was my home, the place I felt most myself, the person I trusted above anyone in the world. Logan was my family now.

Logan

"Why didn't you try to convince me to stay in bed?" Darcy asked as we wandered hand in hand past the stables and toward Badsley House.

Sunday mornings had become both ritual and negotiation. Darcy would insist it was the perfect time for a morning walk to her favorite spot that overlooked Chilternshire, and I would try to persuade her to stay in bed just a little longer. But this morning was different.

The mist swirled across the lawns and the sun was trying to break through. It was a special part of the day, and I'd come to enjoy our Sunday morning walks together.

I shrugged. "It's your birthday, so it's only fair we do what you want to do today. Plus, you stayed in bed with me last Sunday morning—and last night should keep me satiated for a few more hours yet." That was a total lie. There wasn't a time when I didn't want Darcy, even if I'd had her just a few moments before, but I had a surprise for her and everything was in place.

She narrowed her eyes as if she didn't quite believe me, but didn't say anything. "Isn't it a perfect morning? You have to learn to ride, and we can go out together."

"I'm not sure I'm ever going to be a good rider. I think it's like skiing—you can't be great at it unless you learn as a child." I was much more at home boxing or lifting weights.

"You do okay," she said, a compliment considering I'd only been on a horse a handful of times and *okay* was as good as I got.

"We need to make sure our kids ride and ski from the time they can walk."

"*Our kids?* We're not even married yet."

"You of all people should know that just because people

are married, it doesn't mean they're ready for children and just because people aren't married doesn't mean they're not."

She gazed up at me, the soft, pink bloom in her cheeks making her glow. "Are you saying you're ready for kids?"

I kissed her on her head. "With you, I'm ready for anything." Losing Darcy had sent any expectations I'd had about the way my life was going to be up in flames. The day she'd come back to me, I'd started with a clean slate. She was at the center of everything I wanted, and with her, I wanted everything.

She bit back a smile in the most delicious way.

I paused and pulled a scarf from my pocket. We were just a few steps away from her favorite spot and her birthday surprise. "I need you to put this on," I said, holding up the handful of navy blue silk I'd stolen from her dressing room.

"I'm not cold. Where did you get that—"

"I'm going to blindfold you."

She tugged out of my grip. "What are you talking about?"

I cupped her face and skimmed her cheek with my thumb. "Trust me. I have a surprise for you."

She didn't say yes, but neither did she object. She clung to my shirt as I wrapped the silk around her eyes.

Wrapping my arms around her waist, I guided her forward.

"Logan, what are you doing?"

"Shhh, just a few more steps." I paused when we got to the clearing. Everything and everybody was where it was meant to be.

"Okay, promise me you won't scream."

"Logan, I swear, if you—"

I pulled off her blindfold and watched as she took in what was before her. Ryder, Scarlett and their children had arrived last night and slept at Badsley House with Violet and Alexander. Aurora had messaged me before Darcy and I had set off to say everything was in place. My grandmother had been determined to be part of the surprise and with some help from Ryder and Alexander, seemed to have arrived unscathed.

"Happy birthday," everyone chorused.

"I can't believe you're all here." Overwhelmed, Darcy sped toward her friends and family, pulling them into hug after hug. "How did this happen? I thought you were in Shanghai or something?" she asked Ryder.

"Logan made it happen. Organized us all," Ryder said.

She turned back to me and held out her hand. "You did this for me?" she asked as I joined the fray.

I shrugged. "You're not an easy woman to impress. I can't just drop some money on a fancy gift."

"Having all my favorite people around me is better than anything you could ever buy me."

Darcy might have been brought up in an incredibly wealthy family, but what made her rich was how much she loved those in her life, and how they loved her in return.

"Well, I did kind of buy you something, you know, in case seeing this lot was a bit of a let-down." I nodded to the bench I'd placed overlooking the view she loved so much. "I thought as we got older, we'd need somewhere to sit when we came up here."

"Logan, it's *perfect*."

I followed as she smoothed her fingers over the oak curve of its back then rounded toward the front. "Really?"

She traced her fingers over the words I'd had inscribed

on the back of the bench. *"Where Logan Steele fell in love with Darcy Westbury on 12 March."*

"From the first moment I laid eyes on you. It just took me awhile to get used to the idea."

She circled her arms around my waist and pulled me close. "I think I fell in love with you the exact same day. I just didn't want to admit it."

"I think we're both a little stubborn." I kissed her lightly on the lips. "Happy birthday, my love. Let's celebrate."

Lane and Mrs. MacBee had set up some champagne, but refused to join us, so Ryder poured out glasses. I took two and handed one to Darcy.

"I can't, Logan," Darcy said, worry crossing her face.

"I know it's early. I just thought we should start the celebrations early." I brushed her hair from her face.

"No, it's not that. I want to. I just...can't." She took my hand from her face and placed it over her belly. "You said we didn't have to be married to start a family, right?"

My stomach swooped and I tossed the two glasses of champagne on the grass beside us so I could place both hands on her belly. "Are you serious?" I glanced from my hands to her face, trying to take it all in.

"I am. Are you freaking out?" A mixture of hopeful concern crossed her face. My beautiful girl shouldn't have any worries.

I was going to be a father—I couldn't think of anything better.

"Freaking out? I'm fucking delighted." I turned to our friends and family crowded around the champagne table. "Did you hear that?" I bellowed. "We're going to be parents." I fell to my knees and pressed my lips over her stomach.

Shrieks and cheers surrounded us as everyone piled over to congratulate us both.

I'd intended to surprise Darcy on her birthday. Typical, that she'd outdo me. She always did, in every way. As my grandmother said: she gave me a run for my money.

And that was the thing I liked about her best.

Have you read
King of Wall Street - Max & Harper's story
Park Avenue Prince - Sam & Grace's story
Duke of Manhattan - Ryder & Scarlett's story
The British Knight - Alexander & Violet's story

HAVE YOU READ **MR. MAYFAIR**? Stella is shocked when she receives an invitation to the wedding of her newly ex-boyfriend and best friend. There's no way she'll go, is there?

BOOKS BY LOUISE BAY

The Mister Series

Mr. Mayfair

Mr. Knightsbridge

Mr. Smithfield

Mr. Park Lane

Mr. Bloomsbury

Mr. Notting Hill

The Christmas Collection

The 14 Days of Christmas

This Christmas

The Player Series

International Player

Private Player

Dr. Off Limits

Standalones

Hollywood Scandal

Love Unexpected

Hopeful

The Empire State Series

Sign up to the Louise Bay mailing list at
www.louisebay/mailinglist

Read more at www.louisebay.com

KEEP IN TOUCH!

Sign up for my mailing list to get the latest news and gossip
www.louisebay.com/newsletter

Or find me on

www.twitter.com/louiseSbay
www.facebook.com/authorlouisebay
www.instagram.com/louiseSbay
www.pinterest.com/louisebay
www.goodreads.com/author/show/8056592.Louise_Bay

ACKNOWLEDGMENTS

Acknowledgments

I can't believe Darcy's book is finally out in the world! So many people have asked about her book and desperately wanted her to find her happy ever after. I hope I did her justice. I know I'd be happy with Logan if he every wandered into my life! Thank you for asking for this book and thank you for reading it.

Elizabeth—You're the best and it's been so great to see you doing so well this last twelve months when you've helped me more than I could ever have hoped these last four (!) years. You deserve it and much more. This book as been three steps forward, two steps back, but at least it's a net win!

Sophie!! I'm so lucky to be able to rely on you and have you on my team. Thank you for our long calls and you knowing what I need before I do!

Najla Qamber – thank for being all the good words. You're incredibly kind and gracious and talented. You're right at the top of my list of awesome people.

To all the amazing authors that constantly lift me up - thank you.

And lastly to all those bloggers and readers who champion me, spread the word about my books, encourage me when things get tough and lift my spirits every day. I'm so grateful to have you in my life.